TEMPLE OF GHOSTS

J.H. MONCRIEFF

DeathZone Books, Ltd.
Temple of Ghosts
Copyright © 2017 by J.H. Moncrieff

ISBN: 978-0-9877129-7-4

Editing by Chris Brogden, EnglishGeek Editing
Cover design by Kelly Martin
Formatting by Champagne Book Design

OTHER BOOKS BY
J.H. MONCRIEFF

GhostWriters series

City of Ghosts

The Girl Who Talks to Ghosts

☾

The Bear Who Wouldn't Leave

Monsters in Our Wake

Lost

For Christine.

~ CHAPTER ONE ~

Jackson

TAKE MY WORD FOR IT: RUNNING HAND IN hand is not as romantic as it looks in the movies, especially when the person dragging you is terrified.

As we neared Lily's hospital room, I tugged on Kate's arm.

"We can't barge in there like this. We have to chill. Otherwise, we'll freak everyone out, and that's not going to help anyone, especially Lily."

Kate nodded, her eyes wide. To be fair, it was much easier for me to stay calm, since I had no idea what was going on. "You're right."

"Remind me to get that in writing."

"What?" Her tone had a sharp edge I was all too familiar with. *Don't push it, Jackson.*

"Never mind."

We attracted several curious glances when we arrived at the recovery unit. The admissions nurse smiled at us and asked if we'd forgotten something. I wondered what her reaction would have been if I'd said, *"Yes, Kate forgot to tell me she saw a creepy-ass spirit hanging out in our friend's room."* It was just as well I didn't have Kate's gift. If I did, I'd be pulling shit like that all the time.

After mumbling something about needing to speak to Vittoria, we hurried down the hall.

"I hope we're not too late."

Kate wasn't ordinarily melodramatic. If anything, she tended to understate things. "Too late for what? We were here a few minutes ago. Besides, the girl is in a hospital. Hard to get safer than that."

"You haven't learned much, have you? No place is safe."

It was darker outside Lily's room than I remembered, as if the fluorescent tubes weren't operating at full power. Oddly quiet too. Where were the nurses and aides? The visitors, the chatter of other patients? *It was like a tomb,* I thought before shaking it off. Kate's fear was contagious, that was all. It was making me see shadows in the sun.

Still, I breathed a little easier when I confirmed Lily was where we'd left her. She was slumped against her pillows, but brightened when she noticed us. "Hey, you guys came back." After she saw the expression on Kate's face (and probably mine—I'm a lousy actor), her smile faded. "What's wrong?"

Lily's father rose from the chair beside her bed and moved to block our path. "Sorry, but my daughter needs to rest. No more visitors."

"Dad!"

The man scowled at us while I struggled to remember his name. Dan? David? Something like that. I wasn't sure what it was about him that had set Kate off. He looked like your average, middle-aged white dude to me, down to the comb-over and sagging gut. "Sorry, honey, but you heard what the doctor said. Excitement isn't good for you right now."

"But they're my friends. I want to talk to them."

"Is Vittoria around?" Kate had retreated to the doorway. Fear radiated off her—I could almost smell it. What I couldn't understand was why. Lily's father was about the least threatening man I'd ever seen.

"She went home. What business could you possibly have with my wife?"

"That's between me and Vittoria, but I suspect you already know. Don't you, Dennis?"

The man's attention shifted to the corner of the room. "I'm not sure what you mean." But even I didn't believe him. Dude looked as guilty as a cat caught with his paw in the fishbowl.

My gaze following his, I checked out his recently vacated chair and choked, my own breath sticking in my throat. "Kate," I hissed, grabbing her sleeve. "Kate, *look*."

"I see it, Jackson," she said in a nonchalant voice before the meaning of my words sank in. She whirled to face me. "Do *you* see it?"

"Sure, I see it. What the hell *is* it?"

The plastic chair was enveloped in a tunnel of churning darkness. It was as if something were on fire, sending billowing black smoke into the room. Except this stuff didn't react like any smoke I'd ever seen. It curled around and around itself toward the ceiling like a tornado. Lily had noticed it too. Her face paled as she scooted as far away from it as possible. I wanted to run to her, to carry her out of there, but my feet wouldn't move. They were rooted to the spot. My bladder ached with an uncomfortable fullness.

"Kate?"

She faced Dennis again, pretending the thing in the corner, whatever it was, didn't terrify her. Who knows?

Maybe it didn't. Maybe she'd seen a lot worse. But it sure as hell scared the shit out of me. "You realize that isn't your brother. That isn't Bill."

Dennis leered, giving my girl a lecherous look I definitely did not care for. "What do you know about Bill? I don't even know who you are."

"I think you do. I think you know all about me, and that's why you don't want me to talk to Lily anymore."

"Jackson!" Lily screamed, and I saw in horror that the smoke-thing was stretching inky tendrils across the blankets on her bed, reaching for her. Breaking through my inertia, I rushed to her. Her father tried to block my path, but I elbowed him aside.

Kate's voice rose over Lily's shrieking. "Jacks, get away from there. You don't understand—"

Lily jumped into my arms just as one of those tendril things grazed her ankle. Her heart thrummed against my chest like a frightened bird. As her arms wrapped around my neck, the room filled with a sizzling sound, like someone was cooking steaks.

"Jackson!" Kate cried out, but when I looked for her, the only thing I could see was Dennis. His glasses hung askew. He stumbled toward us like some reanimated horror from a B movie.

"Let go of my daughter or I'll call the police." He sounded as if he were talking around a mouthful of marbles or broken teeth. *Police* came out like puh-leeeze. Turning his head to the side, he spit out a bloody incisor.

What in the ever-loving fuck?

Lily squirmed in my arms, holding on to my neck so tightly she cut off my air. "Daddy!"

"That's not your dad," I said, not quite sure what was

going on, but knowing that lump of spitting, leering flesh bore no resemblance to the mild-mannered accountant type we'd met earlier that afternoon. "Don't look at him. Promise me you'll keep your eyes shut, okay?"

She buried her face in my shoulder. I could feel the heat of her tears through my shirt. Sometimes I forgot she was twelve years old. She was so small, I could carry her like a kitten.

The sizzling noise above us intensified and then the fluorescent tubes burst, showering us with glass and plastic. Shards stung my skull, cutting me.

"Jackson." Kate was screaming for me now, terror clear in her voice. "Get out of there. Hurry!"

"I'm trying; I'm trying."

Dennis waved his arms as if he were trying to block a jump shot. I deked left; he deked right. I went right; he matched my moves.

A yelp in my ear made me wince, and then I heard growling. Clutching Lily to my chest, I turned, knowing full well I didn't want to see whatever it was but unable to help myself.

The churning tower of darkness was at least seven feet tall, but it didn't resemble a tornado anymore. As I stared, my eyes straining at their sockets as if they were dying to escape, the glossy head of a huge Doberman loomed over me, foam dripping from its jaws.

My hands slipped and I would have dropped Lily if she hadn't wrapped herself around my torso like a vine. As the giant dog lunged at us, I leapt for the door. Dennis threw himself at me, and my arm shot out, clipping him in the jaw. He went down like a sack of rocks, and the next thing I knew, Kate was yanking us through the door into the hallway.

We fell to the ground, huddled together, Lily's body tucked between us. A surge of energy rushed over our heads, slamming the door with brute force and turning it into wood chips.

"Kate!" I touched her hair, which felt like a cloud of the softest silk against my fingers. "Kate, are you all right?"

She lifted her head, pale and weary-looking. "I think so. Lily?"

Lily raised her tear-streaked face, sniffling. "I'm okay. But what about my dad?"

"I'll check." Shifting the girl's weight to me, Kate staggered to her feet. A nurse came skidding down the hallway at full speed.

"Are you three okay? Are you hurt?"

Ignoring her, Kate crept to the room, avoiding the pile of rubble that had once been a door. She poked her head inside, and then beckoned to the nurse. Though she kept her voice low, I got the gist of it. She was asking for help— help for Dennis.

"Dad!" Lily pushed against me, struggling to free herself, but I tightened my grip.

"Hang on. It's not safe for you to go in there yet. I'm sure your dad's fine." Raising my eyes to Kate's, I searched hers for answers. *Please don't make a liar out of me.*

The hallway soon bustled with medical personnel. Men in green pajamas rushed by with metal carts full of paraphernalia I mostly didn't recognize. I thought they'd get nasty with us for having Lily out of bed, but they didn't appear to notice. No one gave us a second look, which didn't bode well for poor Dennis. I was beginning to wish I'd dragged him out of there too.

Kate kneeled in front of us, resting her hand on Lily's arm. "Your dad's unconscious, sweetie, but a lot of good people are helping him."

"What did you do to him? He was fine before you got here." The bitterness in the girl's voice startled me. It had never occurred to me she'd blame *us* for this mess.

"It may have seemed that way, but he really wasn't. I don't think your dad has been himself for a while now."

"He was *fine.*"

"People thought you were fine too, remember? Appearances can be deceiving."

"You're a liar." Lily's voice broke, and I jostled her a little as if I could shake her out of her tantrum. I was afraid she was going to claw Kate's face off if I let her go.

"Hey, take it easy. I get that you're scared for your dad right now, but Kate doesn't lie. She's your friend. She was trying to help you."

"Some help."

I no longer had to be reminded Lily was twelve. She expressed scorn like a professional teenager. "That's enough."

"It's okay, Jacks." Kate sank to the ground beside us, leaning her head against the wall. "She's right; I didn't help. I didn't see what was going on until it was too late. I don't understand what's happening to me lately. I don't normally make these kinds of mistakes."

At the thought of what I'd witnessed, my mouth dried and my tongue felt thick and useless. "What was that thing, anyway? Please don't tell me it was a ghost."

She shook her head, her eyelids lowering in exhaustion. "No, it wasn't a ghost. Not any kind I've ever encountered before, at least."

"Then what was it?" It had been so real. I'd smelt its putrid breath, seen the fine threads of red blood vessels in its eyes, heard the foam from its muzzle splat as it hit the floor.

Kate sighed, slumping against my other shoulder. Thankfully, Lily's hostility had passed. She wept for her father, the tremors of her body passing through me to jostle Kate.

I forced myself to be patient, not to press too hard for answers. Sometimes Kate needed time to process things, and I wouldn't blame her if this was one of those occasions. The only thing that kept me clinging to sanity was the sense of unreality that attempted to take over my brain, insisting that what I'd seen was a dream. Or a hallucination. Anything but the truth.

"This is going to sound crazy," Kate said, just when I'd thought she'd fallen asleep. "But I think it was Anubis."

~ CHAPTER TWO ~

Kate

WHEN GRANDMA FIRST TAUGHT ME ABOUT The Gift, she'd never mentioned the social work involved. It's traumatic for mainstreamers to encounter the spirit world, even if the interaction is as benign as good ol' Uncle Edward telling you where he hid the will. The brain isn't prepared to deal with it, so it rationalizes, denies, or goes quietly mad.

I usually get the mad ones.

For a change, Jackson wasn't saying much, which was a bad sign, but I wasn't in the proper headspace to explain what had happened yet. I didn't understand it myself. Whatever had manifested in Lily's hospital room was not your run-of-the-mill spirit. And until I had more answers, the silence between us would serve as valuable pondering time.

"I—I don't understand. Why do these things keep happening to us?" Lily's mother, Vittoria, covered her face with her hands. "What did we do to deserve this? We're a good family."

"Of course you are." Awkwardly rubbing her back, I shot Jackson a pleading look, but he was staring at Vittoria's kitchen table in a daze. "None of this is your fault."

There were plenty of recriminations to go around. I kicked myself for not warning Vittoria about the many spirits I'd seen lurking about her home the day we'd met. There were quite a few astral doors in need of closing around here. But to be fair, none of these ghosts posed any threat to the Walkins family, and I hadn't met Dennis until today. Even then, whatever followed him around was a master of disguise. I hadn't realized the danger until Jackson and I had already left the hospital. Thankfully, I'd insisted on going back, but had that improved the situation? Hard to say. It had forced the presence to manifest, but I'm not so sure that was a good thing. Lily, Jackson, and Dennis would forever be scarred.

Searching for the words that would calm her, I reminded Vittoria that her husband would be fine. "They're only keeping him for observation. He could be home as early as tomorrow. I'm sure he's going to be all right."

I couldn't stop thinking of the hideous scene inside the hospital room: how Dennis's face had bloated and contorted as he'd spit his teeth onto the floor. When the presence receded, a lot of that had turned out to be smoke and mirrors. Dennis had lost one tooth, yes, from hitting the floor when he'd fainted. Otherwise, he had fallen unconscious for a while and was exhausted. Which was a normal repercussion of having a foreign spirit use and abuse your body— if anything about this situation could be considered normal.

"Jacks, will you make us some tea? Please?" I'm well aware that tea is not a magic cure-all, but it helps. Sometimes we need to treat gaping wounds with Band-Aids. Sometimes it's all we *can* do.

He startled, looking around at me like he'd realized

where he was for the first time. "Sure. Sorry. Yeah, I'll go."

As he left, I felt Vittoria's shoulders relax under my hands. She was starting to come around. Good. I needed her, as her husband wouldn't be in any shape to answer my questions for a while. And he might not be helpful if he was. People who deny the validity of what I do aren't the most accommodating, in my experience. From what Vittoria had said when she'd first hired me to rescue her daughter's soul, Dennis was one of those "If I can't see it, it doesn't exist" types. Well, maybe he'd seen enough today.

Removing her hands from her face, Vittoria fixed me with her dark eyes. "Did Dennis attack Lily? Tell me the truth."

"No, of course not." *Kind of. But it wasn't him. It was something else wearing a Dennis costume.*

"Then I don't understand. Why was Lily out of her room? It must have hurt so much when she pulled out her IV." Vittoria shuddered, but I could see she was ready to talk, so I pulled out the chair beside her and sat down.

"If it did, I don't think she noticed. In any case, she's fine now. We'll take you to see her after this if you want."

Jackson popped his head into the breakfast nook. "Sugar? Milk?"

Vittoria gave him a grateful smile, and my own shoulders relaxed. Good. Her social graces were returning, which meant I could get to the point sooner rather than later. I needed to find the source of what we were dealing with in a hurry. "Neither, thank you. Black is fine."

"That works for me too. Thanks, Jacks."

She turned to me again. "I still don't understand what's going on. I thought Lily would be fine after you brought her back."

Then you weren't listening to me. I'd told her Lily was the supernatural equivalent of an unlocked door in a bad neighborhood, but apparently that hadn't sunk in. I decided to leave it alone for now. "This really doesn't have anything to do with Lily. It has to do with Dennis."

"What's wrong with him? Is he sick?"

That's what I'm trying to find out. I took a deep breath, and just then, Jackson returned with two steaming mugs. I was surprised Vittoria owned such a thing. She'd always struck me as a porcelain kind of woman. "Thanks, but you should make one for yourself too. Tea is good for nerves."

Jackson collapsed in his seat. "Later. I want to hear this." At my raised eyebrow, he shrugged and said, "It'll save us time on the recap later. And if I'm going to be a partner, I want to be a partner. I don't want you doing the heavy lifting alone anymore."

That was fair. If he was going to uproot his life to live and work with me, he had a right to know what he was getting into. "Okay. Vittoria, has your husband spent any time in Egypt?"

She jerked away from her mug as if she'd burned her tongue, sending droplets of tea down her silk blouse. I handed her a linen napkin from the rack on the table, but she ignored it. "No, never. Dennis hates to travel. It's a miracle if I can to get him over to Boise to see his folks."

Figures. I was beginning to develop a clear picture of her husband. While my mind stumbled around like a drunk, trying to think of what to ask next, she interrupted my thoughts.

"But Bill spent lots of time there. That's where he died, you know."

"No, I didn't know that." I touched Jackson's hand to

get his attention. "Bill was Dennis's brother."

"That's right. They were extremely close. Even if my husband had wanted to go to Egypt—which he didn't—once his brother died there, there was no way he'd ever set foot in that place. My husband..." Vittoria glanced out the window for a moment. "He's a darling man, but he's not very progressive. America is the center of the universe for him, and that's the way he likes it."

"What was Bill doing in Egypt?"

She risked another sip of tea. "Oh, he was part of Operation Star. No, that's not quite right. Operation *Bright* Star, I think it's called. Ever hear of it?"

I looked at Jackson, making sure we were both equally in the dark before I said no.

"American soldiers go to Egypt every two years for training exercises. It's supposed to demonstrate the military might of our great country to anyone in the Middle East who's thinking of messing with us." Vittoria rolled her eyes. "Bill loved Egypt. He went every time the opportunity arose, I think. He was always telling us we should visit him, but he might as well have suggested we dye our hair blue or join the Rockettes. Dennis wasn't having any of it."

"How did Bill die, Vittoria?" I was careful to keep my voice gentle, though she didn't seem to have any difficulty discussing her brother-in-law.

She set down her mug. "You know, they really never figured it out. The coroner listed it as an unexplained death, and there was talk of it being an aneurysm or a heart attack, but they didn't find any proof. The poor man's heart just burst."

"Burst?" Jackson said.

Vittoria nodded. "Exploded. The coroner who did the

autopsy said he'd never seen anything like it."

"Did Bill ever talk about his experiences over there?" I asked.

"Sure, he sent us postcards all the time." Seeing the surprise in our faces, she waved her hand at us. "Oh, I know, it's old-fashioned. But Bill loved sending them, and the kids loved getting them. Even Garrett, who isn't big on reading. He wants to be a soldier now, just like his uncle. I think Dennis appreciated the cards too, though he didn't say one way or another. At least he got to armchair travel."

"Do you still have them?"

"Of course. Garrett keeps them in a box in his room, and I'm sure he won't mind if you borrow them. Probably won't even notice, with everything else that's going on. Would you like to see them?"

"That would be great. I'll get them from you before we leave. Do you recall Bill ever talking about anything strange happening while he was there?"

"Strange? Strange like how?"

Picturing the hideous creature we'd seen, my mind raced. *Would Bill have seen the same thing? Was that what caused his heart to explode?* "Anything you can remember. Anything he might have seen, heard, experienced, that bothered him."

Vittoria was quiet for a minute while she sipped her tea. One of the problems with the human brain is that it often doesn't register experiences as strange or bizarre while they're happening, only in hindsight. And if a person dies, his hindsight dies with him.

The clunk as she returned her mug to the table made both of us jump. "You know, there was something, now that I think about it. Not long before Bill died, he told

Dennis he wasn't feeling well. He planned to go to the doctor as soon as he got back to the States. Since we later found out he must have had something wrong with his heart, we didn't think much of it. Dennis went for a checkup soon after." A sad little smile grazed her lips. "Doctor said he was in perfect health."

I patted her hand. "He was, and he will be again. There's a few things Jacks and I need to look into, but I promise we won't stop until we know your family is safe. Okay?"

"So I'll be keeping you on the payroll for a while."

"If that's all right," Jackson said, and I was relieved when she nodded. I never felt good about taking payment for stuff like this, but a girl's gotta eat. When Jacks witnessed my reluctance, he had offered to take over that end of the business for me. What we did with the money would still be mostly in my hands, but collecting it would be in Jackson's. Which was also a relief.

"All right? Do you know how lost we'd be if we hadn't found Kate? But you must have other clients, other people who need your help."

I thought of the tearful pleas on my voice mail, and it was as if Atlas had told me he was tired and tossed me the world. I shook off the heaviness before it could settle on my shoulders. "No one who's in immediate danger. Those who are always come first."

"So I was right. My family *is* in danger. Tell me what's going on, Kate. Tell me how I can help."

"You already are helping. By talking to us now, you're helping. We'll get working on this right away, and the second we know more, we'll pass it on to you."

She exhaled heavily. "Thank you."

"Can we see Bill's postcards now?"

"Of course."

As soon as she left the room, Jackson leaned over to me. "So what's really going on?"

"I'm not sure yet, but I can tell you this—whatever killed Dennis's brother didn't have a damn thing to do with his heart."

℆

It felt so good to come home that afternoon. Noddy didn't give me the post-travel silent treatment for a change. I suspected a lot of that was due to Jackson's presence. My cat had already bonded with him.

As I returned to the living room with two mugs, heavy on the whipped cream and chocolate sprinkles, I smiled to see the Maine Coon stretched across Jackson's lap like a sphinx.

Jacks brightened when he saw I was bearing gifts. "I don't know what that is, but it looks amazing. Thank you." Reaching for the mug I offered, he breathed in the steam. "Mmm. Irish coffee?"

"I figured we could both use something stronger than tea." Moving Noddy's forelegs aside, I managed to squeeze in beside them.

"You figured right. What a shit show for our first day back. I'm hoping it's a nightmare and we're still sleeping off the jetlag from Poveglia."

As I felt the soothing liquid glide down my throat, I leaned my head against the loveseat and sighed, closing my eyes.

"Feels good to be home, huh?"

"Yes. Yes it does."

What had happened at the hospital was bizarre and terrifying, but at least in Nightridge I was in my element. This
was my center, my heart. I had friends who could help me,
a network of support. In Poveglia I would have been completely alone if it hadn't been for this guy at my side.

"I was thinking of ordering Thai for dinner. I could use
a little comfort food. Sound good?"

"Sounds perfect." Jacks reached across Noddy to caress
my thigh. "*You're* perfect. This was a good decision."

I stuck out my tongue. "Don't lay it on too thick, or I'll
wonder if you're the one who's possessed."

"Seriously, Kate. I'm glad I stayed."

There was a sincerity in his voice that I didn't often
hear. Jacks was a joker and a smartass, which I appreciated,
don't get me wrong, but it wasn't easy to know where I
stood with him sometimes. Okay, a lot of the time. Ever
since I'd had that hunch something was wrong with Lily's
father and dragged Jacks back to the hospital, I'd been half
expecting him to tell me he'd changed his mind about moving to Vermont.

How many guys had claimed to love me, only to run for
the hills when they discovered what my life was actually like?
Though it hurt every time, I couldn't blame them. Living
with me meant accepting that objects would fly through
the air as frustrated spirits demanded my attention, and that
people in desperate need of help would be a near-constant
interruption. My work wasn't 9-to-5, and it would never
be. If an irate ghost is threatening your family, the last thing
you want to hear is a voice mail message telling you to call
back in the morning.

"Really?" I asked, hating myself for needing the reassurance, but needing it anyway.

"I've done a lot of dumb things in my life, but this isn't one of them. When someone as amazing as you is willing to put up with my sorry ass, I don't hesitate."

"Your ass isn't sorry. Far from it."

"I'm trying to be serious, Kate. You're not making it easy."

"Sorry. I'm not used to this side of you yet."

"Well, get used to it."

Blowing gently across the surface of my coffee, I took a sip, promptly decorating my nose with whipped cream. The ideal accoutrement for a serious conversation. Wiping it away, I asked, "Have you talked to your family?"

"Not yet. I need to fortify myself first. Maybe after dinner."

Jackson was extremely close to his family, especially his mother and baby sister. They weren't going to be happy about his decision to move from Minneapolis to Vermont. I hoped they would be supportive of him, and wouldn't hate me.

Reading my mind, he touched my shoulder. "Don't worry. They'll be surprised at first, but they'll get used to it. When it comes down to it, they want me to be happy—they're good people. And they know how I feel about you."

"They do? Even *I* don't know."

"And I plan to spend a lot of my time rectifying that."

"But in the meantime…"

"Bill Walkins and his fondness for archaic methods of communicating."

"Exactly." I settled the box of postcards between us. Noddy showed immediate interest, but thankfully he found Jackson more interesting, at least for now, so he didn't move.

"How about you take half and I take half?"

Dividing the stack of cards in two, Jackson handed me the ones from the bottom of the box. "Sounds like a plan. Let's do this."

"Tell me if you find anything odd, any hint that something out of the ordinary happened to him over there. And tell me when you're ready for dinner."

"Okay, boss."

"Not boss—*partner*."

"I don't mind you being my boss, but okay—*partner*."

"That's better."

The cards smelled musty, like a used bookstore, even though they weren't that old. I suspected that had more to do with Garrett's room than the cards themselves.

They were decorated with stereotypical Egyptian scenes: pyramids, tombs, giant statues of pharaohs. In spite of myself, I felt a prickle of excitement. I'd wanted to visit Egypt since I was a child, but the country's struggles with terrorism had scared me off. It was a dream that hadn't died, though.

Flipping over a card, I was relieved to find Bill's writing was legible. It was a scrawl, but a readable one.

Egypt won the soccer match tonight, and I really wish you guys were here to see it. Cairo's gone crazy! Traffic's come to a standstill, people are hanging out of their windows and honking like mad, confetti and fireworks are all over the place. What a scene! They are such a passionate people, and their joy is contagious. I feel lucky that I'm able to see it. Give yourselves a hug from me.

Miss you,

Bill

Running my fingers along the worn edges of the card,

I glanced at the date. This had been written a year earlier. Someone had handled these a lot in that time. Garrett, or Dennis?

As I read the dead man's words, I reached out for his spirit. It was a phone ringing in an empty house. Nothing.

Went to the market yesterday, and this merchant heard me coughing. He insisted I come to his stall and have some mint tea. Dennis, I know what you're thinking, that he was just doing it for a sale, but you're wrong. That's how people are here. Even the ones who have nothing will give you whatever they have. As far as sales go, he didn't get much from me, but I did buy this postcard. And my throat feels much better. It was a fair trade.

Love you guys,
Bill

Most of the cards were the same. Snapshots of a tourist who missed his family. I hoped Jackson was having better luck. "Anything yet?"

Jackson shuffled through his stack. "Nope, unless you count Egypt is amazing and Dennis's brother was one hell of a nice guy. You?"

"About the same." I stretched my neck until the vertebrae popped. "I'm thinking this was a dead end. Maybe we should order dinner now."

"Wait a minute…hang on. This could be something. Listen to this. 'Did a bit of sight-seeing today and wish I hadn't. Saw the Temple of Waset, which is near Luxor. But afterward I wasn't feeling so good. Still don't. Never thought I would say this, but I wish I could come home. Bill.'"

Leaning closer, I saw the writing had changed. It was messier, as if the man's hand had been shaking. "Didn't

Vittoria say he died shortly after this? We'll have to check the rest of the cards to be sure, but what if whatever he encountered in the temple killed him?"

"Like what, a virus? I once saw a documentary that said there are tons of bacteria and other nasty stuff growing on the walls in some of the tombs. Maybe it's the same with temples?"

"Maybe, if the air can't get to them. Hang on." Pulling out my phone, I typed the name of the temple into the search engine. The results were exactly as I'd expected, but they still made me shiver. "I don't think it was a virus, Jacks."

Handing him my phone so he could read for himself, I wished Bill had written more about his experiences. I cursed the poor man for not using email, where he'd have had the space to go into more detail. Detail we desperately needed.

Waset Temple was the great temple of Anubis.

~ CHAPTER THREE ~

Kate

"YOU NEVER CEASE TO AMAZE ME." JACKSON helped himself to another serving of *kaeng kiew waan,* a spicy Thai-style green curry made with coconut milk. Ordering had been easy. Jacks ate everything, and we had the same favorites. It may seem like a small thing, but relationships had ended after heated arguments over pizza toppings.

"Why's that?" I snagged some more *mee krob* before it was too late. Living with a man meant no more taking it easy at the table. It was everyone for himself, especially when it came to crunchy noodles.

"You know everyone. You're best friends with a psychic, and now you have an Egyptologist in your hip pocket? Who else says, 'Oh, I'll call my Egyptologist'?"

I laughed. "She's not *my* Egyptologist. She's just someone I know. I've taken a few of her classes, and I've been working with her on a project lately."

"You're studying ancient Egypt?"

"Why not? I audit tons of classes at the university. I don't care about getting a degree, and the idea of homework gives me hives, but it's cool to learn new stuff."

"I'd be into that. I think I spent my university years half-asleep. The easiest classes to pass weren't always the most interesting, you know?"

"You're welcome to come with, although I think we're going to be busy until we figure out what's going on with the Walkinses."

"True." Jackson offered me the last spring roll, ensuring my eternal adoration. "So you saw something hanging around Lily's dad right away?"

A memory of the spirit as I'd first seen him, with his features contorted by pain and sorrow, made my stomach churn and growl a warning. Putting the spring roll down, I wiped the grease from my hands. "Yes. It was Bill. He gave me his name, clear as what you're saying to me right now. At least, it was Bill at *first*."

"Did he say anything else?"

"No. He just looked really sad." He'd *wanted* to say something, though. I could see it in his eyes, that beseeching plea to connect that I'd encountered so many times before.

"So how did you know something wasn't kosher? I mean, before the dog-thing appeared and tried to bite my head off, of course."

I thought for a moment, wondering how to best describe a phenomenon that came as naturally to me as breathing. "You know how when you ask a woman what's wrong and they say 'Nothing,' and you know they're not telling the truth?"

He rolled his eyes. "Yep."

"How do you *know* they're not telling the truth?"

"The way they say it, I guess. The steam radiating off them is usually a good clue."

"It's the same in the spirit world. It's all about the stuff that isn't said. It was like seeing a glimmer of Bill, but knowing it wasn't really Bill. Like something else wearing a Bill suit." That wasn't quite it, either. Bill had definitely been there—his emotions were genuine, no question about it. But his spirit was being used as a cover for something else. Rather than a Bill suit, it was a Bill shield.

"Creepy. You think your friend will be able to tell us about this Whaddet-whatever?"

"Waset. I hope so. She's our best chance."

We ate in silence for a few minutes, and in that quiet space, I let my mind wander, searching for Bill. It was akin to strolling through a party, casually skimming the room for that interesting person you'd prayed would show. I didn't dare reach out too intentionally. Bill was welcome, but whatever was clinging to him like a putrid, paranormal parasite had no business in my home. In *our* home.

Jacks cleared his throat, making me jump. "Um, Kate?"

"Yeah?" My eyes slowly refocused on the material realm, and I was unnerved to see the discomfort on his face. *Did something happen while I was gone? Did I say something strange?* Warmth crept up my throat as I realized how odd I must seem to him. Even though he'd been through a lot of this stuff with me before, I don't think anyone can truly get used to The Gift and all the fun things that come with it. *I'm* not used to it, and I've had thirty-five years to adjust. "What's wrong? There's something wrong, right?"

"Not really wrong. I'm just not sure how to ask you this." He looked over my shoulder, at the cat, out the window, pretty much anywhere but at me.

"You should know by now you can ask me anything. When it comes to you, I'm an open book. So shoot." I was grateful I sounded more confident than I felt. Jackson wasn't a beat-around-the-bush type. If he was struggling this much with his question, it must be something awful. Was he regretting moving in with me? Working with me?

"You said you saw 'something' hanging around Bill..." His voice was raspier than normal, as if the words were fighting their way over his tongue.

I exhaled in relief. Is that what was bothering him, the paranormal? *That* I could deal with. "Yes? Go on."

"Well...I guess what I want to ask is...do you still see anyone, um, hanging around me?" This time he did look at me, and his eyes were suspiciously shiny.

With that single question, we were back to tricky territory. My friend Laura always said that what we do for people is more about psychology than the supernatural. When a family comes to you for help finding Dad's will, do they want money or closure? A woman desperate to know her future—why is she asking? This was no different. "You're wondering about Clarke." I kept my voice as gentle as possible when I said the name of Jackson's best friend, who had taken his own life a year before.

"Yeah." He turned away, but not before I saw him swipe at his eyes. "It's stupid. I mean, he's dead. It doesn't matter anymore where he is."

Laying my hand across his, I shook my head. "You're wrong. Of course it matters. You loved him and he loved you. That kind of love doesn't end because one of you stops breathing. Take my word for it."

Jacks laughed shakily. "You're the expert."

"I am." *And how I wish I had better news for you.*

"So? Can you see him?"

"Truth?"

"Always, Kate. You know that. Always truth."

This time I took both his hands in mine. "Then you already know the answer."

"He's gone, isn't he?" His voice cracked, but only the tiniest amount. I doubt anyone else would have heard it.

"Yes, he's gone, which means you were able to let him go. That's a good thing. He wasn't supposed to be here." The old wish intensified into a longing, deep in my gut, that I knew more about what Laura called "The After." I'd love to be able to tell people their loved ones were in heaven, playing poker with the angels. Sadly, my gift didn't extend that far and neither did hers. I don't think we're supposed to know. Not yet, anyhow.

"Yeah, you're right, I guess."

"But you miss him. Jacks, his spirit doesn't have to be present for you to talk to him, or wish him well. He'll still get the message."

He laughed again, and a tear ran down the side of his face. "It's silly, but I started thinking about how much he'd like you. How much I wish he could have met you."

The admission, so unlike Jacks and so without guile, made my own eyes fill. "It's not silly at all. I think it's beautiful. I would have loved to have met him too."

"What you do, it's not really like that, is it? It's not like you *have* met him or anything."

Recalling the sad shadow that had passed for his friend in China, I shook my head. "No. I only experienced his pain. It isn't the same thing at all." The Clarke whom Jackson had grown up with, had shot the shit with and played video games with, was completely unknown to me. He'd been a psychic manifestation of a deep emotional wound by the time I came along, nothing more.

"That's too bad. You two would have hit it off." Taking his napkin, he wiped his face before crumpling the paper onto his plate. "I've told you how I felt about Brandi, his ex. What I didn't tell you is how he felt about the women in my life."

"I'm guessing he wasn't a fan."

"Ha! Hardly. Can't blame him, either. For as much grief as I gave him over the Brandi thing, I made some pretty dumbass choices myself."

"Didn't we all." A parade of losers marched through my mind before I relegated them to the past where they belonged. The guys who accused me of witchcraft or worse, the one who tried to exploit my gift for money, and then there was the charmer who kept taking "long business trips" to cheat on me. To live a life without romantic regrets was to live a life without love. "I did then what I knew how to do. Now that I know better, I do better."

Jackson leaned back in his chair and grinned. "Maya Angelou. I'm impressed."

I raised an eyebrow. Jacks had never struck me as a poetry fan. "You know Maya Angelou?"

"Of course I do. And you can stop looking at me like that. I may not be the most refined guy in the world, but I didn't crawl out from under a rock yesterday. The woman is an icon."

"I'm sorry; you're right. I was making assumptions. And probably being a sexist pig. I just never would have pictured you reading poetry."

"Hey, song lyrics are poetry. Hip-hop is poetry. Maybe Angelou's stuff has less motherfuckers and bitches, but poetry's poetry."

I smiled. "True."

We reached for each other at the same moment, but before our fingers connected, a low growl made us pull back.

"What the hell was that?"

I could have laughed at the panic on his face. Poor Jacks. Living with me meant jumping at shadows for a while, until he accepted that not every bump, creak, or growl in the night was supernatural. "It's Noddy. He probably sees a dog. Or maybe another cat's gotten too close to the house."

Pushing away from the table, I fully expected to see my watch cat on duty, but Noddy was nowhere near the window. To my surprise, he was sitting on his haunches in the kitchen, staring into a corner.

Trepidation crept over me. The only things Nostradamus growled at *inside* the house were malevolent spirits. "Noddy? What's bothering you, buddy? Whatcha got there?" In my experience, malevolent spirits didn't confine themselves to corners. It was the only thing we had going for us at the moment.

I approached my cat slowly, careful not to startle him, but Noddy didn't so much as meow in my direction. He stared at whatever had caught his interest, focusing all of his attention on his new plaything.

"What is it?" Jackson whispered.

A flicker of movement made me gasp, but when I realized the size, the tension left me. "I think it's an insect. Either that or a mouse. But let's hope for the former."

Hunkering down beside my cat, I urged him to move his paw. "What is it, Noddy? Can I see?"

This time he acknowledged me with a mournful meow, like he was trying to tell me something. His worried expression was so human it was comical. "Don't fret; I won't hurt your little friend," I said, smoothing the soft fur along his spine.

My Maine Coon contemplated that for a moment, and must have decided I was a woman of my word, because he lifted his paw. The unfortunate insect, dazed but alive, managed a feeble hop in my direction under Noddy's scrutiny.

Jackson scooped it off the floor and held it up to the light. "How on earth did a grasshopper get in here? You ever have these in the house before?"

Noddy whine-growled, and I scratched his ears for reassurance. I'd never seen him this upset over an insect, which most likely meant it wasn't just a bug, but a message. "Never. I don't even see them in the yard this late in the fall. It's too cold for them. I don't think it's a grasshopper, though."

"Of course it's a grasshopper. What else would it be?" He moved it closer so I could get a better look. Noddy hunched his back and hissed. "What the heck is his problem? Noddy, chill. It's only a bug."

"I think it's a locust."

Jackson stared at the thing crawling on his palm. "As in 'plagues of Egypt' locust?"

"The very same. You have to admit the timing is interesting. Let's hope there's no more where he came from."

~ CHAPTER FOUR ~

Jackson

CONTRARY TO APPEARANCES, I HAVEN'T BEEN living under a rock for the last twenty-nine years. I get that times have changed, and that women don't need (or want) guys to go all heroic on them anymore. And I can respect that. But Kate didn't see the thing Dennis had turned into up close and personal. I did, and there was no way I was letting her get near him until I was certain it was safe.

"I understand your concern, but it's not necessary. I've faced worse." Kate's skin was flushed enough to tell me she was crossing the territory from mildly annoyed into outright pissed. I didn't want her angry with me, but I'd rather she hated my guts than get seriously hurt.

"Worse than that leering monster with the bloody teeth? I don't think so."

"Jacks, I adore you for trying to protect me, but you have to let me do my job." Her fingers tightened on the steering wheel, her knuckles turning white. I'd thought it was smart to spring this on her when we were already en route to the hospital, but perhaps aggravating her while she was driving hadn't been the best idea.

"And you have to let me do mine."

"It isn't your job to protect me."

My jaw clenched. "Then what *is* my job?"

She glanced at me before returning her attention to the road. "Why are you asking that? Your job is writing. I thought you were going to work on your book."

"Fine, but what is my job with *you*? I get that you've been doing this a long time, and finding a place for me might not be your top priority, but I can't sit by and watch you get hurt. I don't want to 'sit by' at all. If I'm going to stay in Nightridge, I need a role."

"A role?" I could almost see her counting under her breath, struggling not to lose her temper.

"Yeah, you know, 'duties as assigned.' I don't want another repeat of Poveglia."

Her eyebrows shot up to her hairline. "What are you talking about? I couldn't have gotten through Poveglia without you. I wouldn't have made it to the island without you."

"I appreciate what you're trying to do, but we both know I did a lot of standing around while you communed with ghosties. If I can't protect you with my sexy black self, I want you to use my brain."

She bit her lip, probably to avoid making some smartass comment. "Use your brain how?"

Studying her features, I attempted to predict how she was going to respond to my request. I should have brought this stuff up before I offered to move my entire life to Vermont; we should have talked about it way before now. But we hadn't, and there was no time like the present. If I was going to work with Kate, I couldn't keep being her sidekick. I needed to be her partner in the real sense of the word. "I want you to teach me."

"Teach you? Teach you *what*, exactly?"

"Teach me to do what you do."

I leaned back, crossing my arms, curious to hear what she'd say. She laughed, but it wasn't her natural laugh at all. Nope, definitely forced, but that was okay. I expected to have to talk her around. Talking people around was one of the things I did best.

"I can't *teach* you to be a medium, Jacks."

"Why not?"

"What do you mean, 'Why not?'" Her voice rose in frustration. "Because you don't have The Gift, that's why."

"Bullshit. There's gotta be a workaround. I've read that everyone has a sixth sense or whatever you want to call it. It's just that most of us aren't open to it. Well, I am...now. And I want you to teach me."

"I'm sure that's true, to a certain extent, but when people say that, they don't mean everyone is capable of doing what I do. It's a little different from learning to trust your instincts or listen to your intuition."

"Are you saying you're special? That you're the only person on the planet who can do what you do?" I knew was goading her, but I couldn't help myself.

"Of course not. There are other mediums out there. But yes, okay, I *am* special, at least in this regard. My gift is one most people would never want. You wouldn't ask for it if you knew what it was like. I've done my best to use it to help people. I don't charge a fortune and I don't make shit up." Her mouth twisted. "I never exploit my clients."

"Hey." I touched her hand, relieved she didn't hit me. "At ease, girl. That's not what I'm saying. I want to be an active part of what we—what *you*—do. I want to help."

She sighed. "I hear what you're saying, and I get it. I wouldn't be comfortable sitting on the sidelines either, and of course I don't want you to feel useless. But there's many things you can do to help that don't require you to have mediumistic ability."

"Like what?"

"Just throwing stuff out here—you're charming, much more so than I am. You should be the first point of contact for clients. You could schedule the appointments. And I always need help in cases of mass murder, you know that."

Remembering how close she'd come to death in China gave me the shivers. "Yeah, I know. And I'm fine with doing that stuff. I just want to do more. I want to *really* contribute."

"This isn't my area of expertise, but if you're serious, Laura might be able to help. She sometimes does consciousness-awakening stuff with clients."

"I'm dead serious. Hook me up." I'd only met Kate's best friend a couple of times, once before we left for Venice and then for a quick chat when we returned, but I liked her. She was smart and funny as hell, once you got past her weird-ass flower child getups.

"Okay, I'll talk to her. I planned to call her when we got back from the hospital anyway. We're going to need her help with this one."

The fact that she'd said *we're* instead of *I'm* wasn't lost on me. "Thanks, Kate."

"No promises."

"I'm still not letting you go into that room until I've made sure it's safe."

"There's no point fighting you on this, is there?"

"Nope. Absolutely none."

She sighed again, looking resigned as she focused on the road ahead. "I guess I should be grateful to have someone watching my back. I'm lucky I'm not a ghost myself, with everything that's happened to me. But I'm used to doing things on my own, in my own way. This isn't going to be easy."

I smiled and squeezed her thigh, already feeling a million times better. "You know what they say. Nothing worth having ever is."

☾

The man in the bed was not the same person who'd guarded his daughter's hospital room with such suspicion. He looked smaller, diminished somehow, a guy who'd had the fight taken out of him. Above his head, machines blipped and beeped, displaying his heart rate and other vital signs I'd need a nursing degree to interpret.

"It's Jackson, right?" He gave me a weak smile, and I was relieved to see he had most of his teeth. It was hard to believe this frail man had been a bloody, snarling monster the day before.

"Yeah. How you feeling?" I offered my hand, noticing how weak his felt. Whatever had possessed him appeared to be long gone, but I had to be certain.

"All right, I guess. I've been better, of course." Dennis's mouth twisted in an expression I understood all too well— dude was trying to wrangle his emotions. "My own daughter is afraid of me. She won't come anywhere near me."

"She's not afraid of you. She's afraid of whatever was... *using* you." I wasn't quite ready to say possessing. "She'll come around. She's a good kid."

"Yeah…" Not meeting my eyes, he stared at the TV, but I knew it was a ruse. If you're going to use a TV to ignore someone, it helps if it's turned on.

I waited him out, watching closely for signs of anything the slightest bit freaky, but all I saw was a sad, middle-aged man. Channeling Kate, I tried to see beyond Dennis's bland shell to his soul, the real essence behind the mask, but I couldn't get past my own feelings.

Truth was, I didn't like the guy. I'd put my own ass on the line to help Kate save his daughter, and while I didn't want to be one of those judgmental fucks who blame everything on the parents, it was hard not to blame him. Lily's mom was a nice enough person—she was kind, gentle, wore her heart on her sleeve. Kate had told me Vittoria was paying us from her own account, an account her husband wasn't aware of, and I had to ask myself why. *Why* didn't her husband know? Why was she hiding money from him? And why did his daughter, a twelve-year-old kid, already hate herself so much she'd carved up her arms for kicks? I got the feeling Dennis wasn't very nice to the women in his life, that what I'd seen yesterday could have been a damn good representation of what the man was like behind closed doors.

And if there's anything in this world that makes my skin crawl, it's monsters masquerading as men.

"Vittoria told me."

"Huh?" I'd been so lost in my own thoughts that Dennis's voice startled me. I'd pretty much forgotten he was there. Obviously I'd done a great job focusing on his soul. Maybe Kate was right. Some people were born with it and the rest of us weren't.

Dennis coughed and then winced, making me wonder

if he had cracked ribs. Those things hurt like a son of a bitch. Almost enough to make me feel sorry for the prick. Almost, but not quite. "Excuse me. What I meant to say is my wife told me who you are. You're not really friends of hers. She hired you."

"I'd like to think we're friends now." If someone had saved my kid, "friend" was probably the least I'd consider him.

"I have to tell you…" More coughing and wincing. "I've never really gone in for that stuff. The *supernatural,* or whatever you want to call it. But I guess I don't have much choice, do I?"

I shrugged, remembering one of the first things Kate had ever told me. *It doesn't matter if you don't believe in the devil; the devil believes in you.* "If there's anything I've learned about this stuff, it's that no one gets a choice."

The man managed an odd little smile, and he muttered something under his breath. Something like, *"I had a choice, all right."*

"Excuse me?"

He was racked by another fit of coughing. Raspy and hoarse, it sounded like it was tearing up his insides. It was enough to make *me* wince.

"Sorry. My wife thinks…that is, she feels…oh, hell with it. She thinks your friend can help me. I haven't felt like myself for quite a while now. Ever since my brother died."

This time the coughing was so bad he doubled over, wheezing. I went to help and then hesitated, not sure what to do. Did I pound him on the back, or ring for the nurse? In that moment of helplessness, Dennis looked up at me, tears streaming down his cheeks.

"Water," he gasped.

"Of course, man. Hang on."

Grabbing the glass from his bedside, I held it to his mouth like he was a child. His hands were shaking too badly for him to hold it himself, though he tried. He drank a huge mouthful before he turned his head and spit it out. Bright red blood sprayed over the sheets and ran down his chin.

"Jesus Christ!" I stuck my head into the hall. "Nurse! Nurse! This man is bleeding."

Kate hurried to my side. "What happened? What's wrong?"

"I don't know. We were just talking when he started coughing, and the next thing I knew, all this blood was coming out of his mouth."

A male nurse in pale green scrubs pushed past us, followed by several others, including a guy in a lab coat who looked like he was still in high school. Shoved to the side, Kate and I waited in the hall while the nurses crowded around Dennis. He was still coughing and choking. A nurse tried to get an oxygen mask on him, but he pushed her away.

"Look at the cards," he yelled between coughs. "The last ones Bill sent. They're...different." Clutching at his throat, he doubled over as a new fit of choking seized him.

Doogie Howser held up the glass from the nightstand, glaring at me. "Where did you get this? Did you give it to him?"

Dennis's water glass was filled with blood.

~ CHAPTER FIVE ~

Jackson

I HAD TO TAKE THREE STEPS TO ONE OF KATE'S IN order to keep up. Girl was practically sprinting, attracting disapproving looks from nurses and visitors alike. Apparently, the only people allowed to hurry in this place were those with initials after their names.

"It was plain water, I swear." Kate would never suspect me of hurting anyone, let alone a client, so my protests were more of a belated response to the young doctor's accusations.

"I believe you. Come on, let's go. We have to hurry."

She gained speed once we left the hospital, flat-out running to her car. Her hands trembled so violently she dropped her keys. Gently nudging her aside, I unlocked the door of the Mini Cooper. "Do you want me to drive? You seem pretty messed up."

"No, I'm fine. It's easier if it's me—I know where we're going. That way I don't have to direct you."

Closing her fingers around her keys, I kissed her knuckles. "Fair enough. Care to enlighten me?"

I was rewarded with a smile. Just a flicker, but it was more than I'd expected, considering her current state. "The enlightening will commence once we're on the road. I promise."

Kate managed to leave the parking lot without squealing her tires, but just barely. Out of reflex I seized the grab handle. Her smile broadened.

"He must have coughed up that blood. What do you think is wrong with him?" I was no Doogie Howser, but even I could tell Lily's dad was seriously ill. My grandma had died of emphysema and her coughing fits hadn't been that severe.

Tightening her fingers on the wheel, Kate shook her head. "I have no idea, but I *do* know he didn't cough up that much blood."

"Where'd it come from, then?"

"This is going to sound crazy." She exhaled in a whoosh. "I really have to stop saying that, don't I? Everything sounds crazy lately. Anyway, I think the blood came from the water. In other words, the water turned."

She hadn't been kidding about it sounding crazy. "The water turned to blood, right there in front of me? You're shitting me, right?"

"I wish I were, but remember the bug Noddy was growling at last night? Both events could be symbolic of the Egyptian plagues."

I braced myself, pressing my feet hard to the floor, as Kate skidded around a corner. "I'm guessing that's not good."

"Water to blood is the first plague, but if that thing from my kitchen is really a locust, whatever's in control of the phenomena has skipped a few pages." The bug in question was along for the ride, blissfully unaware that its fate was in the hands of a woman with a death wish. "Which is good, because I'm in no rush to see frogs rain from the sky."

"Can't say it's on my bucket list either. What are the other plagues?"

"Oh, the usual. You know, boils and sores, animals dying, hail of fire, all that good stuff."

"Hail of fire? This is sounding biblical." I may have been sleeping in church when they covered this. It'd been my ideal place to catch up on some Z's as a young lad, which could be why I didn't remember any mention of Egyptian plagues.

"It is. It was God's way of saying 'Let my people go.' He was telling the Big Bad Pharaoh to release the Israelites from slavery."

Spirits were one thing. I still struggled to accept my new reality, where the dead could pop in any time to say hello. Or worse. But this, this was something else altogether. People who believed God spoke to them usually ended up in a nice padded cell. "Let me get this straight. Are you saying *God* is behind this?"

Kate laughed, and my body sagged with relief. *Whew.* Mom had already had a hard enough time understanding my new career. "Definitely not. That thing we saw in Lily's room yesterday had nothing to do with God."

"So why get biblical?"

"It's a warning. Spirits send bugs all the time. That's nothing new. You've probably heard of the fly swarms at the Amityville Horror house."

"I thought the Amityville Horror was a hoax."

She looked sideways at me. "That's what they want you to think."

I knew better than to ask who *they* were. "What about

the water into blood thing? I thought only Christ did that stuff."

"That was water into wine, but you're right that it's more sophisticated than anything your average ghost can pull off." She gritted her teeth as she took another hairpin turn. "And I suspect that's the point. Whatever this is, it's showing off, telling us it's not to be messed with. You notice that bad things only happen to Dennis when we're around. We're definitely being warned."

"Before everything went to hell today, Dennis told me he hasn't been feeling good for a while. Not since Bill died."

"Not feeling well is one thing. Turning into Anubis and spitting out teeth is another."

"Do you really think he was Anubis?" Something throbbed in the little torture chamber in my brain. This shit was going to give me a migraine if I wasn't careful. I massaged my temples, willing it away.

"Not for a second. Anubis is a mythological figure. We saw Anubis because he was the most terrifying thing an Egyptian ghost could think of. We were lucky it wasn't Sobek."

Remembering how I'd almost lost my shit when that snarling dog reared over me, slavering all over my face, I doubted anything could be worse. "Sobek?"

"God of the Nile with a crocodile's head. Rumored to have a nasty temper."

"Let's not give whatever it is more brilliant ideas. He could have spies." I nodded toward our captive, who was attempting to climb the walls of his jar for the millionth time. That guy never quit. Whoever wrote that fable about the grasshopper and the ant hadn't spent enough time around grasshoppers.

A particularly evil bolt of pain pierced my brain, making me flinch. I moaned under my breath.

"Headache?"

"The start of one, and it feels like it's going to be a bear. I hate to interrupt our regularly scheduled program, but can we stop for a quick bite? Low blood sugar could be the problem." Not to mention that whole water-into-blood thing, but I figured that went without saying.

"We're here." In the time I'd closed my eyes, begging my headache to return to the hell it came from, we'd reached our destination. "We can get something in the cafeteria before we see Eden."

"Where is 'here'?" But before she could respond, I figured it out. The place had a decidedly academic feel, courtesy of the people wandering about with books and backpacks.

"Welcome to the University of Greater Vermont, home to the world's best chicken fingers."

In spite of the throbbing in my brain, I raised an eyebrow. "That's a pretty bold claim."

"Go on, I dare you. See if I'm wrong." Walking around to my side of the car to let me out, Kate studied my face with concern. Her hand on my forehead was cool. Closing my eyes for a second, I leaned into it. "Are you okay? Not that you could ever look bad, but if you were anyone else, I'd say you looked like hell."

"Fitting. That's where my migraines come from."

"Do you want to go back to the house for some painkillers? I assume you brought some from Minneapolis?"

"I've got them with me." I patted the back pocket where I kept my wallet. "But I need water to take them, and food won't hurt either. Let's go, before this sucker gets any worse."

Linking her arm with mine, Kate led me to the front door. One of the awesome side effects of my migraines was that my eyes stopped working right, but from what I *could* see, the university was stunningly photogenic, with its ivy-covered brick and plethora of flower gardens. It had that buzz a place gets when it's filled with young people bursting with optimism and new ideas. Which was about the only thing I missed from my school days. Not that I'd been particularly optimistic *or* filled with new ideas. I'd mostly just wanted a job.

Stepping inside the university was like entering a different world: cool, dim, and quiet. The vise crushing my brain loosened a few turns, allowing me a proper breath. "This is so much better."

"We're here at a good time. It gets a lot busier at lunch. Let's go straight to the cafeteria. We can see Eden later."

"Sounds like a plan."

The cafeteria was louder, but not by much. Kate guided me to a table away from the window and pulled out a chair for me. I was touched by her kindness.

"Relax while I get us some food. What would you like?"

"Those chicken fingers sounded promising. Whatever you're having."

"Gravy?"

"You have to ask?"

Once she was gone, I removed the blister packs of meds from my wallet. Some people resented relying on medication, but I was inordinately grateful my doctor had finally found something that worked. There was no toughing out a migraine. Either you were laid up in a darkened room for seventy-two hours, or you found the right drugs. I glanced at our grasshopper friend, who was now a greenish blur. "How you doing, Cricket? Feeling hungry yet?"

After a quick Google search, Kate had filled his jar with grass and bits of different plants from her garden, but he wasn't interested. Maybe he was holding out for chicken fingers too.

Resting my head on my arms, I closed my eyes, breathing in tandem with my poor, throbbing brain. I'd drifted off by the time Kate set the trays down, nudging my arm. "You all right? We can go home, do this later."

"I'll be fine. This will help a lot. What do I owe you?" Picking up the glass of water she'd brought, I couldn't help but think of what had happened to Dennis's. Hopefully whatever was trying to communicate with us would feel one warning was enough. I washed the pills down with the lukewarm liquid, praying I wasn't too late. Once the migraine got a good enough foothold, even my miracle drug couldn't stop it.

"Are you kidding? Forget about it. I brought you this too." Kate withdrew a can of Coke from her coat. "I thought the caffeine might help. Always works for me when I have a headache."

"Can't hurt. Thanks, Kate."

"No problem."

It's nearly impossible to screw up chicken fingers, but these ones were particularly good, with a crisp, panko-like coating and a tasty seasoning. I squinted at some creamy, pale green stuff in a little paper cup. "What's that?"

"Honey-dill sauce. Apparently it's big in Canada, and I can see why. I'm totally addicted."

Though I normally stuck with ketchup, I was intrigued. Kate hadn't steered me wrong yet. The sauce was good. Sweet, and a little bit cloying, but somehow it worked. "I like it."

"I figure any country that invented poutine couldn't go wrong. How's the headache?"

"Better. I think I caught it in time, and the food really helps. And the Coke." My eyesight had cleared enough that I didn't feel I was going blind anymore, and I wasn't slurring my words like I did during the meanest migraines.

"Good. There's no real hurry, so relax and enjoy. Eden keeps long hours, and it's not even three yet. Now that we've left the hospital, I'm sure Dennis is safe. He's probably sleeping."

If there's no rush, why did you risk our lives on the drive over? Since I knew she was just trying to make me feel better about the unscheduled lunch stop, I left the question unasked. "Why don't we see the bug guy first?" After discovering the grasshopper, Kate had told me that she was buddies with an entomologist. Was there wasn't anyone she wasn't friends with? "I'm worried about the little dude. He doesn't seem to be eating."

"He doesn't, does he?" Kate watched as the grasshopper made his millionth escape attempt. "Okay, we can see if Ben's in, but he might have a class. You ready?"

I crumpled my napkin beside my half-empty plate. The worst of the pain had receded, but the impending doom of an oncoming migraine killed my enthusiasm for a lot of things, food included. "Yeah, let's do this."

She swiped a chicken finger from my plate and demolished it in two bites. "You *must* be sick," she said, and winked at me. "Okay, now we can go."

❦

My navigating isn't too shabby, but the place was a god-damn labyrinth. Kate didn't seem fazed as she led me up one hallway and set of stairs after another. Then again, she'd managed to find her way around Venice, and that ain't easy.

"Wow, they really don't want anyone to find this guy, do they?" I asked as she dragged me up yet another flight of stairs. These ones were cut at an odd angle.

"It's all the additions. It's an old building, and they've kept adding on to it over the years. It's become the academic equivalent of the Winchester House."

"That's where my next book was going to be set." I was embarrassed to realize I was losing my wind, but blamed it on the migraine meds. Still, might not hurt me to start moving my ass a little more. Less takeout food, more exercise.

"I've always wanted to go there. Imagine making contact with Sarah Winchester. It would be fascinating to talk to her." Kate continued to bound up the stairs as if she were a goddamn kangaroo. It would be annoying if she wasn't so cute.

"Do you think you could? That would be amazing."

"I'm not sure. I'd certainly try. But don't get too excited—I have a feeling your next book is going to be set in Egypt."

Egypt had been on my hit list since we'd done a unit on it in sixth grade geography, but after the revolution, I'd relegated it to the back burner. "Is it safe? I kind of figured we'd hash this out from here."

"We'll ask Eden. She'll know, but I assume it's okay.

They still get a lot of tourists."

I was turning this possibility over in my mind when she seized my hand. "Good news; we're on Ben's floor. Let's see if he's in."

Of course the guy's office was at the very end of the hallway. But the door was open, which was a promising sign. A square of yellow light illuminated the drab gray linoleum in front of the threshold. At least one thing was going to be in our favor today.

Kate tapped softly on the frame, motioning for me to come closer. "Ben? Are you free?"

Couldn't say what I'd been expecting a professor of entomology to look like, but it certainly wasn't this guy with his Spider-Man T-shirt and rumpled sandy hair. His face brightened when he saw Kate, but then he noticed our clasped hands. The pleased smile faltered, but it was back in place when he stood to greet us.

"For you, of course. It's always great to see you, Kate. And who's this?"

He sounded friendly enough, but I didn't like the way he was scoping me out.

"This is Jackson. He moved from Minneapolis to be my partner in crime. Jackson, this is Dr. Ben Delambre. He's become a good friend over the years."

Friend, my ass. This guy desperately wanted to find his way out of the friend zone or I'd eat my shorts. "Hey, Ben. Good to meet you." To the guy's credit, he didn't try to crush my fingers when he shook my hand.

The entomologist nodded. "Welcome to Nightridge. Must be quite a shock, leaving the big city for our one-horse town."

He might as well have come out and said, *You don't*

belong here, son. You're not one of us. "Actually, I'm liking the change. The traffic was beginning to get to me. And it's beautiful here. Like a postcard." *A hell of a lot better than Bill's.*

From the way his mouth curled into a smirk, I expected a snarky response, but then he sighed, running a hand through his hair. "Thanks, that's nice to hear. We see a fair number of tourists, of course, especially in the fall, but it's rare that anyone stays. We're desperate for some new blood. Things can get a little...incestuous around here."

Kate smacked his arm. "Ben! You make it sound like we're marrying our cousins."

"Have you seen my cousin? I should be so lucky."

If this guy could unbend a bit, so could I. I gestured at his shirt. "I appreciate the humor."

He checked his chest as if he'd forgotten what he was wearing. "Oh, ah, yes. Entomologists are the ugly ducklings of the science world. We're expected to be a little bit out there. Whenever I wear a suit, people ask me who died." His eyes lit on the jar Kate carried, and he leaned toward her. "This isn't merely a social call, then? You have something for me?"

"We do." Kate passed him the jar, and he rushed over to the window, leaving us no choice but to follow, which was easier said than done. To call Ben's office cluttered would have been kind. Various bug-collecting paraphernalia was scattered everywhere: butterfly nets, tons of those tiny versions you see at pet stores for tropical fish, specimen jars, glass cases. As we passed the cases, I tried not to notice the swarming, slithering occupants until one terrarium *hissed* at me.

"What the fuck?" I managed to catch myself before

tripping over a butterfly net and causing real damage.

"Madagascar hissing cockroaches," Ben said from his position at the window. "Contrary to their name, they don't often hiss. Something has them in a lather this afternoon."

Cockroaches? Memories of my first dorm room came flooding back, making me shudder. *Why on earth would anyone* willingly *keep those fuckers?* Forget the rich—*scientists* are different from you and me. "No problem," I said, trying to sound like a guy who hadn't just been scared by a bug. I could tell Kate was grinning at me, but I ignored her.

"Where on earth did you find this?" Ben rotated the jar in his hands while Cricket scampered on the glass like a hamster on a wheel. "The food is all wrong, by the way. No self-respecting locust would ever eat this stuff."

"So it *is* a locust, not a grasshopper? It was on my kitchen floor last night."

"All locusts are grasshoppers, but not all grasshoppers are locusts. A big part of what makes a locust a locust is swarming behavior, but they can be individualistic as well. I'd have to test its serotonin levels to be absolutely sure. Were there more of them, or just the one?"

"Just the one. Thankfully."

"Well, that's comforting, I suppose. Though this fella is out of season. Can I keep him here, or were you hoping he'd be a playmate for Nostradamus?"

So he knows about her cat. They're closer than I thought. I looked at Kate to see if this question was unusually personal, but she only smiled.

"Noddy has already met him. They don't exactly get along."

"I'm not surprised. Cats have a bad rep in the bug world, being the cause of so much death and destruction.

Can I keep him?"

"Sure. Let us know if you find anything interesting."

It wasn't clear if Ben heard her, as he was already scrambling to introduce Cricket to his new home. At least the poor bugger would get a decent lunch. He was probably starving at this point.

"Nice to meet you," Ben said over his shoulder. "I'm sure our paths will cross again."

"Nice to meet you too." I nudged Kate. "Can we go now?" The guy seemed nice enough, but his office gave me the creeps and the humidity from all the heat lamps made me sweat.

"One sec. Hey, Ben, is Eden around today?"

The entomologist froze, Cricket's jar in his hand. His eyes widened behind his wire-rimmed glasses. "Haven't you heard? Eden is missing."

Kate looked like she wasn't sure whether to laugh or cry. "What do you mean, she's missing? That isn't possible."

"I'm afraid it is. She disappeared about a week ago. No one's seen or heard from her since."

~ CHAPTER SIX ~

Kate

JACKSON JOLTED ME BACK TO REALITY. "ARE you okay?"

Before I could respond, he hurried to clarify. "I mean, it's obvious you're not. You've been sitting here in the dark, not saying anything, for over an hour. I guess what I'm really asking is if you want to talk about it."

Blinking, I let my living room swim into focus. There was enough light to see by, but the sun was going down. The furniture was already in shadow. "There's not much to talk about." Though of course there was. I just had no idea where to start.

"I'm sorry about Eden. Were you close?"

His sympathy made the tears flow. Memories of the Egyptologist, her dark hair pulled into its customary ponytail, her whip-smart brain, threatened to overwhelm me. "Not at first. At first, she thought I was crazy. But by the end, yes, I think we were."

Jacks walked over, toting Noddy. I'd purposely sat in the armchair so he wouldn't touch me. I didn't want to be comforted by anyone; I didn't want physical contact. When he settled the cat on my lap, Noddy immediately got comfortable, kneading his paws against my thighs and purring. My tears fell on his ebony fur.

"When was the last time you saw her?"

"A little over a week ago." I remembered it well. It had been an extremely productive session, the best one we'd had yet. Then I thought about what Ben had told me and it felt like ice water trickled over my spine. "My God, I must have seen her right before she went missing. What if I was the last person she talked to?" *What if our project caused this? What have I done?* Envisioning the scientist with the pale, serious face, I tried desperately to pull her to me.

Nothing.

At least she wasn't dead. Or, if she was, she was somewhere I couldn't reach.

Jackson knelt in front of me. "If that's true, you should probably talk to the police. I'm sure they'll want a statement from you."

"I can't do that. She didn't want anyone to know what we were working on. She was adamant about it. If I go to the police, it'll come out. And they won't believe me anyway. They never do."

They believe Laura, a voice in my brain whispered, and it was true. Laura had been consulted a few times in missing-persons cases, but always under a veil of secrecy. God forbid anyone knew law enforcement was willing to do whatever it took to bring people home. *Laura.* Wherever Eden was, Laura would find her.

I leapt to my feet, sending a disgruntled Noddy hurtling into Jackson's lap. "I have to get Laura."

"I thought she was already coming over." Jackson's hands smoothed Noddy's fur as he did his best to soothe my cat.

"It's not soon enough. I need her *now*."

(

Laura's hand was raised to knock when I opened the door and pulled her inside. "What's going on? I thought we were—" As my fingers closed around her wrist, the confusion in her eyes cleared. "Ooh, something's happened to Eden. Why didn't you tell me on the phone?"

"I haven't been thinking straight. I've been messed up ever since we talked to Ben." Laura didn't know Ben, but as I still had my hand touching her skin, explanations wouldn't be necessary. One of the benefits of having a gifted psychic for a friend is it eliminated the need for small talk.

"Hi, Jackson." Laura disentangled herself from me so she could give my new partner a hug. She had to stand on her tiptoes to do so, the beads in her braids clicking. "It's great to see you again."

"It's great to see you too. I'm glad you're here." You didn't have to be a psychic to see how relieved he was. It was written all over his face. I must have really freaked him out. Poor Jackson. He hadn't known what he was getting into when he signed up for this.

"Of course I'm here. Kate and I have been best buddies for years. I heard her call for help clear across town long before she phoned." In the guise of comforting me, she whispered in my ear. "Would you stop worrying? That man is madly in love with you."

In spite of everything, I couldn't help but smile. My friend made herself comfortable, taking the cushions off the couch and arranging them on the floor. Rubbing her hands, she looked at both of us with bright, expectant eyes. "Okay, what's first? Eden's disappearance? Lily's uncle and whatever lovely thing he brought back with him from Egypt? Or opening a doorway in Jackson's mind?"

"I think we're going to need a lot more than a doorway." Jackson glanced at me. "We better figure out what happened to Eden first."

"Agreed. Kate, do you have anything of hers?" Turning her attention to Jackson again, Laura said, "I don't need it, but it makes it a lot easier."

Thinking over my meetings with the Egyptologist, I racked my brain for anything that might be able to help. "I'm sorry. I have some papers she wrote, but they're all electronic. Nothing she's touched."

"That's okay; it doesn't matter. *You* know her, at least a bit. Come sit with me."

Eyeing Jackson, I wondered what he was going to think of all this. If he thought what I did was odd, Laura's abilities would send him over the edge. My friend waved off my fears before I could express them. "Don't worry about him. It'll be his turn soon enough."

Jacks stood awkwardly in the middle of my living room. "What should I do? Do you want me to leave?"

"No, honey, you sit next to me too." Laura patted a teal cushion on her left side. "Just be careful not to touch me. Right now, I need to focus on Kate."

As Jackson lowered himself to the floor beside us, I felt overwhelmed with gratitude that he was so willing to go along with whatever I asked, even things that must have seemed bizarre or crazy to him. He used to be a lot more resistant. Was it seeing the thing in Dennis's hospital room that had changed him? Or something else?

Now wasn't the time to ponder Jackson's path to enlightenment, though. Laura reached for my hands, and I closed my eyes, picturing Eden and the last time we'd worked together. Her hair had been in a messy ponytail, as always, and she'd had a drafting pencil tucked behind an ear. She wore her lab coat and jeans, and there were the usual dark shadows under her eyes. Had she seemed more harried than usual?

"Hmm...this woman is strong. Smart. I like her," Laura murmured.

Smart was putting it mildly. Eden had so many degrees they'd covered her office like wallpaper. But, unlike most of the academics I'd met, she was people smart too. Once she'd decided you were worth her time, she could be incredibly charismatic.

"She's with a young woman."

"You see her?" I asked stupidly, before I could think better of it. My fingers tightened around Laura's. For some reason, even though I hadn't been able to reach her, some part of me had been convinced Eden was dead. There was a sense of irretrievable loss whenever I thought of her, a deep sadness that weighed on my shoulders until I was so exhausted I wanted nothing more than to curl into a ball and weep.

"Sorry, a young man. The makeup threw me. He's got some kind of fabric wrapped around his waist, but his chest is bare. He's smiling at her. She cares about this man, and she's afraid for him." Laura clicked her tongue. "He's so familiar to me. I've seen this guy somewhere before."

"Can you get his name?"

There was a long moment of silence while my friend's energy flowed over me in waves. I wondered if Jackson could feel it too. Sometimes it gave me the sensation of floating.

"It's not coming through. It's a long name, though, and it's definitely not English."

"But he's wearing makeup?"

"Yes, his eyes are lined. It appears to be a costume of some kind."

This didn't make any sense. Eden was one of the most conscientious people I'd ever met. She was dedicated to her students. Why would she have taken off to be with a young man? "How young are we talking?"

"Hmm…hard to say. Eighteen? Nineteen? I don't get the sense they're romantically involved. Her feelings toward him are motherly more than anything. He's a kid."

Whew. "Can you get anything else? Anything that will help us find her?"

Laura's hands vibrated in mine. Wherever Eden was, it wasn't easy to access. "It's…really difficult to make anything out. Wherever she is, it's morning, but it's still dark. It's like they're in a cave. I can see artwork on the walls, but it's too blurry. Just a lot of bright colors. Crimson, turquoise, yellow."

"But she's definitely alive?" Jackson asked.

I'd expected Laura to answer immediately, but instead I heard her breath catch in her throat. "Yes and no."

"She's not in the spirit realm." I realized my voice was rising, but I couldn't help it. "I would have been able to see her."

"No, but she's not in this realm, either. She's not anywhere the police will be able to find her. Her heart is beating, she appears healthy, but she's beyond our grasp."

My mind spun out of control. I couldn't comprehend

what she was saying. Alive, but not here. *Oh Eden, where are you? What happened to you?* For once, talking to Laura hadn't helped. I was more confused than before.

"Is she hurt?"

In spite of my growing panic, I was touched by the concern in Jackson's voice. He'd never met Eden, but he cared about her. And he'd asked the question I hadn't dared.

"No, not hurt, but…"

I tugged gently on Laura's hands. "What is it? What's wrong with her?"

"She's terrified. She's trying her best to hide it, but it emanates from her. Something has scared her half to death. She feels trapped. She wants to come home, but for some reason, she's not able to."

"Has she been kidnapped?"

It was a logical question for any mainstreamer to ask, but I could have told Jackson that wasn't the case even before Laura answered. This was far beyond the realm of a normal abduction. Whatever Eden had stumbled into, it might be too much for Laura or me to help her with.

"No, but whatever this is that's scaring her, it's very dark. And sadly, I feel it's connected to what's happening to Lily's father."

"Is it an entity of some sort?" My voice trembled, betraying my own terror. Had I inadvertently summoned something that was attacking anyone I came in contact with? First Lily's family, and now Eden? *Was this my fault?*

My eyes were still closed, but I could tell Laura was shaking her head by the sound of the beads in her braids. "No, it's more powerful than that. A lot more powerful."

"She's alive, though. That's good, right? That means we can help her."

Trust Jackson to look on the bright side. I wrestled with the implications of Laura's words. A lot more powerful than an entity? My God, what were we dealing with?

"Maybe, but we're a bit too late to help her friend."

I was shaken out of my morbid thoughts. "What are you saying, Laura?"

"I'm saying the young man she's talking to is dead."

~ CHAPTER SEVEN ~

Kate

LAURA STARED AT THE CEILING, HER LIPS PARTED. Her chest hitched with every breath. Jackson pressed a cool, damp cloth into my hands, which I draped across my friend's forehead. Her skin was clammy to the touch.

"Are you sure we shouldn't take her to the hospital? She seems really sick," Jackson said.

"She's okay. Spending that long with Eden took everything out of her. She needs some time to regain her energy, that's all." He looked so worried I wanted to hug him, but settled for squeezing his hand. "Please trust me. If there were something actually wrong with her, she'd already be in an emergency room. I've seen this before."

That was both true and not true. I'd seen Laura drained before, but never quite like this. She was nearly catatonic. "I'm sorry, Jacks. I know you had your heart set on it, but I'm not sure she'll recover her energy enough to help you tonight."

"That's okay." He ran a hand over his head. "After what I've seen today, I think I'm fine with my doorways staying the hell shut."

"Can't say I didn't warn you."

"You did, and I saw what you went through in China and Italy. I get that. I just—I want to help."

This time, I did hug him. Pressing my head to his chest, I could hear the comforting rhythm of his heart. "You do help. You *are* helping. I don't think you have any idea what it means for me not to have to go through this stuff alone anymore. Thank you."

"You're welcome," he said, his voice gruff, as if his throat were sore. "Well, I guess we should get to work, huh?"

My brain spinning from everything that had happened in the last few hours, I pulled away enough to get a glimpse of his face. He was as serious as I'd ever seen him. "Work?"

"Dennis told us to check out the last postcards his brother sent; he said they were different. Laura may be out of commission, but at least we can do that ourselves. We obviously missed something."

In my anxiety over Eden's disappearance, I'd temporarily forgotten about Lily's father and his weird choking fit at the hospital earlier that day. And now that we knew Dennis's illness and his brother's death were somehow connected to what had happened to Eden, it was even more important for us to figure out how they were related.

Dread loomed over me at the thought of contacting Bill. Though I was sure he'd been a nice enough guy in life, whatever had glommed on to his spirit was darker than anything I'd encountered before. I wasn't sure I was up to it, and what if it manifested here? What if it attacked Laura while she was in her weakened state? I checked my friend, grateful to see her eyes were closed now. She was breathing deeply, and appeared to have fallen into an ordinary sleep with Noddy curled on her lap. When she woke up, she'd have more energy than a carload of marmosets on a sugar rush. I only hoped Jackson would be able to handle it.

Before I could confess my fears, he'd left to get the box of postcards. Seeing the battered shoebox in his hands, I cringed as a series of cramps twisted my stomach.

"What's wrong? You look like you're about to throw up." He set the box on a chair and touched my arm. "Is it Eden?"

Fighting back the foul-tasting bile that had flooded my mouth, I didn't trust myself to speak. I ran to the bathroom, where I spat the mess into the sink. As the cramping increased, I knelt before the toilet. My stomach heaved and I retched, but nothing came. Exhausted, my forehead beaded with sweat, I closed the lid and rested my head on it.

There was a soft tap on the door. "Kate, are you all right? Can I come in?"

It wasn't my finest hour. My hair was plastered to my scalp with sweat, and I was sure I looked like shit. But once Jackson had moved in, the illusion of forever presenting myself in the best possible light had gone out the window. He'd seen me first thing in the morning, and now he was going to see me sick and wretched.

"Sure," was the most I could manage.

He eyes widened when he saw me crumpled beside the toilet. "What's going on? Are you sick?"

It was a cramped space, but somehow he found room to sit next to me on the floor. He stroked the damp hair off my forehead, and I closed my eyes. It was so wonderful to be touched, to know for certain that another person cares about you. "Honestly? I'm scared to death. I think this is my body's way of sending me a warning."

"Should we stop? Do you want to go through the cards another day?"

I could hear it in his voice—he didn't *want* to stop. He was super protective of Lily, and until we figured out what was going on with her father, no one in that family was safe. Jackson's stubbornness was one of the things that made him attractive; it was a trait we shared. Couldn't fault him for it now. "No, we can't waste any time, especially after what Laura told us. I need to give my stomach a minute to calm down, and then I'll come out. Okay?"

"Why don't we look at them in here?"

"In the bathroom?" I smiled in spite of the nausea. I'd worked in some strange places before, but never crouched beside a toilet.

"Why not? That way, if you feel sick again, you're already here."

Jackson's seeing me with a sweaty face or stringy hair was one thing. I was *not* about to let him watch me vomit. "I'm not going to throw up in front of you."

"Hey, if you so much as start to lift that lid, I'll be out of here like a shot. I promise." His hand was smooth against my cheek. "Kate, you've done the same for me. Let me be here for you."

Even though the immediate need to empty my stomach was gone, I didn't feel confident enough—or strong enough—to leave the toilet just yet. Jackson's solution, as bizarre as it was, made sense. "Okay, but you *promise* you'll leave?"

Placing one hand over his heart, he held up the other in a Scout's-honor sign. "You have my word."

"Okay. Bring them here."

As he left the room to retrieve the box, I prayed Laura wouldn't wake up and catch us huddled around the toilet. Some things you just don't want to have to explain.

"I've started sorting them by postmark." Jackson handed me a stack of the cards, which looked more faded than I remembered, as if they had aged overnight. "That way, we don't have to guess which ones Bill sent last."

"Good idea." Leaning against the bathtub, I forced myself to focus on the blurry dates. Some were impossible to make out, and I laid those aside to examine later. Soon we'd separated the most recent cards from the oldest. Feeling lightheaded, I rested while Jackson flipped through them.

"I don't get it."

"What?" I'd hoped he would be able to figure this one out on his own. The more time that passed, the more my energy flagged. I'd have liked nothing better than to crawl to my bed.

"There's nothing different about these. Aside from that one where he talks about visiting the Temple of Waset and feeling sick afterward, there's nothing out of the ordinary. The usual chitchat about how wonderful Egypt is and how generous the people are, et cetera." He tossed the cards back in the shoebox with an exasperated sigh. "Damn it. I was hoping to avoid another visit with Dennis. Did I mention I don't like the guy? Because I really don't like that guy."

"You didn't have to mention it. It's obvious." Gathering the cards that were piled beside me on the floor, I handed them to Jackson. "Maybe he meant these ones."

"What are these?"

"They were at the bottom of the ones you gave me."

My words were mumbled, slurred, like I was talking around an ice cube, but I couldn't help it. My eyelids drooped, heavier and heavier. *Sleep…would be so nice to go to sleeeeep.*

"Kate!" Jacks shook me. "Snap out of it. I think these are the ones he was talking about. They have to be."

Rubbing my eyes, I examined the postcards he shoved into my hands. At first it was like trying to read through gauze, but at last the writing swam into focus.

Dear brother,

Egypt is a remarkable place. So remarkable that I've decided to extend my visit. Would be great if the family could join me here. Lily will really love all the history, especially the great temples and tombs. I'll gladly pay for your tickets—all you need to do is take the time off. Let's make it happen.

All my love,

Bill

I read it over several times, not understanding what Jackson wanted me to see. What was I missing?

"I'm sorry," I said, handing the card back to him. "I'm not getting anything. It seems normal to me, albeit extremely generous." *Wish I had a brother who would send me to Egypt.* Ha! Talk about fantasies. The closest my brothers had come to Egypt was watching reruns of *The Mummy Returns*, and that's the way they liked it.

"Read the next one." Rather than sound disappointed, he evidently still had faith I'd pick up on whatever he'd discovered. Trying not to seem as beleaguered as I felt, I studied the next card, which featured the Great Pyramid of Giza. This time Bill had crammed so much text into the writing space that the message was continued under the side usually reserved for the address.

Dear brother,

Did you receive my last message? I'm feeling quite at home here, but it's not the same without my beautiful family. Please come. You've been due for a vacation for a long time, and this is the thing Lily needs to snap out of her funk. Maybe she could even stay with me for a while.

I understand you still have some concerns, but I assure you, Egypt is quite safe. I've been here for ages and have never had a problem. I'll send you the tickets as soon as you say the word. Please respond.

All my love,

Bill

Hmm…okay, that part about wanting Lily to stay behind with him was a little over the top. Is that what had bothered Jackson?

"Did you see it?" There was that light in his eyes again. It was the same light he got when his writing was going well.

"Are you talking about the creepy uncle thing? 'Leave your daughter with me—I'll show her a great time'?"

"Nah. It sounds a bit off, especially in this day and age, but maybe Bill and Lily were close. And we know Lily has issues. I could see a caring uncle thinking a change of scenery might help."

The competitive streak in me took over, and I looked harder at the two cards, but to my frustration, everything was pretty much the same. No discernable difference in the handwriting, tone, or message. "I give up. He sounds a bit desperate, but he was probably lonely, especially if he'd been there a while. What am I missing?"

"I missed it too, the first time. When we had the cards out of order, these ones blended right in. They didn't jump out at me at all. Whatever we're dealing with is sharp as hell." Taking the postcards from me, he laid out the last two on the toilet seat, along with the one Bill had sent about feeling sick after visiting the Temple of Waset. He touched each card with an index finger as he talked. "In this one, Bill feels like shit. He's tired of Egypt, wants to come home. But look at the postmark on this second one. Two days after he talked about leaving, he's saying he plans to stay indefinitely?"

Picking up one of the cards again, I noticed other differences. "He never used a salutation before, but in the last ones he starts with, 'Dear brother,' almost as if he doesn't know Dennis's name."

"I know, right? It's too formal. Same with the 'All my love, Bill' stuff—it's only used on the last two cards. I checked."

That horrible feeling of creeping dread returned, along with the foul taste in my mouth. "I think you're onto something, Jacks."

"It was the fixation on Lily that caught my eye. Why doesn't he mention Garrett? Why only Lily? I get that she's the one who's struggling, but he doesn't focus on her in any of the other cards—just these two."

The dread intensified as the skin on my arms puckered into gooseflesh. "Lily is the one with The Gift. As far as I know, it's passed down through the women in their family."

"It really seems like someone was trying to lure her to Egypt. Do you think Bill wrote these?"

Wishing fervently that Laura were awake, I examined the cards again. "The writing looks the same to me, but that doesn't mean he wasn't being controlled by someone...or *something.*"

"You mean possessed?"

I'd be willing to bet Jacks was picturing Linda Blair's head spinning around while pea soup spewed from her mouth.

"Not in the way you're thinking. That doesn't happen."

"What about Abbandonato? He pulled it off pretty well," he said, referring to the doctor who'd dragged Lily's soul to Poveglia, the world's most haunted island. Basically, the reason we were involved in this mess in the first place.

"Yes, but Lily had to be willing, remember? Spirits can't take over any old body they want, whenever it suits them."

"Maybe spirits can't, but what about demons?"

I sighed. I knew he'd been thinking about *The Exorcist*. Damn that movie. "Religious mythology. They don't exist. Hey, don't look at me like that. I was raised Catholic, re-member, but trust me. Demons are biblical boogeymen. If there were any truth to them, I'd know."

Jackson leaned against the bathroom vanity, lapsing into silence. No doubt he was thinking about his own Baptist childhood. It's difficult not to fall back on a belief system that's been hardwired into you.

Finally, he spoke.

"The plagues of Egypt *are* biblical, Kate. You said so last night. Shouldn't we at least consider that this is too?"

"I don't think God is turning Dennis's water into blood or sending a locust to my house. The plagues may be biblical, but there's another explanation for what's hap-pening here."

"I'd love to hear it. What, then? Ghosts?"

"It would be unusual, but not necessarily impossible. Some spirits can exert tremendous control over the physical realm. My scars are testament to that." I lifted my chin to display the white ring that wound round my throat like a necklace.

Jackson averted his gaze. He'd never been comfortable with the more...*physical* part of my job. "I get that. As much as I can. And I'd never presume to tell you anything about ghosts, or the spirit world—"

Why do men always say they're not going to force their opinions on you right before they do? Not having the patience for it, I cut him off. "Thank you."

He wasn't deterred, of course. "But you admitted that thing in Lily's hospital room wasn't a ghost."

Ah, so now we were getting down to it. I'd wondered when Jackson would get around to asking me about that nightmare brought to life. I'd assumed he needed time to process it. Hell, *I* needed time to process it, and I'd been dealing with the supernatural since I was a child. Only a year ago, Jackson hadn't believed in ghosts, let alone any of the other stuff he'd experienced since we'd met.

Seeing the open skepticism on his face, I conceded defeat. "Okay, okay, maybe it's not your average, everyday Aunt Martha kind of ghost, but some spirits are capable of projecting an image much more terrifying than their own."

"It turned Dennis into a monster, Kate."

"It's extremely powerful. I'm not denying that." I didn't like where this conversation was going. At all. Of course we needed to have it—Jackson was a full partner now, and that meant he was entitled to the truth. But I'd been avoiding even thinking about it much, and for very good reason. What if I wasn't strong enough to handle whatever this was? Sure, my best friend was a formidable psychic, and Jackson would do whatever he could to help. But what if it wasn't enough? What would happen to Lily and her family then?

"What would make Bill that powerful after death? Do you think he has The Gift, like Lily?"

"This isn't Bill. It's something that's attached itself to Bill. *Attached*, not possessed," I insisted when Jackson opened his mouth. "There's a difference. Bill's spirit still exists as Bill—it's just harder to get to. Imagine you're trying to talk to a shy girl at a party, but her mouthy friend keeps pushing in front and cutting her off. It's like that."

"Hey, I never *try* to talk to girls at parties. They come to me." He stuck his tongue out at me in an attempt to be playful, but his smile never reached his eyes. Still, I was grateful to him for at least trying to lighten the mood. The atmosphere in this bathroom was getting damn heavy.

"Consider yourself lucky I'm too nauseous to make you pay for that remark, you conceited ass."

"Jealous?"

"Of you, you misogynistic pig? Hardly."

Jackson clutched his chest and slid to the floor. "You wound me, woman."

"I'm going to do a lot more than wound you in a minute."

"Promises, promises."

Just when I believed I could relax my guard, he asked me the mother of all questions. "So, this thing that's attached itself to Bill...if it's a spirit, who is it? Or who *was* it?"

"I don't know. I haven't...haven't been able to figure that out yet."

"Well, at least there's an easy way to find out."

"What are you talking about? What easy way?"

Jackson shrugged. "Ask Bill. Bill's got to know."

Closing my eyes, I took a deep breath. "Jacks, if I reach

out to Bill, there's a good chance he'll bring that…other thing with him."

"I guess that's a risk we'll have to take. What other choice do we have?"

Before I could answer, there was a loud thump from the other room, followed by an ear-shattering scream.

~ CHAPTER EIGHT ~

Jackson

LAURA'S FACE WAS SO CONTORTED BY TERROR that she looked like a different person. As I burst into the living room, she was staring at something on her lap, her shrill shrieks blistering my brain. Scared though I was, I was grateful to see she was still alive. From the sounds of it, I'd thought an ax murderer had broken into the house.

"Laura, it's okay." Realizing she couldn't hear me over her own screams, I moved closer, putting a hand on her shoulder. She stared up at me with wild eyes, but she stopping yelling instantly.

"Help me," she whispered.

Fear prickled the back of my neck, and the last thing I wanted was to see what had frightened her so badly. The urge to run, to grab my shit and flee to Minneapolis was strong, strong enough that I didn't think it was only coming from me. Something didn't want me here. Knowing that gave me the courage to look.

Revulsion swirled in my gut when I saw the thing on the afghan. It resembled a greenish-brown piece of rubber. A *slimy* greenish-brown piece of rubber. "What the fuck?" Bending to get a closer look, I saw it had once been a frog.

Equal parts annoyance and relief swept over me. *This* is what Laura had been losing her shit over? A tiny frog, and a dead one, at that?

Before I could speak, her hand clamped around my wrist. She shook her head, beads clicking, and opened her mouth as if to speak, though no words escaped.

"Laura? What is it? What's wrong? It's just a frog. It can't hurt you."

Thump. Thump thump THUMP!

"What the fuck is that? Kate?"

But Kate was already there, pushing past me to open the blinds. As soon as the window was exposed, something slammed into the glass right in front of her face. "Oh my God. It's happening. It's actually happening."

The three of us stared in horror as frog after frog hit her window with such force I was terrified it would shatter. Kate's garden and driveway were filled with glistening, hopping creatures. I stood paralyzed, watching amphibians fall from the sky like croaking pieces of hail. This couldn't be happening. It had to be some weird mass hallucination.

Something brushed against my ankle and I flinched, only to see large blue eyes staring at me. Noddy cowered against my legs. I picked up the cat and cradled him, but as soon as another frog struck the window, he leapt out of my arms with a yowl and ran down the hallway.

"He's scared," Kate said.

"Well, that makes all of us. What the fuck are we going to do?"

She turned away from the window. "Please shut the blinds. I can't stand to see any more."

At least that was simple enough. While I yanked them closed, Kate sat on the floor beside the couch and held out her hands to Laura. "Let's fix it."

Pale, her blue eyes as guileless as a child's, the psychic slipped her hands into Kate's. Both women bowed their heads as if praying, leaning toward each other. Almost immediately, the skin on the back of my neck and arms tingled. I couldn't see anything, but I could feel it. My stomach dropped as if I were on a roller coaster. Backing away from them, I winced at the intensified pounding on the house's roof and walls, hoping the ceiling wouldn't cave in.

Thump-thump-THUMP! Thumpthumpthumpthumpthu mpthumpthumpthumpthumpthumpthumpthumpthumpthumpth umpthumpthumpthumpthumpthumpthumpthumpthumpthumpt humpthump.

Then, as suddenly as it had begun, the noise stopped.

I'd been driven back as far as I could go while remaining in the same room. Kate and Laura slowly pulled away from one another, keeping their fingers entwined. Kate's hair stood out from her head like a cloud of fire, and whatever wisps had escaped Laura's braids were sticking straight up.

"You've gotten stronger," she said. "I didn't think that was possible."

"I'll take that as a compliment, coming from you."

Okay, enough was enough. "I hate to interrupt this love fest, but will someone please tell me what the hell is going on?"

Kate laughed at my exasperated outburst, but kindly. Laura still looked too shaken to see the humor in anything. "Sorry, Jacks. That must have seemed really strange to you."

"Nah, what's strange about two chicks creating a force

field that stops frogs raining from the sky? Seen it a million times."

"Oh, Jackson." I was happy to see the fear had vanished from Laura's face. She was paler than normal, but her smile was genuine. "Have I mentioned how glad I am you moved here?"

"I think so, but I'm happy to hear it again." Crouching beside Kate on the floor, I reached out to smooth her hair and got the shock of a lifetime. A bolt of static electricity shot through my hand. "Ouch!"

"Oh God, I'm so sorry. Are you okay?" Kate patted my hand and I recoiled, but whatever power had coursed through her was gone. I felt the slightest tingle move up my arm and then dissipate. "I should have warned you."

"I'm fine." Embarrassed, sure, but I'd live. "That's one hell of a party trick. You girls would make a killing on YouTube."

"Maybe we should consider that. It would be a lot easier on the heart." Laura leaned back on the cushions. "Whew. I am all in, Kate."

"I know. Me too." She returned her attention to me. "It wasn't a force field, though I can see why you might think that." Now that she wasn't holding on to Laura, Kate's hair was lowering back to her shoulders. She was almost normal again. Or at least what counted as normal with Kate.

"What was it, then?"

"That phenomenon was created by negative energy. We needed to generate enough positive energy to override it."

"Phenomenon? That's what you call it when frogs fall from the fucking *sky*?"

"If you'd left this house during the commotion, you'd

have seen it was an extremely focused frog rain. I'm willing to bet no one else in Nightridge noticed anything the slightest bit unusual."

Before I could argue, Laura laid her hand over mine. "It's true, Jackson. I know it seemed real—it did to me too. Remember the dead frog on the blanket?"

"Yeah." Thinking I should toss the poor, shriveled thing before it started to stink, I looked over to where I'd last seen it. "Where is it? I'll throw it out."

"It didn't exist. That's what we're trying to tell you."

"Nah. No, I *saw* that thing. It was real." It wasn't that I thought they were lying. I knew Kate would never lie to me. It was more that I couldn't get my mind around it. I'd seen the glistening, rubbery skin, its glazed eyes, the way its little mouth was parted and its tongue was partly visible. It was as real as any frog I'd ever encountered, save for the fact it was dead.

The women didn't try to convince me. They just waited me out. They'd no doubt dealt with jerks like me before. What must it be like to have no one believe you? To have people argue with everything you say? It had to get exhausting after a while.

"It does get tiring," Laura said, even though I hadn't said a word. "But we're used to it. Right, Kate?"

"Used to what? The frog rain was a first for me."

"Used to people not believing us."

"Oh, that. Yes, sadly. Comes with the territory. But Jackson believes us—he needs some time is all."

Making a show out of shaking my head as if to reset it, I said, "Okay. I get it. The frogs weren't real. So what exactly are we dealing with here?"

"Before we get into that, I need to ask how much you

guys care about this family."

"A lot. Why?" There was something about the way Laura wouldn't meet my eyes that bothered me. "You're not going to tell us they're not worth it, are you?"

"Calm down, Jacks. Some clients can't be helped, and she doesn't know how much Lily means to you," Kate said.

I doubted that, since she'd already proven she could help herself to my thoughts whenever she felt like it. Realizing Laura probably also knew how I felt about Kate, a warmth crept into my cheeks. I cleared my throat. "What do you mean, some clients can't be helped?"

"While it's great you care about the girl, and I understand from Kate she is extraordinary, my main concern is, and will always be, my friend. I don't want her to risk her life for a client. There are limits."

But that's what Kate does. That's what Kate had always done since I'd met her, and it had never occurred to me that it was a choice, or—if so—to question whether or not it was a fair choice. Should Kate keep risking everything for others? I remembered the way Lily had trembled in my arms when I'd rushed her out of the hospital room with that thing on our heels. If we turned our backs on the Walkins family, what would happen to her? We might as well have left her soul in Poveglia with that damned doctor.

"I'll be okay, Lore."

"I think it's time you told him what we're dealing with here. He deserves to know, Kate."

My temper bristled at the suggestion I'd been deliberately kept in the dark. No one likes being the last to know, least of all me. "Yes, please enlighten me. I'd *love* to know what we're dealing with."

"It's a demon," Laura said, in the same matter-of-fact

way other people would announce what they're having for dinner.

"Laura!"

"What would you call it?"

"Not that. You know I don't believe in that stuff." Kate folded her arms across her chest. "There are no such thing as demons."

"It's not a spirit. This thing isn't, and never was, human."

Seeing my opportunity, I jumped in. "How do you know? What's so different about…whatever this is?"

"You're a perceptive guy. You know this isn't an ordinary haunting as much as Kate and I do."

I wasn't so sure. I'd seen some pretty freaky shit over the past year. If spirits were capable of causing physical harm and even killing people, what was a little fake-frog rain? "So, if it isn't a demon, what is it?" I directed my question to Kate, since she was the one in the anti-demon camp.

"It's an entity of some sort, an extremely powerful one."

Laura snorted. "Talk about the understatement of the year."

Kate glanced at me, her discomfort clear. "Whatever it is, it seems to be getting stronger, which worries me."

Stronger than the thing that nearly killed us in the hospital, blew the door to smithereens, and turned water into blood? Grrrreat.

"Have you tried to contact the brother?" Laura asked.

"No, not yet. I've been afraid of what he might bring with him."

"Understandable." Laura clicked her tongue against the roof of her mouth. "I think that was a wise decision. I'd better see those postcards now."

Still feeling like they were speaking a different language, I retrieved the shoebox of cards from the bathroom.

"Thanks, Jacks." Laura smiled when I handed her the box, but then caught my hand before I could walk away. "Please be patient with us. I know it's frustrating when it sounds like we're talking gibberish, but it won't always be like this. You have an open mind, you're willing to learn, and that's all you need. Think of this as the growing pains a person experiences when starting any new job."

Giving my hand a squeeze, she let me go, but her empathy had done its work. "I just wish there was something more I could do. I feel useless."

"Don't worry. There's soon going to be plenty for you to do, so much so you'll look back on this day with wistfulness."

Closing her eyes, Laura laid her hand on the cards. Kate beckoned me to a chair, and I sat beside her, trying my best to be patient while the psychic did her thing. Mom and Roxi had always teased me about my lack of patience. I pictured them laughing at my current situation, telling me it was for my own good.

As the minutes clicked on interminably, the excitement of the day caught up to me. I rested my head against the back of the chair, my eyelids closing against my will.

Dennis lumbered toward me, spitting blood. I held his daughter in my arms, and even though she was thin and frail, my upper body shook with the effort of keeping her safe. I wasn't sure how much longer I'd be able to hold her. Lily pressed her face into my chest, unwilling to see the monster her father had become, but I forced myself to meet his red-rimmed eyes. This time I wouldn't look away.

The tomb...the tomb...you'll find it in the tomb, the thing that was Dennis whispered, baring what was left of his teeth.

"Find what?" I asked, and my voice had a strange echo, as if I were in a cavern instead of a hospital room.

"Let's go, Jackson," Lily begged, whimpering against my neck. "Please just go. Don't listen to him. It's a trick, a bad trick. He wants to hurt you."

The answer is in the tomb. Go there, and you will find what you seek.

"Jacks? Jackson?"

I didn't want to leave, not before I figured out what that abomination meant. He was telling me the truth this time. I could feel it, no matter what Lily said. The hand on my shoulder became more insistent, shaking me until my head lolled forward. My eyes snapped open, and I glared at Kate, who drew back at my unexpressed anger. Thankfully, I managed to bite my tongue before saying something I'd regret.

"What's wrong?"

Again, I had to stifle my urge to snap at her. What was my problem? I must be overtired. "Nothing."

"Sorry to wake you, but Laura's ready to tell us what she knows. I thought you'd want to hear it."

Who's Laura? It took me a second to remember the blonde psychic, who was studying my face a little too closely for my liking. The irritation I'd felt when Kate first woke me stirred and continued to build.

"What's poking at you, Jacks?" she asked, and I was instantly ashamed of my hateful thoughts. I liked Laura. I liked Kate. Damn, I was well on the way to *loving* Kate. What the fuck was wrong with me?

"Nothing. I'm tired, is all. Think I'm finally losing steam."

Her scrutinizing gaze didn't waver, and I was careful to keep my mind blank.

"Are you sure?"

"Yeah, of course I'm sure." I ran my hand over my scalp, stretching my neck as an excuse to avoid that unnerving stare of hers. "Sorry if I was pissy. Like I said, I'm tired."

"Okay, but if you have any strange dreams that are unusually realistic, let us know. It could mean something is trying to get at Kate through you."

What a crock of shit, the vile new voice in my brain piped up, and Laura's head drew back slightly, a look of shock upon her face. She was still digging around in my thoughts, then. My fingers tightened into fists. *I'll show that bitch what happens to people who mess where they don't belong.*

I shook my head to clear it, jamming my palms into my eyes. What was wrong with me? I'd never hit a woman in my life, and I wasn't about to start now.

"Jackson? What's going on with you? It's okay to tell us. We can help."

Looking at Laura's kind, open face, I realized I had to be honest, even though that awful voice screamed at me to keep my big, stupid mouth shut. "I don't know. I was having a dream about that moment in the hospital when Dennis went crazy. Only this time he was trying to tell me something."

"What did he tell you?"

None of your business, you whore. "I can't quite remember." I raised my voice, almost yelling now. Kate grimaced, but it was the only way to keep the other voice—the ugly one—quiet. "Something about a tomb, and finding the answer there."

Laura tilted her head to the side. "Interesting. Anything else?"

"No, that was all he said. All I can remember, anyway."

"Anything strike you as strange about the dream, Jacks?"

"No…" I looked away, struggling against the part of myself that wanted to shrug and convince her everything was normal. "Except it was extraordinarily real, like you said. And I didn't want to come out of it. Ever since Kate woke me, I've felt these surges of irrational anger, almost rage."

"Thank you for being honest." Laura turned her attention to Kate. "It's what I was afraid of. Something's been poking at him."

I squeezed my eyes shut against a vision of seizing Laura by the throat and slamming her skull into the wall until it cracked open like an eggshell. It was so real I could feel her smooth skin under my fingers, the muscles in her throat contracting as she fought for air, the sharpness of her nails as they clawed at my hands. My chest tightened. Why was I imagining such horrible things? *What's wrong with me?*

"You don't really want to hurt me," Laura said. "Something else is trying to use you. Don't let it. Fight it—force whatever it is out of your head."

Holding my breath, I pushed at the dreadful thoughts, pushed *hard.* A migraine flared along my temples, setting them on fire, and I felt the blood vessels burst in one eye, but I didn't care.

Smooth, cool skin touched my face—Kate's hands, holding my head. "Whatever you are, let him go. Let him go, goddamn you! He's not yours."

I took her hands and stared into her beautiful green eyes, barely noticing that tears were running from my own. "Help me, Kate."

"I've got you, Jacks. It's okay. You're going to be just fine." Climbing onto my lap, she leaned forward until her forehead pressed against mine. I felt a bit of the same energy that had made the walls hum when the women had linked hands. It drove the last of that horrid voice from my brain. Kate slumped against me as though exhausted, and as I held her, I felt an overwhelming rush of gratitude.

"Thank you. I don't know what you did, but thank you. That was awful."

Laura shook her head. "Kate's the most powerful medium in the state, maybe even the country. It should have known better than to mess with her."

Since Kate was in no shape to explain, I directed my question to her friend, who was relaxing on Kate's couch with the shoebox in her hands as if nothing untoward had happened. "What was it? What was happening to me?"

"It's the entity. I would call it demonic, but as you've heard, our medium friend here disagrees. But demonic or not, whatever you want to call it, it's up to no good. We both agree on that."

The idea that something evil could invade my brain that swiftly, that easily, made me shudder. What if it had made me hurt Laura? Or Kate? I'd never have forgiven myself.

"It's not powerful enough. Not yet. But you're right to be concerned. We have to teach you how to guard your mind. Your openness is one of the most appealing things about you, but unfortunately, in this situation it puts you at risk. And in turn, it puts Kate at risk."

"Was it that thing I saw in the hospital?" The memory of the black dog, jaws slavering, made my stomach roil.

"I didn't get a look at it. I could only hear its influence over you and that was enough, believe me." The expression on Laura's face told me she'd seen my thoughts, seen herself murdered by my hand. The realization filled me with shame. "Kate will probably be able to tell you more."

Kate's head moved against my chest, nodding. I drew her closer.

"But that doesn't make sense," I said. "I thought that thing was…attached, or whatever you want to call it, to Dennis. Or Bill."

"It attaches itself to whomever it needs to in order to get what it wants, and what it wants is a medium, someone with powerful abilities it can control. I'm guessing it wants Lily, but since Lily is being kept away from her father, Dennis was no longer of use to it. Now it has its sights set on Kate, and when you went to the hospital today, it was simple enough for it to jump ship from Dennis to you."

"But I didn't feel anything at the hospital."

"That's why I don't think it's too powerful yet. It needed to wait until your conscious mind was at rest in order to strike. That's a good sign."

"If you say so." The next thought made my pulse quicken. "Could it have transferred to Kate now?"

"Not a chance." Laura grinned. "My girl kicked its ass and sent it back to hell, at least for now. She'll be okay. She just needs to rest."

I sagged in the chair, cradling Kate in my arms like she was a little girl. "She's not the only one. My brain hurts."

"It's been a rough night. But before you get too freaked out, let me tell you our lives aren't normally this exciting."

"Really? Because everything I've seen so far says otherwise."

"Oh, I have visions and Kate communicates with spirits," Laura said with a shrug. "But evil entities are another thing altogether. This is my first encounter with one, and I'm almost thirty-six years old. So I'm thinking they're pretty rare."

I was curious in spite of myself. "If you've never seen one before, how did you know what it is?"

"Remember when we first met, and I told you your aura was pink?"

Recalling the memory, I smiled. Things had been much simpler then, even though Kate and I had been headed to Italy to rescue a girl's soul. To rescue *Lily's* soul. Funny how that could seem like a simpler time, but it did. "Yeah."

"Well, whatever this thing is, it doesn't have an aura. That's how I know it isn't human. Even spirits have auras, assuming they were living creatures at some point."

"So it's what, dead?" Sometimes talking to Laura was like speaking in riddles. My brain felt sluggish trying to keep up with her.

"Not dead, but not alive in the way we understand, either. It just *is*. That's why I call it a demon, or an entity, as Kate prefers. It's not organic, and it's not a manifestation of energy the way human spirits are. That's why it needs to attach itself to someone in order to communicate. It doesn't have its own energy, so it needs ours. At least until it gets stronger."

Recalling the terrible visions that had invaded my brain, I shuddered again. Some communication. If that's what the thing had to say, it could bloody well keep its thoughts to itself.

Thinking about it felt like tempting fate, as if my own thoughts would give it power. "Can you stop it from invading my mind?"

"No, but I can teach *you* to stop it." The confidence in her voice gave me hope. Laura wouldn't lie.

I exhaled in a rush. I hadn't noticed I'd been holding my breath. "Good. How?"

"Let's give Kate another minute or two. I'm going to need her help for this." Laura rearranged the cushions on the couch until they were to her liking. "I'm really glad you asked, though. It's important you know how to do this, especially where you're going."

"What do you mean? Where am I going?" But even before I asked the question, I knew what she was going to say.

"To Egypt, of course. Isn't it obvious?"

~ CHAPTER NINE ~

Kate

I'D NEVER SEEN SO MANY GHOSTS IN MY LIFE.

They pushed past the living, indifferent to the existence of gawking tourists as they went about their business: carting food, bringing offerings for the gods, or fussing over their wigs and makeup. The spirits were so vivid here that their bronze skin glowed and I could smell the scented oils they'd used to perfume their hair. It was intoxicating.

"Kate? Everything okay?"

Reluctantly, I stopped watching the spectacle in order to focus on my new business partner, whose brow was furrowed with concern.

"I'm fine. Just taking it all in."

Even beyond the bustling population of indifferent spirits, Luxor's Temple of Waset was extraordinary. Limestone columns too wide for me to get my arms around gleamed in the blazing sun. Two massive statues of the dog-headed god himself guarded the entrance, and dozens of people leaned against his well-muscled legs and beamed for the camera. Or, most often, the smartphone.

The spate of recent terror attacks hadn't dimmed the world's fervor for Egypt in the slightest. A surging wave of humanity flowed in and out of the temple, and the resulting bedlam was deafening. Surprising when you considered this was once a church for the ancient Egyptians, a reverential place. It was enough to make me glad the spirits couldn't see what had become of their magnificent temple, or watch the selfies taken with their beloved god.

But was *Anubis beloved*? The ghosts, as intent on their once-earthly business as they were, still eyed the towering statues warily as they passed. There was something in their manner—their quick step and hunched shoulders—which betrayed their fear. Then again, who wouldn't be afraid of a dog-headed god of death?

"It's not…dangerous for you here, is it?"

While I would have preferred exploring the site on my own, at least until I got over the worst of my awe and culture shock, I understood why Jackson had insisted on coming with me, and why he was so worried. He was all too aware of my proclivity to take on the pain and suffering of spirits, to the point where it threatened my own health and even my life in some cases. The Temple of Waset was a recent excavation, and new chambers were continually being unearthed. Not a lot was known about its history.

Thankfully, I had detected no mass deaths or tormented souls thus far. Wherever the lively ghosts had met their end, it hadn't been here.

Save for one. And that was the one I needed to contact.

"Don't worry. It's perfectly safe."

I watched a lot of tension leave Jackson's features. A lot of it, but not all. We were both on edge, unnerved by our government's warnings that non-essential travel to Egypt was to be avoided. Of course, if saving Lily and her family didn't count as essential, what would?

"I still don't like leaving Lily," he said. "Do you really think she'll be safe?"

"You heard what Laura said. Our being here is the best chance of *protecting* Lily. Laura's used the most powerful wards she can find to shield her, and she'll contact us if anything happens. You can trust Lore, Jacks. She won't let anything happen to Lily while we're gone."

A man gestured at us and, seeing he had caught my eye, hurried over. Extending an arm to better display the hundreds of necklaces dangling from it, he launched into his spiel without pausing for breath. "Necklace, beautiful lady? Real stone! I have lapis, malachite, amber, and obsidian. Very beautiful, very cheap. I make you good price."

Unable to hide my smile, I shook my head. "No thank you."

Far from being discouraged, he withdrew a packet of postcards from the long *galabayya* he wore, and draped the colorful scenes over the necklaces. "Souvenirs? Something for your family back home?" Undeterred by my silence, the man snapped his fingers. "You like cats? I have just the thing." Again his hand disappeared into the folds of his robe, only to reappear with a new treasure—a small cat statue in brilliant shades of green. "Bastet. Very important goddess for women. You like?"

"You heard her. We're not interested," Jackson said in a tone that should have brooked no argument, but it was too late. The man made his living reading tourists' faces, and he'd spotted a flicker of interest in mine. Game over. Daring to take a step closer, he pressed the figurine into my hand.

"You want the kitty god, miss? I give you very good price."

"It's lovely," I said before Jackson could scare him away. "What's it made of?"

"One hundred percent malachite," the man said, withdrawing yet another statue from his robe, this one of Anubis. He smashed the two together so violently that I flinched. "See? No damage. This is pure stone."

Bending to get a closer look at the cat, Jackson snorted. "That's not stone. Stone should chip or crack. Besides, you can see the seams. Nice try, dude."

Undaunted, the man pressed Bastet into my hands again. I'd always been a sucker for Egyptian mythology. Any culture that worshipped cats couldn't be wrong. "I give you very good price, pretty lady," the man promised.

"Of course you'll give her a good price. She's probably going to be your only sale of the day. This is cheap crap," Jackson said, rolling his eyes.

Argh! What did men know about shopping?

"Is not cheap! Is not crap."

"What's it really made of, then? Because we both know it's not malachite."

If the man felt defeated, he didn't show it. I had to hand it to him—the guy was good. I was tempted to buy it for the performance, if nothing else. "Hokay! It's one hundred percent imitation malachite. Made of genuine resin. Won't scratch or crack. Won't break in your luggage. It's perfect for the lady."

"How much?" Jackson asked. He didn't have to ask if I wanted it. He knew me well enough by now.

"For the beautiful lady, special price of one thousand Egyptian pounds."

"One thousand pounds! That's over fifty bucks. Kate, give him his statue back."

"Wait!" the man said, and for the first time I noticed his forehead was beaded with perspiration. In spite of myself, I felt sorry for him. "Even more special price of eight hundred pounds."

"That's over forty." Jackson shook his head. "More than forty bucks for a piece of plastic. We must look real stupid."

"Is no plastic, is resin. Very good quality." The man bashed the two statues together again. "No break, no chip, no problem."

"How about two hundred?" I asked. I hated to admit it, but Jackson was right. Forty dollars was way too much for a trinket, even if it had been made of malachite. With Lily's family taking up the majority of my time, money hadn't been exactly pouring in the door. Her mother would cover our expenses, but that wouldn't help pay the mortgage when we got home. Cat statues, while charming, were not a necessity of life.

The merchant winced as if pained. "No, miss. Please, I have to feed my family. That is too low. Please give me fair price."

"Okay, four hundred. And that's my final offer."

Jackson sucked in his breath. I could feel the disapproval radiating off him, but I didn't care. Would I have paid over twenty bucks at home for a figurine of a cat? No, but this was Egypt, and who knew when I would return? It was worth it for the experience alone.

The man's face brightened. "Sold, to the beautiful lady. And, to show you my appreciation, I throw in Anubis for free." He displayed both statues on his palm, and as much as I didn't want any reminder of the death god, I had to admit they looked great together. "Puppy god and kitty god, gone to good home."

Tissue paper and a plastic bag appeared from his sleeve, and before I could blink, my purchases were expertly wrapped, bagged, and hanging from my hand. My two hundred pounds disappeared as quickly. As I thanked him, the string of postcards dangling from his arm caught my eye.

"You want postcard? Very, very special price." He grinned, clearly having fun with us now that he had a sale under his belt.

I nudged Jackson. "Do you see that?" I tilted my chin toward a card that featured a close-up of one of the Anubis statues' heads. "I'm pretty sure that's one of the ones Bill sent."

"That doesn't mean anything. There are probably hundreds of people selling the same postcard. Besides, Bill was here months ago."

It didn't matter. When you're born with The Gift, you come to realize there is no such thing as coincidence. Giving Jackson the bag with my statues, I rooted through my purse, which sent our vendor friend into paroxysms of excitement.

"Only twenty pounds for the card, miss. You like the puppy god? Or, I sell you the whole collection for one hundred pounds. Great souvenirs for friends and family back home, yes? You need stamps? I have stamps."

"Of course you do," Jackson muttered, earning himself a dirty look.

Finally I found what I was looking for. "Sorry, I'm more interested in the man who bought this card." As I handed the merchant the photo of Bill that Vittoria had lent me, Jackson groaned.

"He must have seen about a thousand—"

"I remember this man," the merchant said, tapping Bill's face with his finger. "I know him."

His excitement was too instantaneous, too ingenuous, to be suspect. I couldn't resist smirking at Jackson. He needed to learn to trust a woman's intuition. Especially when that woman was a medium.

"All of us remember," the vendor went on, signaling to the small crowd of eager salespeople who had surrounded us. "We will never forget."

A tall man with an astonishing array of scarves hanging about his neck and arms bowed his head, looking down at his feet. Thrusting his hand forward palm out to ward off the evil eye, he shook his head. "Such a tragedy."

"What tragedy? What happened?" Feeling chilled in spite of the heat, I was tempted to ask how much the scarves were.

Our original seller's mouth turned down, his lower lip trembling. When he hesitated, his colleagues waited him out, perhaps believing that since he'd spoken to us first, it was his right to tell the story. "Are you his family, miss? If so, this will be difficult for you to hear."

"No, we're not family. But this man's family *is* in trouble, and we're trying to help them. Please tell us everything you can," I said.

Squaring his shoulders, the vendor took a deep breath that seemed to come all the way from his toes. As he prepared to speak, a spirit appeared behind him—a kind-looking elderly man with sparkling eyes undimmed by death—and rested a hand on his arm. Whoever the friendly ghost was, his presence gave our merchant strength. The man faced us with new resolve.

"At first, this man not so different, but I notice him because he is military. I can tell he is American soldier. His hair is cut very short, and he is wearing the clothes soldiers wear when they're off duty."

As if his words were magic, I saw Bill as clearly as though he were standing among us. Wearing a light brown T-shirt and camouflage pants, a camera hanging about his neck, and an excited smile on his face. Even if the day had ended in tragedy, at least it had started off well.

"How did he act that day? Did he look troubled?" Jackson asked, and I was relieved to hear no remaining trace of skepticism in his voice. While the vendor might misrepresent his wares in order to make a sale, he wasn't lying about this.

"Not at all. I mostly remember him because he re-member me. He greet me by name, saying he buy post-cards from me many times before. He bought one from me that day, before he go inside the temple." He glanced at the temple in question and his robes swayed as he shivered. The other vendors made protective gestures, carefully keeping their backs turned to Anubis's place of worship. "I try to get him to buy more—two for one, very good deal—but he says he won't need it because he will be home soon."

My instinct was to give the troubled salesman a hug, but I resisted. Since he was a Muslim man, I assumed such affection was not permitted with women aside from his wife and family. Though he was acting brave, it was costing him greatly to tell this story. It was in his troubled expression, the way he labored over every word. The spirit now had both hands on the man's arm and his smile had been replaced with an expression of concern. *What on earth had happened here?*

Jackson nudged me. When I looked over at him, I could tell there was something I was missing, something he'd picked up on, but I wasn't sure what it was. We'd have to talk about it later, when we were alone.

The merchant continued his story. "He buy postcard, and go inside. I'm thinking maybe I will sell him some souvenirs for his family before he go." His cheeks colored. "It is only my job, you understand. I must provide for my family."

"Hey, no judgment," Jackson said. "I take it he didn't buy any souvenirs."

"No. No, he did not. He gone for such long time, for a moment I think he leave without me seeing."

The other men muttered something in Egyptian Arabic and made their hand signs in unison.

"Fine, he not want to buy, there are other customers. I sell, sell, sell. It is not a great day, but not bad. There are some Chinese, I think, and some British who wish to buy from me. Soon I forget about the man."

To my surprise, his voice broke, and he buried his face in his hands. Stepping forward, the tall scarf seller continued the story. "The man runs out of the temple. Everyone hear him scream. It was a terrible thing."

No wonder the Egyptians remembered Bill. It was obvious the incident had traumatized them.

"He trips on the steps and falls to his knees in the sand, crying out." Our vendor friend, recovered slightly, lifted his hands to the skies as Bill must have done, his face contorted in a silent scream. "It was the sound of a man who has lost his mind. I hear it in my nightmares to this day."

"Any idea what scared him so badly?" Jackson asked.

"It not fear so much as pain. You see, his face—" The vendor swallowed hard, turning away for a moment. "His face, his hands, everything. They were covered in sores. Big, weeping sores full of blood."

~ CHAPTER TEN ~

Kate

I'D PUT IT OFF LONG ENOUGH. IT WAS TIME TO talk to Bill.

There was no way to do it with hundreds of people cramming the temple, but luckily our new vendor friend Ahmet had a solution. It turned out some of the guards could be persuaded to let people in after visiting hours, provided the price was right.

While we waited for dusk, Jackson and I shared some kebabs and mint tea at the adjacent tourist café and talked strategy. I loved the Egyptian custom of bringing an entire mint plant to your table so you could flavor your own tea. Our little plant was quite diminished, as Jacks had decided the leaves were an acceptable substitute for dessert.

By unspoken agreement, we'd avoided discussing Bill's fate while we were eating, but our food was long gone. Hoping the mint would soothe the nausea I felt whenever I thought about what had happened to the soldier, I chewed on some leaves myself.

"It's strange Vittoria never mentioned this thing with Bill's skin," Jackson said. "It doesn't seem like the kind of thing a person forgets."

"No, it doesn't. But the coroner's report didn't mention it either. I wonder if the skin condition went away before his heart burst."

"Could be."

While I'd done my best to push the vendor's chilling story aside for the time being, it had nagged me like a toothache. "Boils."

"Whaa?"

"Boils. Another word for sores is boils."

"As in one of the plagues of Egypt," Jackson said.

"You got it."

"I wonder if Bill experienced any of the others before he died."

"If he did, that would at least partially explain what happened to his heart." The rain of frogs had been dreadful, but at least Laura and I had known it wasn't real and how to stop it. For a man like Bill, whom I assumed was a mainstreamer with no second sight, a similar event could have been cataclysmic, off-the-charts terrifying.

"Hey, check it out. It's show time." Jackson signaled at someone behind me, and I turned to see a security guard waving us toward the temple's back entrance. My stomach clenched at the thought of facing whatever was tormenting Bill's soul.

Lost in thought, I jumped at the touch of Jacks's hand on mine. His eyes were warm with admiration. "You've got this, Kate. You're the toughest chick I know. And I'll be right there with you."

Taking a deep breath, I clung to his hand as I left the table. *He's just another spirit, and you've been communicating with spirits all your life. Jacks is right; you've got this.*

But that's the problem with lying to yourself. You never

quite believe it. "Hey, Jacks?"

"Yeah?"

I smiled as he awkwardly dug in his wallet for the required pounds with one hand so he didn't have to let go of mine, like we were a couple of kids in high school who couldn't bear to be parted from each other.

"During Ahmet's story, you nudged me. I got the feeling you wanted to tell me something."

He was quiet as we left the café, but after a moment, he remembered. "Oh, right. Yeah, that was weird."

"What was? Whatever you picked up on, it must have gone straight over my head, because I didn't find anything weird. Besides the obvious, of course."

"Ahmet said Bill told him he needed one postcard because he would be leaving for home soon."

Going over the conversation in my head, I nodded. "That sounds right, I think. But what's weird about that?"

"What's weird is that was *before* he entered the temple. Remember the postcards we read? Bill talks about wanting to come home after visiting the temple, but before that, he was talking about staying for a while. Remember?"

Jackson's voice rose in excitement, and I realized he was onto something. Either Bill had changed his mind about staying shortly *before* he visited the temple, after he spoke with Ahmet, or…

"Maybe he said that to get Ahmet to back off." The sellers could be aggressive, but it didn't ring true. Bill had been an honest man, an ethical and moral man who'd loved Egyptian culture and who had treated the vendors with kindness.

"Nah, Ahmet and him were friendly. I think he was telling the truth. You should ask him about it."

Now he'd lost me again. "Ahmet?"

"No, Bill. Once you're in contact with him, ask him what happened to change his mind about staying here before he visited the Temple of Waset."

I was sure there would be no shortage of things to discuss with Bill, assuming Bill was here. All right, that was another attempt at lying to myself. I *knew* Bill's spirit was around; I'd been able to feel him as soon as we got off the bus. But would he be willing and able to communicate with me? That was another matter altogether.

"I might not be able to reach him. Even if I can, he might not want to talk to me. Or be able to."

"You'll reach him, Kate. He'll talk to you."

I couldn't detect the slightest hesitancy in Jackson's voice. There was no doubt in his mind. Unfortunately, there wasn't much in mine either. Perhaps the question should have been if *I* wanted to talk to Bill. Of course, we both understood it wasn't actually Bill I was afraid of.

The best thing about the back entrance was being able to avoid the towering statues of Anubis, which resembled the monstrosity in Lily's hospital room a little too closely. Instead, the guard guided us into a communal area where people had mingled after paying their respects to the great god of death and mummification. With its stone path and lush grass, the courtyard could have been a park. The only hint we were in Egypt was the stone edifices on either side, crammed from top to bottom with hieroglyphs. Seeing them reminded me of Eden, and my chest tightened. I hoped my friend was okay.

The spirits I'd noticed earlier were present, chatting and greeting each other with no respect to the late hour. I wondered what time it was in their realm, or if the worship of

Anubis had no end. The thought made me anxious. Jackson linked his arm with mine. I wondered if he'd acquired some of Laura's mind-reading ability after all. He'd certainly mastered her mind-guarding exercises with ease.

"You've got this," he whispered in my ear.

The security guard had weathered skin that was heavily pockmarked. Acne? Measles? Some unidentified childhood disease? In spite of this, he appeared to be quite young, perhaps in his early to mid twenties. Once he'd led us far enough into the courtyard that we wouldn't be spotted from the road, he held out his hand. This time Jackson let go of me long enough to retrieve two hundred pounds from his inside pocket. The guard had originally asked for five, but since tourism had taken another hit after the terrorist attacks, he'd agreed to our price. I was grateful Jackson had done the negotiating. I didn't have the heart for it, not with Eden missing and Lily in danger. My energy was at an all-time low, in spite of the kebabs.

The man counted Jackson's bills and scowled. "This is not enough."

"What do you mean, it's not enough? It's two hundred. That's what we agreed on."

The frown on the guard's face deepened. "I changed my mind. It's not enough. I think five hundred."

"And I think you're out of your mind. There's no way we're paying five hundred."

"Then you leave." He thrust a finger in the direction we'd come. "Makes no difference to me."

"Come on, man. A deal is a deal. Two hundred pounds tax-free. That's what we agreed upon. We shook on it."

"I am sorry, but this is big risk for me. My job is on the line, maybe my life. Two hundred is not enough."

Before Jackson could respond, I jumped in. "What do you mean, maybe your life? Would someone hurt you for this?"

I'd learned about ancient Egypt in junior high, and had audited some of Eden's classes, but I knew next to nothing about contemporary Egypt. Was letting us into a temple after hours an actionable crime? So intent was I on picturing a cruel boss, I was completely unprepared for the man's response.

"It could happen," he said, lowering his voice as he checked over his shoulder. "Maybe Anubis." He hissed the mythological god's name as if it were a curse. Squirming, I waited for Jackson's laughter, the mocking, "Oh, come on!" that was sure to follow.

Surprisingly, it never happened. His face so serious it could have been carved from stone, my partner removed another hundred pounds from his wallet. "Three hundred."

Then I remembered. Jackson had seen Anubis, or at least whatever was masquerading as him. And he'd been a hell of a lot closer to those teeth than I had.

The man shook his head, still extending his hand. "Five hundred. I am the only guard who will stay here after sundown. Everyone else is too afraid."

Jackson sighed, and I could see the fight had gone out of him. We'd both been through so much in the past two weeks, and if I was struggling with it, I couldn't imagine how difficult it was for him.

"What is your name?" I asked the guard, whose eyes narrowed. "It's okay; you won't be in trouble. I only want to know what we should call you."

"You can call me Mohammad."

"Okay then, Mohammad. Can you tell me why everyone

else is afraid? Did something happen to them?"

The man surveyed the grounds again before answering. I couldn't recall the last time I'd seen someone this anxious. He may have had an unethical way of achieving his price, but he wasn't lying about the fear. I'd stake my reputation on it. "If I tell you, maybe you not give me the money."

"Oh, we'll pay you. I promise." I nudged Jackson, who grumbled under his breath before slapping two hundred more pounds into the man's hand.

"Not cool, buddy," he said. "The next time you give your word, try harder to keep it."

Holding my breath, I waited for the explosion of anger that was sure to follow. But once again I was surprised. Blushing, the man ducked his head as he folded the bills into his wallet. "I am sorry. When I spoke with you earlier, I was under pressure. My supervisor was nearby; I was not thinking clearly. I forgot about the risk."

"What risk?" I was nearing the end of my patience. As much as I dreaded talking to Bill, I also longed to get out of this place. The desert wind had picked up, and the temperature had already dropped dramatically. The last thing I wanted was to encounter Anubis in the dark.

His eyes darting left and then right, the man leaned closer, so close I could smell cloves on his breath. "The men and me...we believe this temple is haunted, miss."

Biting my lip, it was everything I could do to keep from laughing. Around us, at least a hundred ghosts went about their eternal business. It was haunted, all right. "I understand how frightening that can be," I said as kindly as I could, trying my best to see the situation from a mainstreamer's point of view. "But these ghosts can't hurt you.

I'm sure they don't even realize you're here. You're safe."

"You don't understand. It isn't the ghosts we're afraid of. It's Anubis."

He made a gesture so quickly it was impossible to follow, but I assumed it was an Anubis worshipper's version of crossing oneself. He'd said the name of the god with no irony.

"I thought Anubis was an old legend. Mythology. I didn't think any modern-day Egyptians believed in him," Jackson said, and I could tell he was striving to sound casual. He almost pulled it off.

"I assure you, Anubis is no myth. He is very much alive, and here especially, he is powerful. We fear him much more than any human spirit."

"Have any of the guards seen Anubis?" I asked. "Has anything happened?"

"You spoke to Ahmet. I understand he told you about the American soldier. Days later, that man was dead." Looking over his shoulder again, the man then stared into my eyes as if trying to impress upon me the seriousness of his words. "That is what happens when you cross a god."

Cross a god? "I'm sorry; I don't understand. How could that man have angered Anubis? He was a tourist, here for a visit."

The guard sneered. "You are a fool if you think he was a tourist. For many, many years, American soldiers have come to Egypt, but they do not belong here. They are messing with something they do not comprehend. I am trusting you not to do the same."

"What are they messing with, Mohammad? Please tell us what's going on. We're not with the government. We're trying to help that soldier's family. He has a niece, a young

girl, and whatever he encountered over here is now threatening her."

"I'm sorry; I've told you everything I can. But I will
pray for her."

"No offense, but it's a little late for prayers. Something
has already attacked this girl. She's just a kid. If it was your
child, wouldn't you want someone to help you?" Jackson's
jaw tightened, and I could see a muscle twitch in his temple.
When it came to Lily's safety, he was the proverbial mamma
bear.

The man's face flushed, but with anger or shame, I
couldn't be certain. "I've already said more than I should.
I'm a security guard. What do I know of the American military and its dealings? I know nothing."

Jackson wasn't buying it. "I think you know plenty.
What's going on, Mohammad? What did the soldier do
during his visit? Surely coming here to the temple wouldn't
offend your god."

"He is not my god!" the man said in a harsh whisper,
his voice breaking. "He is an abomination, worshipped by
those who cherish darkness. My god is Allah, only Allah.
May he protect me from evil."

"We apologize, Mohammad. We didn't mean to offend
you." I gave Jackson a pointed look. "Of course you have
only one god. Please understand, we're worried about Lily,
the child. We promised her family we'd do whatever we
could to help her. Please tell us what you've seen."

The guard hesitated, parting his lips as if to speak, and
for a moment, I thought he was going to help us. But then
he closed up again. "The sun is setting. I do not want to be
here after dark, and neither do you. You have twenty minutes before I ask you to leave."

"Come on, man," Jackson tried, but the guard returned to his post across the courtyard. Jacks turned to me with a pained expression. "I'm sorry if I buggered that up. I thought we were getting somewhere for a minute."

Taking him by the hand, I led him toward the temple. "It's not your fault. Something's obviously frightened him, and frightened him badly. I think we're lucky he told us as much as he did."

"What does Operation Bright Star have to do with this, though? I thought that was a chest-puffing display of how awesome we are."

"I don't have a clue, but I know someone who does."

Empty of tourists, the temple was eerily silent. Huge stone pillars stretched to the sky, so tall we had to crane our heads in order to see the ceiling. Small floodlights cast an otherworldly glow.

"Whoa," Jackson said. "Check that out."

The walls were covered with murals of Anubis carrying out his godly responsibilities: standing before a mummification table, holding a vessel of embalming fluid over the corpses of assorted pharaohs, accepting offerings.

The highly detailed scenes, startling in their intricacy, were similar to those we'd seen in other temples. But those paintings had faded to shades of sand, muted over thousands of years. These, with their lurid shades of cobalt, turquoise, ochre, and crimson, could have been completed yesterday.

"Were they restored?" Jackson asked, reaching to touch a particularly vivid image of Anubis and then thinking better of it.

"I doubt it." I racked my brain for anything I'd read about the temple, but couldn't recall a single mention of mural restoration. "Some of the temples did keep their colors

better than others. The temple of Queen Hatshepsut is supposed to be extraordinary."

I couldn't see how the queen's resting place could be
more spectacular than this, though. The colors were so
bright they shimmered.

"Is this a good place?"

"Huh?"

"To contact Bill. Is this a good place, or should we go
somewhere else?" Jackson asked. We both whispered, as if
we were in a library.

Or a tomb.

"Let's try the shrine."

There were few spirits in here with us, but I had a feeling there would be even fewer at the shrine. Besides, self-
ishly, I wanted to see it. The Great Shrine of Anubis was
one of only two that had managed to remain intact over
thousands of years. When we'd first arrived that morning,
the crowds of tourists had clustered so thickly around it
there'd been no hope of getting a glimpse.

Jackson grinned, his teeth flashing in the dim light. "I
was hoping you'd say that. I want to see it too."

The shrine was a tiny, suffocating square, protected
from the public by a rope stretched across its entrance. At
the chamber's heart was a stone platform bearing a statue of Anubis striking the ever-popular Sphinx pose. This
Anubis was all doggy, and aside from the preponderance
of gold chains around his neck, could have been mistaken
for a particularly regal-looking Doberman pinscher.

"This is it? This is what people were trampling each
other to get a photo of?"

"It *is* one of the only remaining shrines in the country," I said, but that wasn't it either. There were absolutely

no spirits here, either in the chamber or anywhere around it. I considered mentioning this to Jackson, but wasn't sure if the news would frighten or comfort him. It sure as shit frightened me. Something wasn't right. "I don't like it here. Let's go somewhere else."

"Wait...did you see that?"

I'd already turned away, searching futilely for a place that wasn't dominated by an Anubis image, but the doggy god was everywhere. Jackson's hand caught mine and tugged. "Kate..."

I saw them, all right. Hundreds of ghosts, but not in the chamber—trapped beyond it. There was a room behind the shrine that had yet to be discovered, and something was keeping the spirits from leaving. They panicked, rushing the stone wall in a frantic bid for freedom. Watching them pound their useless fists against it was heartbreaking. A gloomy, sweltering prison was no place to spend eternity. There had to be something I could do to help.

Temporarily distracted by this new predicament, it took me a moment to remember Jackson couldn't see them. So what had caught his interest?

"Jacks?"

His hand trembled in mine. His entire body was vibrating. *What did he see?* Had The Gift rubbed off on him in some strange way, enabling him to view the shrine's secrets? But the spirits within were too terrified to be frightening. As I regarded them again, powerless to look away, they noticed me and screamed to be rescued, their cries silenced by time and space.

"Kate, that statue," Jackson whispered, staring at the likeness of Anubis as if in a trance. "Its eyes moved. I'd swear it."

There was a ludicrous, *Scooby-Doo* feel to his words, and it would have been amusing if we weren't standing in a creepy-as-fuck ancient temple surrounded by ghosts. "Any chance it was a trick of the light?"

"Nope. That fucker *looked* at me." Finally, he was able to tear his attention from it long enough to study my face. His features mirrored the panic I'd seen on the imprisoned spirits'. "What's going on? Do you see anything?"

Against my better judgment, I regarded the statue. Its eyes had darkened into interminable pits, completely black against its narrow head. No trick of the light, then.

Energy, more powerful than anything I'd ever felt, throbbed under my feet, charging the air with static electricity. My hair rose off my shoulders, and I could hear a faint humming coming from the shrine. The trapped spirits, their faces paler than death, stopped their screaming and fled, melting into nothingness.

"Kate? What's happening?"

"We need to get out of here. *Now*."

"Wait! Miss Carlsson, don't leave me here."

A man hovered in front of the shrine. Dog tags hanging from a chain around his neck glowed silver. A nice touch, lest I had any doubt who he was. I didn't, though he appeared much younger than I'd expected. Wasn't he supposed to be Dennis's older brother? He didn't look over thirty.

"Holy fuck." Jackson gaped at the apparition. Whatever energy flowed through this place, it was stronger than any Gift.

"Don't worry; he can't hurt you." Glaring at the fallen soldier, I raised my voice. "Lay a finger on him and I'll send your sorry ass back to the spirit realm."

Bill drew back, wounded. "Why would I want to harm you or your friend? I'm hoping you will help me."

He sounded sincere, but in light of what we'd learned, I wasn't convinced. If I had a dollar for every ghost who'd lied his paranormal ass off, I'd be sitting on a lovely beach in the south of France. "I'm more interested in helping your family, Bill. You know, your *living* relatives. Who would prefer to stay that way."

The aura that enveloped the soldier flickered, growing dim. Bill's spirit was harnessing the power of this place, but he wasn't able to absorb it for long, which told me that he'd been, without a doubt, merely human. Pathetically mortal like the rest of us.

"I can *see* him," Jackson said, sounding equal parts thrilled and shitting-his-pants scared.

"It's the shrine. The energy around it amplifies everything, even the dead." I hoped he wouldn't look around. If he saw how many spirits occupied the rest of the temple, it might blow his mind. And not in a good way.

"Is he *fading*?"

"Yeah. He can use it, but he can't hold on to it. 'Fess up, Bill. What were you involved with in Egypt? What did you get yourself into?"

The soldier extended his hands, palms raised, in an unconvincing parody of innocence. "I have no idea what you're talking about. I need your help, Miss Carlsson. All I want is to move on. Let me out of here and you'll never see me again, I promise."

Uh-huh. Sure. Never heard that before, either.

"I can *hear* him," Jackson said.

"Your family isn't doing too well with your parting gift, Bill. You get that, right? You get that you nearly killed

Lily and that your own brother is in the hospital with his children too afraid to visit? That okay with you?"

The spirit wavered. "I didn't do anything to them. I'd never hurt them. I love them."

"If that's true, tell me what happened here. Why did the government keep sending you to Egypt? What were you involved in?"

The floor rumbled under our feet, sending us stumbling into one another. "What the fuck was that?" Jackson steadied me. "An earthquake?" He eyed the soaring ceiling of the temple, and it was everything I could do to stave off a panic attack at the thought of being buried under mountains of ancient Egyptian stone.

Keeping my voice strong and centered, assuming a don't-fuck-with-me vibe, I focused on the wavering spirit. The chickenshit, pasty-faced, clueless soldier who had messed with something he shouldn't have. "I'm thinking Bill's boss isn't happy about him talking to us. That's my guess. Who's your boss, Bill?"

"You don't understand. What's happening to Lily and Dennis has nothing to do with me."

I laughed. "Yeah, right. That's rich. It's obvious you were never a great liar. You had a traumatic experience in this very temple, so traumatic that every fucking vendor in an eighteen-mile radius remembers it in great detail, and yet it's a coincidence that something out of an Egyptian tomb attacked your niece? Give me a break."

Bill's face went slack with horror. "What are you talking about?"

"What do you think she's talking about, man? *Anubis.* Why the hell do you think we're here?"

In spite of the energy building around us, threatening

us with its power, I had to smile. Jackson, smarting off the dead. I'd definitely picked the right partner.

"You saw Anubis? Where?" The soldier's innocence may have been a ruse, but his anxiety was not. He ran a hand through his crew cut. "Jesus, it's worse than I thought. Miss Carlsson, you have to help Lily."

Resentment bristled along my spine, and with difficulty I stifled my first response, which would not have been conducive to further discussion. "That's what I've been trying to do. That's why I'm here. But I need your help, Bill. I need to know what you were messing with in Egypt. Because whatever is threatening your family is not an ordinary spirit."

"Anubis isn't a spirit." Flustered, Bill's likeness wavered in and out of focus. Luckily, I could still hear him, even when I couldn't see him.

"Tell us something we don't know," Jackson said.

It was a trick, this entire thing, and it made me furious. I couldn't believe Bill was so selfish, or perhaps blind to duty, that he'd put his family at risk, even now. Even after what had happened to him.

"I've heard some incredible stories, but an Egyptian god who deigns to visit hospital rooms in middle America? That's a new one."

"No, you don't understand. Anubis isn't a god. He's a—"

A loud *crack* made everyone duck for cover, including Bill.

"Christ, what was that?" Jackson eyed the ceiling again. "That didn't sound good."

"I've said too much. You've got to get out of here." Bill's spirit flickered in and out at greater speed now. "Hurry."

"What is he, Bill? Tell me."

Low rumbling, like boulders rolling across a stone floor, shook the temple.

"Kate!"

Shaking Jackson off, I concentrated my energy on Bill Walkins. *Stay put, you bastard. Stay put and* answer *me.*

"Miss, you've got to get out of here."

Rumble.

I could hear Mohammad, the security guard, calling for us too. He sounded a million miles away.

Rumble.

"Let's go, Kate. Come on." Jackson yanked on my arm, pulling me off balance. "I do not want to get buried alive in here."

Rumble.

"Please, Miss Carlsson. Your gift can't protect you here. Nothing can. And if you die, you won't be able to help Lily."

Rumble. CRACK.

"Jesus Christ, Kate. Do I have to pick you up and carry you out of here? Let's go, *now.*"

The spirits around us shrieked at a decibel far more painful than Jackson or Mohammad could achieve. I felt the breeze created as they rushed past, disturbed from their eternal duties by the impending destruction of the great temple.

I ignored them. I ignored everyone, pulling away from Jackson every time he attempted to drag me to safety. I ignored the constant stream of dust pouring onto us, the heavy tiles shifting upward, creating stone tents at our feet. Jostled from side to side, I staggered, struggling to stay up-right as I focused on Bill.

Tell me.

His face anguished, his eyes darted from side to side, taking in the destruction. *Miss, please. I'm begging you. Get out of here.*

Not until you tell me. What is Anubis?

Please tell my family I'm sorry. I didn't mean for any of this to happen. I didn't understand…I didn't believe.

What is Anubis, Bill?

Anubis is…

CRACK.

What? For fuck's sake, Bill, spit it out. We're running out of time.

Anubis is REAL.

In an earsplitting cacophony, every floodlight in the temple exploded, plunging us into darkness. Splinters of glass stung my face and arms like a swarm of bees. Over the cries of the spirits, I could hear Jackson screaming.

~ CHAPTER ELEVEN ~

Jackson

IN TERMS OF FUN THINGS I LEARNED IN EGYPT, the fact that it's possible to go out of your mind with fear wouldn't exactly top the list. Thankfully, you *can* recover your lost sanity.

At least, I hope so.

Then again, if one were to ask the people who know me best, they'd say it's hard to tell.

Fuckers.

Shamefully, I admit that when Mohammad grabbed me, trying his damnedest to drag my sorry ass out of the temple before it collapsed, he almost got knocked out for his troubles. Not only did I have no idea who he was, I had no idea where I was. I'd turned into a babbling idiot.

That's what I get for trusting a redhead to know when it's time to give up the ghost.

"Are you okay? Do you need ambulance? Miss? You need to go to hospital?"

Spooked, I looked over at Kate, whose hair glittered with a million tiny pieces of glass. Her face was scratched in about as many places. She gave the guard a slow, lazy smile, as if drugged. "I'm fine. It's just a scratch."

"You look like you've been in a fight with several pissed-off cats, and the cats won," I said.

She smiled again and shrugged, her chin sinking to her chest. Completely drained. It was going to be some work getting her out of here.

"She's fine," I said to the anxious security guard, who was no doubt picturing his cushy job coming to an end. His once-spotless uniform was coated with a layer of gray dust. "Just tired. Sorry about destroying your temple. It wasn't intentional."

Mohammad gave me that lovely look I'd seen so often in China, that one that says someone was questioning my sanity. "What are you talking about? The temple, she is fine. She's withstood greater quakes than this."

My head whipped around like I was pulling a Linda Blair, which is ill-advised when you've recently been rescued from a collapsing temple. Mohammad had told the truth. The temple was pristine. The two great statues of Anubis towered over us, staring off into the distance as if we were too lowly a concern to bother with.

"But—" I shook my head to clear it, and then groaned with pain at the crick in my neck. Again, not the smartest idea. "What about the broken glass, the dust, that cracking noise?"

The guard brushed off the sleeves of his uniform, which accomplished nothing. He remained coated in dust. "It was an earthquake. Sure, we lost some lights, but they are easily replaced. It's you two I'm worried about."

"We're fine. It was a bad scare, but we'll get over it." Kate was slumped beside me. When I leaned closer, I could hear a delicate snore. Cute.

"Good. If you come back tomorrow, I will be happy to

let you in. During business hours. No charge."

The idea of returning to that temple of horrors was enough to make me scream again, but then I thought of something worse. *Would Kate want to come back?* She'd obviously connected with Bill—I'd seen my first ghost, aside from Yuèhai. But had he told her anything useful? I'd never seen her that furious with any spirit. She'd gone easier on Italy's Doctor Death, and that guy was a piece of work. Bill must have really pissed her off.

With the girl in question softly snoring beside me, I couldn't speak for both of us. But I could speak for myself. "Thanks, but no thanks. I think I've seen enough temples for a while." *Like, the rest of my life.*

"I see. This one, though—this one different from the rest."

I couldn't help but notice the guy avoided looking at the Anubis statues in a manner that was almost comical. He kept inching away from them.

"How so?"

Mohammad traced patterns in the dirt with the toe of his now filthy boots. "You've seen what it can do. The guards working here, they've...seen things. Heard things. I am the only one who will stay here after closing, and I prefer not to linger too long after sunset."

Several smartass replies sprang to my lips, my favorite among them featuring Anubis as some kind of vampire. But after nearly dying in the temple, I was less inclined to be my usual skeptical jerk self. Too bad Kate slept through my admirable restraint. "What kind of things?"

The man shuffled farther out of range of the statues, which was both amusing and sad. I didn't have the heart to point out that, if he was afraid of their coming alive and seizing him, he'd have to move a lot farther away than that. Like fifty miles away. As of now, they'd barely have to shift before they'd be on him. "I shouldn't say. Not here. He doesn't like it when we talk about it."

"Who, Anubis?"

Mohammad wrinkled his nose at me. "No, my boss."

Shit. I'd been hanging out with Kate and Laura too long. Pretty soon I'd be warning people about the boogey-man. "Oh, right. Of course. Guess your boss isn't going to be happy about the busted lights, huh?"

"He is used to it. Like I say, this temple is different. Many strange things happen here. We deal with it." Mohammad wiped the grime from his watch. "It is time for me to go. I am late. How did you get here?"

"We were on a bus tour, but we parted ways with them so we could return after hours."

The temple parking lot, if you could call it that, was a vast expanse of sand. Only one vehicle remained, and I bet I knew whom it belonged to.

"Where are you staying?"

I had to retrieve the hotel's business card from my wallet in order to tell him. Rather than butcher the name, I handed it over.

"That's in the city center. I go past there on my way home. I could take you...if you don't want to go to the hospital?"

He looked at Kate again, and I appreciated the concern in his eyes. In spite of my earlier reservations, this was a good man. A kind man. Dude was only trying to make a little extra scratch for his family. It wasn't his fault he worked in the creepiest temple in Egypt.

"A little disinfectant and a lot of sleep, and she'll be fine."

I hoped I wasn't talking out of my ass. Her wounds didn't look serious, but what if she were bleeding internally? What if she had one of those concussions where people seem fine, but then they go to sleep and don't wake up? What if she was, I don't know, *psychically* injured? Was that even a thing? There was still so much I didn't understand about Kate's "gift." Which is to say, almost everything. "If you wouldn't mind dropping us off at the hotel, that would be great. I can spot you some more cash."

Mohammad waved off the suggestion. "No, I want to do this for you and your friend. It is my pleasure. No money, please."

Fine by me. "Kate?" I gently touched her shoulder, careful not to jostle her. "Kate, Mohammad is going to take us to the hotel. Are you ready to go?"

She moaned under her breath and her eyes fluttered partly open. "Jacks?"

"Yeah?"

"Are you okay?"

I laughed, which caused a burst of pain to flare in my side. *Fuck.* Felt like I'd bruised some ribs. Which is never fun at the best of times, when you can get away with doing nothing but lying around all day, eating ice cream. However, under the circumstances, I wouldn't complain. It could have been a lot worse. "I'm fine, darling. I think you should be more worried about yourself. How are you doing?"

She rubbed her forehead. "I've been better, but I'm okay. I've got an awful headache."

"I have stuff for that at the hotel. Let's get out of here."

Kate let me help her to her feet. She stumbled on the way up, noticeably enough that the guard rushed to help, but once standing, she seemed fine. "Thank you, Mohammad. You've been incredibly kind."

"It is absolutely no problem. Your friend says you don't need the hospital. Do you agree?"

Her smile was a pale imitation of the Kate standard, but I was glad to see it. "I agree. All I want right now is some painkillers and a hot shower, followed by bed."

We made slow, painful progress across the sand to Mohammad's car, the security guard holding up one side of Kate while I supported the other. She was either hurt, drained, or both. Otherwise she would have told us to fuck off and stop treating her like a goddamn invalid.

When he left Kate in my arms while he unlocked his aging coupe, I took the opportunity to whisper in her ear. "Are we done here? Did you get everything you needed?"

I held my breath while she hesitated. *Please don't say we have to come back. Please don't say we have to come back.* Watching paint dry in a cubicle forest sounded pretty damn good right now. At least no one had tried to kill me when I was an office drone. Unless you counted death by boredom.

"Everything I need? Ha, hardly. But I did learn something very important."

Kate always did love her cliffhangers. It was one of the most intriguing yet frustrating things about her.

"What's that?"

As Mohammad helped her into the car, she paused to stare at me. "Bill isn't dead."

~ CHAPTER TWELVE ~

Jackson

Y*OU ADORE THIS WOMAN. SHE'S EVERYTHING you've been looking for and never thought you'd find. You uprooted your entire life for her, sent your family into paroxysms of worry, to follow this person into an inarguably fucked-up line of work.*

Sometimes I have to remind myself of this stuff so I don't throttle her.

"What do you mean, Bill isn't dead? I saw his ghost. I *talked* to his ghost."

Finally, after surviving twenty minutes of banal small talk in Mohammad's car, plus waiting while Kate had her shower, got patched up, and ate a room service dinner of lentil soup and tabbouleh, she was ready to explain her unbearably cryptic comment.

Well, kind of.

"That wasn't his ghost."

"What are you talking about? Of course it was his ghost. It was spooky as shit. It was translucent. Not to mention the dude is dead. What else could it have been, a hologram?"

Kate leaned against the pillows, closing her eyes. She looked so much better now that the blood had been washed from her face and the glass was out of her hair that it was easy to forget she was still recovering.

"Sorry. Obviously you know a lot more about ghosts than I do," I said. "If you say he's not dead, he's not dead. I'm just confused."

Taking a deep breath, eyes still closed, she asked, "Jackson, was Yuèhai translucent?"

"Hells no." Yuèhai had been as real as me, able to move things and touch them and—ugh, let's not go there. That was one of the reasons I'd found it so difficult to believe she was a ghost.

"Exactly. And since she's the spirit you've actually seen, in the flesh so to speak, why would you think Bill's translucency meant he was a ghost?"

"Who knows? Too much *Scooby-Doo* as a kid? Come on, Kate. Old beliefs die hard. Give a guy a break."

"All right, you're forgiven for believing in cheesy stereotypes."

"Thank you. But this doesn't make any sense to me. Bill's heart burst. His family saw the coroner's report. They have the death certificate. Are you saying the documents were faked?"

Kate bit her lip. "Not exactly, although if I'm right, whomever Bill was working with is certainly capable of falsifying death certificates."

The words she'd yelled in the temple came ricocheting back to me. "Yeah, what was that stuff about him messing somewhere he didn't belong? Is this about Operation Bright Star?"

"I think so. Or maybe it was called something else. Bright Star might have been a cover for what he was really doing here."

"Which was?"

She frowned. "I don't know. He wouldn't tell me."

Great. Perfect, in fact. "But he admitted he was mixed up in something."

"Yes, and he definitely feels guilty. He never thought whatever he was doing would affect his family. He probably didn't expect it to affect him, either. He told me he didn't believe."

"Believe in *what?*"

Kate sighed. "That's the ultimate question, isn't it? I wish he'd said more, but something was holding him back. Either he was afraid, or he's the consummate soldier, obeying orders even now."

Soldier. That had to be the key to the whole thing. Hell, I'd read enough Tom Clancy. I could do this. "Let's go over what we know. Bill was a soldier, sent to Egypt on a regular basis. Something happened to him while he was over here that either killed him or...changed him somehow. And now whatever it is has threatened his family. And looks like a gigantic fucking dog with the body of a tornado."

For the first time since we'd returned to the hotel, Kate looked hopeful. "What are you thinking, Jacks?"

"Well, as far as I know, there are only two reasons our government messes around in the Middle East—or anywhere, really. Money and power. So it has to be one or the other."

I could feel the energy building in the room as I spoke, the skin on the back of my neck prickling. I was close to the truth; I could feel it. Our eyes met, and for a crazy moment, I wanted nothing more than to throw her down on that bed and kiss her until she lost control of her senses.

Sadly, now was not the time. Not when I was so close. Clearing my throat, I forced myself to concentrate.

"I don't think it's money," she said, her voice low, and for once I was pretty sure she felt exactly the same way I did.

"Please stop looking at me like that. Makes it hard to focus." I stared at the wall for a moment, bringing myself back to center. "I don't think it's money, either. Everything we've seen points to power. What if during these Operation Bright Star maneuvers, our government found out Egypt had developed a new weapon? A game changer."

"A weapon of mass destruction?" I could hear the tease in her words, but I wasn't playing.

"Exactly. Even though Egypt is an ally, Uncle Sam wouldn't like that. Not one bit. These people are brown, and if there's anything that raises Sammy's ire, it's well-armed brown people."

"Go on."

"So what does Sammy do? He's not about to leave the Egyptians alone to play with their new toy. He'll want to keep an eye on them. And here's Bill, this aw-shucks American soldier who loves Egypt and who is in no hurry to go home. I bet they gave him a promotion, put him in charge of the babysitting operation. That's why he wrote that postcard, saying he was going to 'stay on' for a while."

"Makes sense. And he obviously wasn't too worried about the weapon if he encouraged his family to visit him. He told me he didn't believe in it, whatever it was."

"You got it. But this weapon is the real deal, and my guess is, right before he went to that temple, there was an accident of some kind, a mishap. Something went wrong. It caused the sores on Bill's skin, maybe even his heart attack." Remembering Kate's conviction that Bill wasn't actually dead, I corrected myself. "Or whatever."

She was quiet for a moment. "What kind of weapon do you think it is?"

"Good question. Chemical, would be my bet. Bill's skin problems, what happened to Dennis in the hospital..."

"What about what you saw in the hospital, though? That tornado thing with a dog's head? You weren't under the influence of any chemical."

"Maybe I was. Maybe the Egyptians got worried about what Bill was telling the folks at home, and sent them a little taste on the last postcards."

Kate shook her head. "That wouldn't work. Postcards are too open. If they'd put something on them strong enough to make people aggressive or have hallucinations, it would have affected a lot of people before it ever got to the Walkinses."

Now we were both quiet for a bit, lost in thought. I felt an actual strain on my poor brain. We were close, though. So close. What were we missing? How did the Egyptians—or the Americans, for that matter—transfer the weapon to Vermont to destroy Bill's family?

"Maybe there was a package Vittoria didn't tell us about. Or wasn't aware of. Some Egyptian souvenir that was tainted."

"Could be, but I'm sure she would have remembered when we were asking about Bill and she told us about the postcards. Unless Dennis received something from his brother and didn't tell her about it."

That was it. I snapped my fingers. "His last effects. Dennis would have received his brother's personal effects. Some of Bill's stuff had to have been contaminated. It might not have been deliberate at all."

"Of course. Why would the government want to unleash its new discovery on the public? They'd want to keep it hush-hush."

"Exactly."

We grinned at each other, smug in our certainty we'd figured everything out. But all too soon, Kate's smile faded.

"Uh-oh. I know that look. What do you got? What are we missing?" I asked.

"It's not that. I think we're close, very close. Thanks to you, we've figured out a lot more than I thought we would have at this point, especially considering how reticent Bill was."

"Blame Tom Clancy. He taught me everything is a conspiracy." Joking aside, her admiration warmed me. I wanted to be a full partner, to *really* help rather than just be the muscle, and for the first time, I felt like I was.

"The only thing I think we're getting wrong is the age."

Whaa? "The age of what?"

"This weapon. Hear me out. What if the Egyptians haven't discovered a new source of power, but an ancient one? The Temple of Waset is a recent find, and there are chambers that haven't been uncovered. They're not done digging yet. Archaeologists unearth incredible things in Egypt all the time."

As usual, I was unable to keep the influence of the movies I'd seen and books I'd read from interrupting my thoughts. *The Mummy. Stargate. Raiders of the Lost Ark. The Da Vinci Code.* Every single one featured an ancient source of power contemporary governments lost their shit over.

"I suppose it's possible. Tons of people have tried to sell us that story. What are you thinking, the Ark of the Covenant?" I was only half-teasing. Something biblical in nature would explain the weird shit that had happened lately. I felt that jolt of excitement I got whenever I thought about ancient mysteries. Imagine being the dude who discovered the Ten Commandments. What a kick that would be.

"You're on the right track, but the ark, if it exists, belongs to a Christian god. And we're in Egypt."

In spite of my misgivings about the religion I'd been raised in, I'd fallen into the trap of believing our god was the only "real" one. Whether I truly had faith in him, her, or it, was another story.

We'd been led in one consistent direction throughout this entire adventure. "You're talking about Anubis."

"I realize it sounds crazy, but what if Anubis isn't a myth? What if, like Bill said, Anubis is real?"

"What are you saying, Kate—that the weapon isn't chemical, or mechanical, but an ancient Egyptian god? Something we've been taught to believe was a cute little story primitive people told themselves to explain thunder?"

"Or some way to summon him. Think about it, Jacks. I get that this is the most bizarre thing you've encountered so far, and trust me, you're not alone. But what you saw in that hospital room wasn't a cute little story. It was real."

I could still smell the stink of its breath, feel the heat of it on my face. "Well, it wasn't a fucking fable, that's for sure. But the gods of Egypt, Kate? Really? That's a bit hard for me to believe."

"Maybe they're not gods."

"What, then?"

"I don't know." Her voice rose in frustration. "This is

beyond what I do, what I'm capable of. I'm completely in the dark."

"Hey." I took her hand. "Hey, that's not true. You're doing great. You contacted Bill, and now look how close we are to figuring this out. I think we're on the right track, as crazy as it seems."

She took a deep breath, managed a smile. "Me too."

"What about demons? I get that you don't believe in them, but like you said, this is the most bizarre thing you've encountered. Don't we have to at least consider the possibility?" I'd never been sure what to think about demons. My parents believed in them. When we were kids, they'd filled our heads with this stuff about how to deter them and avoid them. And the first time I'd seen *The Exorcist*, it had scared the crap out of me. But actually existing, in the cold light of day? Hard to stomach. Then again, maybe Anubis wasn't a god *or* a demon. Maybe he was something we didn't have a word for yet.

"I've never believed in demons, but Laura does. She believes in angels too. I was always convinced she was just communicating with particularly strong spirits, but she's never bought that. Said whatever these beings are, they were never human." Kate shrugged. "She also says that 'demon' is how religions refer to another religion's gods."

"From my personal experience with the church, I'd buy that. There's only one god, as long as it's ours. Everyone else is living a lie."

"Been there, done that. So, going on what we know so far—Bill said Anubis is real. We both saw something that looked like Anubis at the hospital, and it had incredible power. And we've been experiencing supernatural phenomena that would be beyond an average spirit's capabilities. Even an exceptional spirit's capabilities." Kate settled against the pillows. "People have no idea what they're asking when they beg for 'signs' from the dead. It takes an enormous amount of energy for a spirit to flicker a light, let alone tip a table."

A chill ran over me as an idea popped in my head. "You mentioned the weapon might not be Anubis, but some means of summoning him...*it*. Say this god, demon, or whatever it is, does exist. He's obviously not walking around Egypt, because people would have noticed him. Hell, the *National Enquirer* would be all over this shit."

"True."

"So, what if the weapon, for lack of a better word, was something that allowed Anubis to leave whatever world or dimension he's in and come into ours?" As I said the words, it took everything I had not to cringe in embarrassment. It sounded like the plot of a sci-fi movie, or a video game, not real life. But I'd seen the thing with my own eyes. That was impossible to discount.

"Like *Stargate*."

Ah, we'd watched the same movie. I knew there was a reason I loved this woman. "Kind of, except the soldiers in the film used the Stargate to enter the gods' world. The gods didn't come back through it. And the gods were aliens." Man, come to think of it, that was a really fucked-up movie.

"I hate to say that makes sense, but at this point, who knows what to believe? Gods, demons, aliens—everything is alien, isn't it? Anything we don't understand or can't wrap our heads around is, by definition, alien."

"That thing wasn't a shriveled old extraterrestrial wearing a dog costume, though. That I'm sure of." Whatever it was, it had immense power. *Physical* power.

"If we're right—and I think we're pretty damn close, even if we don't understand everything fully yet—why on earth would our government want to summon Anubis? What would give them the audacity to think they could control something like that, bend it to their will?"

I laughed, even though the situation was far more unnerving than funny. "You need to read more Tom Clancy. Our government thinks they can control everything. It's their greatest downfall."

Kate's eyes widened as if something had pinched her, which was well within the realm of possibility. I understood without asking that her reaction wasn't in response to anything I'd said. Our government had been called power hungry so often it was practically a cliché. Certainly nothing startling about that.

"Do you hear that?"

I tuned into a noise that had been slowly growing in intensity for a while. It was a zapping, sizzling sound, kind of like you'd hear when a mosquito gets caught in one of those bug lights.

Only louder. *Much* louder.

As the sound gained volume, I could hear a rhythmic pounding behind it, almost like drums, but a lot more destructive.

"What the—"

Outside our window, a woman screamed, and we both scrambled off the bed, hurrying to see what was going on. It wasn't difficult to locate the source of the screaming. A woman flailed in the street, crying out in Arabic, her robes and headscarf ablaze.

"Oh my God, she's on fire. Why isn't anyone helping her?" Kate's voice broke.

We soon saw why no one had come to the woman's aid.

Tiny stars were falling from the sky.

Pinpricks of fire, they alighted whatever they touched. Whenever a man would run out to help the woman, he would be struck and burned by the missiles. The stench of burning hair and skin permeated our room as smoke rose from wherever the pellets hit, singeing arms and legs and clothing.

"What the fuck is going on, Kate?" *Was it terrorists? Would the hotel be hit next?* Though I hadn't accepted it yet, I already knew the hotel was under attack. The destructive thumping, sizzling sound had grown deafening as the missiles pounded against the roof.

"Hail of fire," she yelled, holding on to the windowsill. "The seventh plague of Egypt."

"But—this isn't localized, Kate. Those people are getting hurt. There must be something we can do to help."

A group of Muslim women had at last dragged their blazing sister to safety. I hoped she would be okay, but I had my doubts. That cooked-flesh smell hung heavy in the air. While my stomach turned, I was about to bolt out the door when Kate took hold of my arm.

"We're on his turf. He has a lot more power here."

"Who, Anubis?"

She turned to me with a wild light in her eyes I'd seen before. Inwardly, I groaned, knowing that Kate was about to do something crazy, something I'd have absolutely no chance talking her out of.

"We've got to go down there," she said. "We've got to stop it."

On the way out the door, she grabbed the statue of Anubis.

~ CHAPTER THIRTEEN ~

Kate

AS I RUSHED DOWN THE STAIRS TO THE STREET, not daring to take the elevator, it dawned on me that I had no idea what to do. In Nightridge, I'd been able to stop the rain of frogs, but only with Laura's help. Here I had no psychic to stand beside me, and I desperately needed one. Pushing past the spirits who called to me, begging for help, I hurtled toward my death. For surely that's where I was going. Who could step into fiery hail and expect to live?

"Yes, you do."

A diminutive woman appeared in front of me from the darkened stairwell. Her English had the lovely lilt of a native Egyptian's, and soulful eyes dominated her tiny face. Though she'd startled me, I liked her immediately.

"Sorry?"

"I don't mean to intrude on your private thoughts, but I felt honor bound to correct you. You believe you have no powerful psychic to stand beside you, but you do. You have me."

Before I could respond, Jackson came pounding down the stairs. "Kate, please think about this. You can't go out there—it's suicide."

The strange woman appraised him. "Your friend will come to no harm, I promise you. You must let her fulfill her purpose."

Jacks, not given to social niceties at the best of times, was understandably flustered, given the situation. "Who the fuck are you?"

"I am Fatima." She returned her attention to me. "I heard about what happened at the temple, and I've been tracking you ever since."

More screams from outside made me stiffen. "I have to go. I don't know how to help, but I have to try."

"You *do* know," she said, slipping her small hand into mine. "And I will be with you."

As Fatima's skin made contact, an electric current shot through my body, staggering me. The strength went out of my legs and I sagged against the stairwell.

"What the fuck did you do to her? Let go!" Jacks lunged at the psychic, but thankfully I was able to summon enough strength to call him off.

"She didn't do anything. She's just…very strong."

How could I explain that whatever was going on with Fatima was about a million times more intense than Laura's abilities? Until then, Laura had been the most powerful psychic I'd ever encountered. Alone, I didn't have much of a shot, but with Fatima by my side, I was galvanized.

She pulled me to my feet as if I weighed nothing. "Let us go."

I'm not sure how many guys would have willingly plunged into a hail of fire, but as Jackson's jaw tightened and he lowered his head, I saw that's exactly what he intended to do.

"Jacks, you don't need to do this. Stay here. I don't

want to see you hurt."

"I'll be fine," he said, gently shaking me off. His words belied the fear in his voice. "If you're determined to kill yourself, the least I can do is be there to make sure your body gets a decent burial."

"I appreciate that."

We were grinning stupidly at each other when Fatima tugged on my arm, giving me another jolt. "Please, no more talking. We have already wasted too much time."

Guarding the bare skin of his scalp with his arms, Jacks darted out the door in front of us, heading to a woman and child who stood in the line of fire, wailing, either too frightened or too injured to run for cover.

After that, I lost sight of him.

Mesmerized by the endless rain of sparks, I gazed at the glowing orbs that arced around us, sizzling near our faces close enough to make me flush before landing harmlessly at our feet.

"Wow." As others were hit and cried out in agony, we continued to pass through the worst of the firestorm untouched, the hail lashing at us and then as quickly falling away. It was like we carried an invisible shield.

"You see," Fatima said, and it wasn't a question. "Together, we are very strong."

Energy coursed through me, making it difficult to speak. I'd never felt anything quite like it before. My grandmother, bless her soul, had called it *reaching*. I could reach outward to talk to difficult or uncommunicative spirits. When Lily's soul had been kidnapped and taken to Poveglia, I'd used reaching to speak to it. But rather than project this energy outward, I now felt it growing inside me, building and building. To what purpose, I had no idea.

My hair felt weightless as static electricity lifted it off my shoulders. My arms and neck prickled with goose bumps; my nipples hardened. Unable to form the words or shout loudly enough to be heard over the shrieking mob, I hoped Fatima would not need me to. *What's happening?*

Do not be afraid. Her thoughts had the same softness as her voice. *You are about to discover what you are truly capable of. This is your destiny, Kate Carlsson.*

What I'm capable of? I communicated with spirits. As far as I knew, that was my only gift, and it was more than enough. I wasn't sure I wanted to discover any other destiny. I resolved not to ask Fatima any more questions.

You are wrong. You are so much more than you have ever believed.

What if I don't want to be more? The thought leapt to mind before I could help it. It was foolish as well as selfish. I couldn't turn away from The Gift any more than I could change my eye color or my hair's tendency to frizz in high humidity. It was a part of me, and if I was something else as well, something that could put a stop to the torment these innocent Egyptians were enduring, who was I to refuse or resist it?

That said, I was scared beyond belief. Fatima's fingers tightened around mine. "We are almost there. Can you see him? He is not a spirit, so you may have to look harder. Search with your heart, not your eyes."

She'd led me into the middle of a town square. All around us market stalls burned, throwing off so much light it made my eyes water.

And then I saw him.

Fatima no longer had to show me the way. Holding tight to her hand, I walked toward him.

"Hello, Bill."

The soldier appeared more solid than he had at the temple, but I could see the fire through him, as if the flames were consuming his organs while I watched. The effect was unnerving. He inclined his head politely, dog tags jangling around his neck. "Ma'am. It's a pleasure to see you again." His eyes flicked to Fatima and then quickly away.

"Are you the cause of this, Bill?"

"No, ma'am." His deceptively youthful face crumpled. "This is not my doing. It's his."

New strength and confidence flowed through me. There was no doubt where they were coming from. "I think I need to meet him. Can you summon him for us?"

Even with the fire casting a warm glow against him, I could see how pale he'd gone at my request. "No, ma'am. That is a bad idea. You would not like for me to do that."

"Yes, we would," Fatima said, but he ignored her, which pissed me off.

"Christ, Bill. People are dying. They're suffering. The people of this country, the country you loved so much, are hurting, and it's all because of you and whatever you got involved with."

"No, not me. I'd never hurt them. That's why I'm here. I want to help."

Was this guy thick? How on earth did he think he was helping by standing here watching the show? "Then summon the bastard responsible. I want to talk to him." It's amazing how forceful I can sound when I'm terrified out of my mind.

"I'm afraid I cannot do that, ma'am. I'd be signing your death warrant."

"You signed a lot of other people's, didn't you? Without

so much as a twinge of conscience. There's a woman near our hotel I'd love to introduce you to. If she managed to keep any of her skin, I'd be surprised."

As I'd hoped, I hit a nerve. The soldier winced. "I told you, I didn't know. I didn't believe. By the time I did, it was too late to stop it."

"To stop *what*, Bill?"

"This man is too weak, too afraid. He will not do what you ask," Fatima said. "You will have to do it."

Her words surprised me enough to draw my attention away from the soldier. "Do what?"

"Summon him."

Before I could react, Fatima reached into the pocket of my pajama pants, withdrawing the cheap statue of Anubis. She handed it to me. "Do it now. There is no time to spare."

I gaped at the ferocious face of the dog-headed god before lookingfink I could summon an Egyptian god with a cheap, dime-store souvenir? How did one summon a god, in any case? It wasn't like I could slap my knee and call, "Here, puppy. Here, Anubis."

"Center yourself, Kate," Fatima snapped, jerking my arm. "Focus. Remember what I told you. You are more than you have ever believed." She closed her eyes, raising her other arm so it appeared to float on the air. The energy I'd felt build in me went crazy, crackling and popping, tingling in the fingers that were linked with hers. If I'd touched anyone at that moment, I would have given him one hell of a zap.

Following Fatima's lead, I closed my eyes, feeling a bit silly. But then I began to get angry. How dare this thing, whatever it was, torture innocent people? How dare it fuck with our lives in this way? It didn't belong here. It could take its stupid plagues and go back where it came from.

My blood heated; my chest tightened. Laura's face floated into view, and as from a long distance, I could hear her chanting a protection spell. My heightened emotions had awakened her, then. We'd always had a close bond.

Fatima squeezed my hand. "It is working. He is drawing near. Do not falter. Stand strong."

The wind howled around us, gaining in intensity as it whipped my hair back from my face and tore at my T-shirt. Though my eyes remained closed, the heat from the fiery hail made my forehead drip with sweat, and I could tell the pellets were circling us too, faster and faster.

The air grew heavy, as if something had seized me around the ribcage, crushing me. When the pressure grew unbearable, I dared to look. Fatima's eyes were closed, her dark hair flying around her head like an aura. She mumbled something under her breath, brow furrowed with concentration. I had the strangest feeling she and Laura were saying the same words in different languages.

A tower of black smoke blocked my view of the square. As I watched, gritting my teeth, it moved closer, undulating like a tornado so I could see the glittering spheres of fire within.

He's here. I pushed the thought at Fatima, not trusting she would hear my voice.

Stay strong. Her eyes remained closed; her focus never faltered.

Turning back to the smoke, I was startled to see it was gone. In its place was an exceptionally muscular man. His skin was charcoal, making the gold of his kilt gleam. His massive chest bare except for an extravagant collar-style necklace, he towered above us, stretching at least ten feet tall.

Craning my head to see his face, I was horrified but not surprised to see it was that of a dog, with a narrow, sharp muzzle and cruel eyes.

"You would dare speak to me, mortal?"

His words blasted through my brain like an aneurysm, making me wince in spite of myself. The pain was so great I wanted to sink to my knees, but Fatima jerked my arm again.

No. He is afraid of you. Do not falter.

Afraid of me? I found that highly unlikely. He was every bit as imposing and terrifying as you'd expect a god to be. In one motion, he could wrap a hand around my neck and crush the life out of me.

And yet, he kept his distance.

My mind raced. In spite of everything I'd seen, everything that had happened, I'd never believed this moment would come. I never thought the thing in front of me could actually exist.

I felt new sympathy for the soldier.

"I demand you leave this place." My voice was as loud and powerful as I could possibly make it. Fatima gripped my hand with the strength of a prizefighter, encouraging me to hold my ground. Whatever this creature was, we couldn't show fear.

The man tilted his canine head (or did the canine tilt his human neck?) before emitting a harsh sound that was half laugh, half bark. "What right do you have to make demands of me? I can destroy you."

If he could destroy you, he already would have.

Steeling myself, I hoped Fatima was right. "You do not

belong on this plane. We demand you go back to your own realm."

Another laugh-bark. "You are merely an amusing obstacle in my path, but you will not remain one for long," Anubis continued, white spittle flecking his muzzle as he spoke. "I am here for the girl. Let her fulfill her destiny and all this"—he lifted his hands to the sky, letting the hail bounce harmlessly off his enormous palms—"will end. Peace will return to your miserable planet. As much as it ever has."

My stomach dropped, for there was no doubt in my mind which girl he referred to. Unbelievable. First the Doctor of Death, and now an ancient Egyptian monster. How much trouble could one twelve-year-old girl get into? *Lily, what in the hell did you do this time?*

"The child is not to blame. If you must direct your ire at a target, turn it toward the girl's uncle, who willingly sacrificed her in return for my participation in this foolish experiment." Anubis shrugged his massive shoulders in a surprisingly human gesture. "As this cost me nothing, it was an easy trade to make."

"It wasn't like that. I didn't say you could have her."

The weak protests reminded me that Bill was still here. "I would never give her up. I love her."

I'd suspected Bill was misguided. Stupid, even. But evil enough to offer his own niece to this demon? The depths of human depravity never failed to astonish me.

"What experiment?" As terrifying as Anubis was, he was more forthcoming than Bill. It was worth a shot.

The dog-man roared. "Ask your friend. I am sure he would love to fill you in, since it was his discovery. Isn't that correct, Lieutenant?"

Bill edged closer to us, sidling behind Fatima. What a hero. "I had nothing to do with this, ma'am," he said, the pitch of his voice rising in near hysteria. "You have to believe me."

Anubis snorted. "His whining grows tiresome. I will leave him here with you. If you kill him, ensure he suffers. You will soon learn he well deserves it."

Lowering his great head, his eyes glowing, the dog-man continued. "Take heed, mortal. The girl belongs to me. She has been promised. Interfere with me again, and I will set forth the tenth plague."

His voice deepened to a growl that was almost indiscernible from the thunder that raged in the sky. "Next time, you will not see me coming."

A flash of lightning, unbearably close, seared our skin. As we fell to the street, I lost my grip on Fatima's hand. The energy that had circled around us in a maelstrom flickered and faded.

"Kate! Kate, are you all right?"

Jackson leaned over me, his face streaked with soot. Unable to speak, I nodded as he scooped me into his arms. "I'm fine...I think. How are you?" The heady smell of smoke clung to him. "You look hurt."

He cradled my head to his chest. The familiar rhythm of his heart relaxed my own. "Got a little burned, but I got everyone off the street. That's the important thing." He stroked my hair. "That woman was pretty bad, Kate. I don't think she's going to make it."

The shock of seeing Anubis in the flesh had temporarily distracted me from the horror that had unfolded outside our hotel. Remembering the screaming woman, my stomach roiled. "You did what you could, Jacks. This is no one's fault, especially not yours." *Well, maybe Bill's.*

"I wish I could have done more. I felt so helpless. And then I saw you with that…that *thing*, and I couldn't get anywhere near you, couldn't help you. It was like something held me in place." His voice cracked. "I'm so glad you're okay. I thought—well, never mind what I thought."

"Of course she is okay. Kate is a woman of great power." Fatima's dress was rumpled and dirty, and her headscarf was nowhere to be seen, but she hadn't lost any of her spirit.

"Tell me something I don't know." Jackson offered her his hand. "Guess I should thank you properly for helping us, even if I don't really understand what you did. I'm Jackson, Kate's…."

Seeing his hesitancy, my heart broke a little. "Jackson is my partner in crime. Among other things."

"Fatima. I am happy to assist you. As you have seen, we share a common problem."

"I hate to break up this little love fest, but if you plan to save my niece, shouldn't you be getting to it?"

Jacks's eyes widened when he noticed Bill sitting in the dirt behind us. "Where the fuck did he come from?"

"Anubis tired of him, I guess. I think he wants us to torture the truth out of him." Shooting the soldier a look of death, I continued, "Let's hope it doesn't come to that." While I'd known Bill wasn't dead, it was still a shock to have him here, as a flesh-and-blood man. Jackson's reaction was understandable—I only hoped he didn't expect me to explain it, because I couldn't. At least, not yet.

Bill raised his hands in surrender. "Hey, I never lied to you. You tell me how you'd explain what you just saw."

"Gee, I don't know, Bill. How about something along

the lines of, 'You know Anubis, the ancient Egyptian god of mummification? Well, me and the guys were messing around and we managed to lure him here to earth by offering my niece on a silver platter.' That would have been a start."

"He gave Lily to that thing?" Jackson's arms tightened around me, and I knew I didn't have much time to diffuse the situation before my partner beat Bill to a bloody pulp.

"It wasn't like that. It was never like that. He's lying. They all lie." The soldier's attention darted to each of us in turn. "You'll find that out soon enough."

Before I could ask the obvious, Jackson was on it. "What do you mean, they *all* lie? Are you saying there are more than Anubis?"

"Of course there are. Dozens more, and Anubis is hardly the worst." Bill spit on the ground, his features twisting in disgust. "If you think he's bad, you should see Set."

"But that's impossible," Jacks said. "How are the four of us supposed to stop an army of Egyptian gods?"

"They are not gods." Fatima shook her head. "They are monsters."

Great. That makes it so much better.

~ CHAPTER FOURTEEN ~

Jackson

NO LONGER TRANSLUCENT, THE SOLDIER WAS now very much a man. A foul-smelling asshole of a man who was lucky to be alive once the truth of what he'd done to Lily had been revealed. Only Kate's calming influence kept me from murdering him. For now, I had to content myself with giving him death glares across the room.

With the cluster of ambulances and dozens of paramedics rushing around, no one had given our sorry little group a second glance when we trudged back to our hotel room. Fatima seemed okay enough, I guess, but it was weird to have this relative stranger in our personal space. Bill, on the other hand, could have been left on the street for all I cared, but the women insisted we needed to get what information we could from him. The soldier was the only one who had any answers, assuming there were any answers. I would love to know how he planned to explain the thing we'd just seen. Couldn't wait.

I'll say one thing for the guy. He must have had some mind-reading tricks of his own. Meeting my eyes, I was surprised to see him flush. "I'm sorry for stinking up your room. I can barely stand myself, to tell the truth. I hate to impose, but any chance I could have a shower before I spill my guts?"

"I thought we were running out of time."

"Jacks, we've been through a lot tonight, and it's not over yet. Let's order some room service and let Bill wash up. Fatima too, if she likes." Kate patted my arm, giving me the most exhausted smile I'd seen yet. "We're a team now, for better or worse."

I'd rather be left on the bench forever than have to play ball with that guy, but I shrugged. "Go ahead," I told the soldier, since he appeared to be waiting for my permission. Another thing to dislike about him—Kate's word wasn't enough. I hated guys like that.

Bill tipped his head before disappearing into our bathroom, taking his miasma of stench with him. "Thank you."

Once he was out of my sight, some of the weight I'd been feeling left my shoulders and I slumped into the nearest chair. "Sorry, I'm just worried about Lily."

I could feel eyes burning into me, and was startled to find Fatima assessing me, her expression bright and her head tilted. She reminded me of an inquisitive rodent, but not in a sharp, pointy-snout way. She was definitely one of the cute ones. Still, no one likes being gawked at. "What?"

"You're a good man. You really care about this girl."

"Of course I care about her. She's like a sister to me." That wasn't quite it, though. As much as I loved my little sister, I didn't feel the same drive to protect Roxi. But then again, Roxi's soul hadn't been kidnapped and no dog-faced ghoul was threatening her.

"You had it right the first time."

I looked up to find Fatima smirking at me. "You

shouldn't overthink things so much. If you followed your initial instincts more often, you'd find they lead you to the right path. That enhanced clarity you desire? You already have it. You just don't trust it."

Shit, this chick was as cryptic as Laura. Psychics drove me crazy. "What are you saying?"

"Lily is not an ordinary girl. I believe you've both figured that much out by now. She may be a child, but already she is attracting the wrong element, those who would use her extraordinary abilities for dark purposes. She needs a protector, a guardian." Fatima's dark eyes shone as she nodded at me. "*You* are that guardian, Jackson. That's why you feel like you would move heaven and earth to save her. You would."

I thought back to when I'd met Lily—or Lily's soul, to be more accurate. Since I'd been unable to see or hear her, we could only communicate through writing. Sometimes I'd felt the lightest pressure on my hand when she'd tried to warn me about things. I cared about her, sure. She was a kid caught in a life-threatening, wretched situation, and Kate had been hired to save her. There was nothing supernatural about it.

"See, there you go—second-guessing yourself again. Why do you do this?"

"It's called critical thinking. I don't swallow every lump of shit a stranger dishes out."

Kate winced at the anger in my voice, but for once I didn't much care. I was so tired of hearing these fucking fables. "Anyone would care about Lily. She's a kid whose father attacked her while she was lying helpless in a hospital bed. This may come as a great shock, but I'm a decent guy. I'm not going to sit around and let that happen, but

I wouldn't let it happen to anyone. That doesn't mean I'm some mythical guardian, like something out of *The Lord of the Rings*. Give me a fucking break."

Fatima smiled. "You are absolutely right. Those things do not indicate anything except basic human decency. It is the lengths you will go to in order to protect Lily that sets you apart."

Before I could think over the few times I'd had to step in to help, the woman raised her hand. "It's too soon for you to accept the truth of what I am saying, but it won't be long before you realize I am correct. You are Lily's guardian. It's one thing you both have in common." She looked over at Kate. "Neither one of you has any idea what you're capable of, or how to use it."

"Yeah, speaking of…I meant to ask you, what exactly did we do out there?" Kate asked. "Why didn't the hail hit us? Why didn't Anubis rip us apart while he had the chance?"

I had a sudden urge to knock on wood or cross myself. That's the thing about gods—or monsters, as Fatima called them. What was to stop Anubis from returning and trying again? It's not like some drywall and a few sticks of timber were enough to keep us safe.

"You're right again, Jackson. But *she* is enough." Fatima nodded at Kate.

"What's going on? Why does she keep responding to stuff you didn't say?" Kate wrinkled her nose, and I could see she was getting annoyed. I was glad I wasn't the only one.

"Apparently my mind is an open book."

"You heart is as well. You need to learn how to better close them both, or Anubis and the others will take advantage of this." Fatima sucked in her breath, as if something had spooked her. I couldn't imagine what, after she'd stared down an Egyptian god like it was no big deal. "I suspect you've already been tampered with."

Tampered. Now there's a nasty word no one wants to hear about themselves. It brought to mind Yuèhai and a particular night in China I'd love to forget. "Tampered with how?"

"One thing at a time. You need to use what the other psychic taught you to create a wall, and you"—she turned to Kate again—"have to open your eyes."

Uh-oh. My girl was a redhead, with a temper to match. As the saying goes, you wouldn't like her when she's angry. But Kate only leaned closer to Fatima as if to say, "Tell me more."

"What is it? What am I missing?" she asked.

"You and I are very similar. We both commune with spirits. We absorb their pain, their torment, their violent deaths," Fatima said.

That much I knew. I'd seen this ability, this "gift," as Kate called it, almost kill her at least once.

"Have you ever tried releasing it?"

"Releasing it?" Kate wrinkled her nose again, but this time she looked more confused than angry. "Releasing it how?"

Fatima gestured to the scar around Kate's neck, the lovely parting souvenir Isabelle had given her when Kate was just a kid. Normally it was a faint, white line against her pale skin, almost invisible. But as the Muslim woman pointed to it, I could have sworn it flushed purple, a recent wound. "The girl who gave that to you. Can you feel her pain?"

"Yes. Every day." Kate's eyes welled with tears. She'd told me the story of Isabelle in China. As always, her pain was difficult for me to watch. There was so much of it.

"Good. Gather it within your core, as if you were taking her pain and winding it into a ball in your gut." Fatima pounded her stomach with a tiny fist. "Take all of it, every little bit. Let me know when you have it."

Kate closed her eyes. The lights flickered, and I felt the air in the room take on weight, like it had when Laura was trying to communicate with the missing Egyptologist. Shifting in my chair, I thought of my family back in Minneapolis, probably watching some inane sitcom or getting ready for work. I loved them, but I'd always thought their lives were small, boring. Having nothing more to look forward to than that evening's dinner had scared the shit out of me. I'd been determined not to sleepwalk my way through life, but at that moment, I would have killed for some boredom. As it turned out, being scared all the time wasn't much fun.

Kate's breathing was audible now, raspier. The only other sound was the patter of running water hitting the bathtub, which irritated me. We were in the desert, for Christ's sake. Water was at a premium. When was the soldier going to get his ass back out here and give us some answers?

"Okay."

She seemed exactly the same, except for her eyes. Her pupils were dilated like a cat's in a dim room. Sparks of static electricity crackled in her long hair, and I knew that if I touched her, I'd get the shock of my life. That was actually a good way to sum up what Kate had been to me.

The shock of my life.

But God help me, I loved her in spite of it. Or maybe because of it.

"Push it out the window with everything you've got," Fatima said. "Get rid of it once and for all."

Kate narrowed those creepy new eyes of hers at the window. The chair vibrated under my butt, and then I realized I could feel a similar tremor under my feet. The entire fucking room was shaking.

I had a bad feeling about this.

"Wait—"

Something flew out of my girlfriend's chest, speeding toward the window. It moved too fast for me to get a good look at it, for which I should probably be forever grateful. All I know is it was dark and ugly. When it hit, it was like a volcano erupted.

The window, frame and all, blasted from the wall, glass shattering. The blowback was enormous, as if every particle of oxygen had been sucked out of the room. Cracks ran along the walls, sending a shower of paint and plaster to the floor. The floor bucked under my chair, and I had to hold on to avoid being flung to the ground. It barely lasted a couple of seconds, but in those seconds, I was convinced I was going to die, and that death would be preferable to the agony and fear I currently felt.

"Holy shit."

We turned to see Bill standing in the bathroom doorway, a towel wrapped around his waist. His mouth hung open as he stared at the hole in the wall where a window had been a moment before.

"Jacks?"

Kate gazed up at me, her pupils normal again. Tears trickled down the sides of her beautiful face in a constant stream. I'd given up trying to wipe them away. There were always more.

It hadn't taken much convincing to get Bill and Fatima to give us a little space. The psychic had taken the soldier to get a bite to eat, and I trusted her enough to bring him back if he tried to do a runner. As much as it pained me to admit, we needed him. He was the one person who had any idea what was going on.

"Shh, don't say it. Try to relax; get some rest. They'll be back soon enough."

Too soon for my taste. Even though I was eager to do something, to take active steps to protect Lily, I was happier with them gone. In their own way, they both gave me the creeps. And Fatima—wow. I get the impact of a live demonstration, but she should have warned us.

How were we supposed to pay for the damages? Our room looked like it had survived a nuclear blast.

Kate pushed herself up and wrapped her arms around me, burying her head in my neck. "I'm not tired," she said, her voice muffled against my skin. "I've actually never felt better."

She radiated heat, which was welcome, because Egypt got chilly at night. Shockingly cold, especially when you considered how hot it was during the day. The temperature in the room was about the same as your average freezer's. We'd have to hang a blanket over the hole in the wall soon if we planned to get any sleep.

Adjusting my arms so I could hold her, I cradled her head against my chest. Now that I could touch her, I relaxed.

She was magic that way. "I'm not surprised. She's gone now, isn't she?"

Kate ran a tentative finger along the scar on her throat, which was once again a thin, white line. "I think so."

"You've been carrying Isabelle's pain around for years. No wonder you feel great. A huge weight's been lifted off your shoulders. Does this mean she can't hurt you anymore?"

"I'm not sure. I don't know anything about this." She pulled away slightly to look at me. "I've never felt anything like it before. And it was so easy, like scratching an itch."

I took in the destruction of the wall. Great chunks of plaster had fallen out, exposing the bare boards beneath. It was hard not to be scared of that kind of power. I couldn't wrap my head around what I'd seen, that this extraordinary burst of energy had come from the woman in my arms.

"What didn't you want me to say?"

"Huh?"

"When I first said your name, you shushed me. You said, 'Don't say it.' Are you a mind reader now too?"

"You know me—I hate to be left out. No, it's not about reading minds. It's about spending enough time with you to be able to predict what you're going to say."

"Oh, really. This should be interesting. What was I going to say, Jacks?"

I sighed. "You were going to ask if I wanted to leave you, if I'd changed my mind. The same thing you always ask whenever something crazy happens. For Christ's sake, Kate. What is it going to take to get it through your thick skull that I'm not going anywhere?"

She turned away from me, but not before I saw tears shimmer in her eyes again.

"I'm sorry; that was a bit harsh."

"A bit?" Keeping her face averted, she wiped it with a corner of the bedsheet.

"Okay, a lot. I guess it bugs me that you don't have any faith in me, in this. What am I doing wrong? Am I such an asshole that you think I'm going to cut and run the second things get a little challenging?"

She laughed—a dry, bitter sound—as she gestured to the battered wall. "I think they're more than a little challenging, Jackson. I'm a freak."

"So what? We're all freaks." What Kate had done had scared the crap out of me, but I was afraid for *her*, not for myself. I only wished she could understand the difference.

"I'm more freakish than most." She gave me one of her patented "Don't patronize me" looks. "We're not talking about your average quirk here. It's not like you've discovered I snore or that I always misplace my keys."

"No, and you also don't play games. You don't get pissed at me, expect me to read your mind, and then say you're 'fine' when I ask you what's wrong. You don't lie. You haven't killed anyone that I'm aware of, but if you did, I'm sure they deserved it. You're not afraid to speak your mind." I tucked a lock of her fiery hair behind her ear. "Actually, that last one is both a blessing and a curse. But the other stuff? That's all to the good."

"Are you saying none of this scares you? Because I find that really hard to believe."

"Of course it scares me. We've got Egyptian gods wandering around, fire and frogs falling from the sky, and a dead soldier who suddenly isn't dead. If none of this made me shit my pants, I'd be seriously concerned about my mental state."

She smiled. "You have such a way with words. Nice image."

"Part of my charm. I think what you're actually asking is if any of this has scared me away from *you*, and nothing could be further from the truth. You could shoot lightning bolts from your ass and I'd still be here. My only request would be that you point that lovely posterior in the opposite direction."

Leaning against me again, she sighed until her entire body shook. "Where did you come from? Other guys, they couldn't handle a couple of ghosts. When the first frog hit, they would have been running for the hills."

"Well, despite all appearances to the contrary, maybe your taste in men has improved. Did you ever consider that?"

This time I felt her smile rather than saw it. "Actually, no."

"Maybe you should. I'm not going anywhere, Kate. Not unless you want me to."

~ CHAPTER FIFTEEN ~

Kate

AFTER A SHOWER AND PROBABLY THE FIRST HOT meal he'd had in months, Bill finally looked more human than ghost. The wraithlike grayish tone had vanished from his skin, though the haunted expression remained. I suspected it always would. No matter what he ended up telling us, it was clear to me that he'd seen things no mainstreamer was supposed to.

Ever since Fatima had sprung that "guardian" stuff on us, the soldier hadn't been able to look Jackson in the eye.

"Let's get on with it," Jacks said, an edge to his voice I hadn't heard since his scuffles with Harold in China. He'd never liked the soldier—that much was obvious—but I was afraid his connection to Lily had curdled that instinctive dislike into hatred. "We've wasted too much time as it is."

Bill ran a hand through his hair and hunched forward, as if the weight of his story crushed him. "Before I begin, you have to know I didn't mean for any of this to happen. And I didn't sacrifice Lily. I wouldn't do that. I love that girl." His voice cracked, his eyes pleading. "I'm her god-father, did you know that? She's had my heart wrapped around her little finger since she was this big."

The soldier spread his hands apart to indicate something the size of a loaf of bread. A *small* loaf of bread.

"We believe you, Bill," I said, even though I wasn't sure I did. Not yet. But it was what he needed to hear. "Just start from the beginning. Tell us everything you remember."

The soldier gazed toward the broken window, which was now blocked by the wool blanket he'd hung to keep the chill out. "It's not like I could ever forget. And not for lack of trying."

Jacks made an exasperated sound, and I pinched his leg. As much as I wished Bill would get on with it too, people needed to tell their stories in their own time. It did no good to rush them.

Folding his hands between his knees, Bill cleared his throat. "I've been coming to Egypt as part of a military exercise called Operation Bright Star for a long time. It's no secret I love this country. My superiors noticed I was always reluctant to leave and eager to return. I started learning the language, and well…I guess my enthusiasm made an impression.

"During the last operation, my colonel asked if I'd mind staying on for a bit. Said the Egyptians had discovered something big, and they wanted a guy to stick around and see if there was anything to it. Though I'm far from fluent, I already knew more Egyptian Arabic than anyone else on my team, and my colonel said it would be an asset. I felt I was finally being recognized." He paused to swipe at his eyes, keeping his head lowered. "I was such a dumbass."

"None of this was your fault," Fatima said with such conviction it startled me. "You must not blame yourself."

The soldier lifted his red-rimmed eyes to hers. "That's

easier said than done, ma'am. Anyway, it was mostly a waiting game for a while. It took so long for anyone to contact me that by the time they did, I'd thought they'd forgotten all about me. They asked me to come to a new archeological site one night. A team of Egyptologists had stumbled across something they thought our government would be interested in."

"Interested in buying, you mean," Jacks said, and I was relieved to hear the harshness was gone from his voice.

"Most likely. Things have been tough around here since the revolution. Lots of people are suffering."

As Bill continued his story, I realized the dig site he was describing was none other than the Temple of Waset. "But that's impossible. Yes, there are some undiscovered chambers, but that temple would have taken decades to uncover. How could it have been a new site that recently?"

"Let's just say that once the archaeologists unveiled their great discovery, things progressed pretty rapidly." There was a coldness in his eyes that made me shiver. "Some people called it a miracle, but there was nothing miraculous about it. That place was evil. I could feel it the first time I saw it, but back then, I was a simple guy. I shrugged it off as my imagination."

Fatima made the sign of protection from the evil eye. I could feel waves of energy radiating from her. In her own way, she was protecting us, even now.

"They'd discovered a shrine. It was the second intact shrine to the ancient gods discovered in the entire country, so everyone was pretty excited." Bill cleared his throat again, looking at each of us in turn. "I wondered why they couldn't feel what I was feeling."

"Which was?" Jacks asked.

"I can't really explain it. It was dread, I guess. I just knew it was a bad place. As soon as I got there, I wanted to leave."

"Why didn't you?" I asked, though I already knew the answer.

"Orders are orders. I'd been charged with finding out what this discovery was, and I wasn't going to leave until I did. Besides, I kept telling myself it was all in my head. Just fatigue, maybe a bit of PTSD left over from Afghanistan.

"Anyway, they didn't call us in to see the shrine itself. It was the statue of the jackal in the middle of the chamber that had caught their attention. They wanted to study it, but they couldn't remove it, you see. Every time they tried, someone got hurt. And with every attempt, the injuries were more serious. The last guy nearly lost an arm when the jackal shifted and crushed it, but before that happened, he'd managed to dislodge the statue from its pedestal a bit. Enough to hear a noise coming from inside."

Bill paused long enough to drink from the bottle of water he'd brought back from the market. "Turned out the statue was hollow, and when the archaeologists took a closer look, they found the base of it was filled with these little statues. Figurines. One for each of the Egyptian gods. They weren't canopic jars. They were too small, too skinny, to hold organs, but their heads were made to come off just the same.

"Before my colonel contacted me, a scientist opened one. Blew his fucking head off."

Wincing, I wondered why I hadn't sensed the hapless scientist's death. That kind of tragedy tends to leave a deep impression on a place.

"The radiation levels in that chamber were off the charts.

Pardon my French, but it made the hair on your balls stand on end to go anywhere near it. The archaeologists were dropping like flies. They lost their teeth, their mouths filled with blood, their skin was covered in sores. You can see why my superiors thought it might be some kind of extraordinarily powerful chemical weapon."

"What was it really, Bill?" I asked.

"I think it was a warning system. When that jar took the guy's head off at the neck, splattering his brains over the walls—" Seeing Fatima cringe, he apologized. "Sorry to be so graphic, but that should have been enough for them to leave it alone. Of course, that's not human nature. We're always going where we're not wanted, where we don't belong. And we never give a shit about what harm we cause."

"Sounds funny to hear a soldier concerned about causing harm."

I wanted to give Jackson another not-so-friendly pinch, but thankfully Bill didn't appear to be offended. "I'm not a soldier anymore. I'm just a guy trying to figure out how to clean up the mess I made."

"Did they open the rest of the jars, Bill?" I kept my voice deliberately soft, suspecting he was nearing the most difficult part of his story.

"Not them, no. But they figured the opened one had been defused, so they took it to a lab in order to study it, maybe isolate some of the chemicals that had made it go boom. Problem was, it wasn't empty. Like I said, the first blast was an early warning system. What followed was worse...a *lot* worse."

"Anubis," Fatima whispered, holding up a hand against the evil eye.

"Yeah. After the initial blast, the jar was found several

meters away, its cap back on. They used a robot to pry it off. I guess they must have been prepared for more fireworks. They certainly weren't ready for that...*thing*."

Bill dragged a hand over his face, pulling at his skin until it looked like melting candlewax. "It killed everyone. It exploded from that jar and tore everyone to pieces. All that was left was shredded meat. But the security footage had survived, and that's what my colonel wanted me to take a look at.

"I couldn't fucking believe what I was seeing—sorry, ladies. You've seen him now too, so you know our brains weren't meant to process stuff like this. It's enough to drive you right out of your mind. Creatures like him don't exist. They just don't."

"Except they obviously do," Jacks said.

Fatima's eyes met mine, and I didn't have to be psychic to read her mind. "It's a little different for us," I said. "We've always lived with the understanding that there's much more to the world than science would have us believe. Since we were children, we've had to accept we could see things other people refused to acknowledge."

"Since birth," Fatima added. "When I was an infant, I reacted to things no one else could see. My mother knew then I had the second sight."

"Then you tell me, ladies. What *is* that thing?"

The sincerity in the soldier's voice startled me. My great hope that Bill would point us in the right direction faded. So much for getting answers. "You mean the military doesn't know?"

He shrugged. "If they do, they're certainly not telling me. Whatever the creatures are, they're not from Earth, I can tell you that, but I don't think they're alien, either. I don't believe in that Area 51/Roswell crap. Wherever they were keeping me, it was like Egypt, but not Egypt."

"They were keeping you in the past," Fatima said, and I thought of what Laura had told us about Eden.

She's not anywhere police will be able to find her. She's not in the spirit realm, but she's not here either. She's beyond our reach.

Could Eden have somehow gotten hold of one of those figurines? Was she in the past? Is that why neither Laura nor I could get to her? I'd never heard of such a thing, outside of books and movies, but it made terrible sense.

"What happened to you, Bill? If you were only watching the security footage, I don't understand how you were captured." The soldier was still the key to this mess, I was convinced. Buried somewhere in his brain were the answers we needed.

The man leaned back in his chair. "The United States Army isn't known for its imagination. When my superiors saw footage of some creature with a humanoid body and a dog's head tearing the scientists apart, they believed it to be some kind of elaborate hoax. Terrorists using chemicals to mess with our minds. Animated robots. A highly realistic costume. About the only thing they could agree on was that it had immense power. And that this power had to be contained."

It struck me then how much bravery this man had. The evidence of this had been there all along, in his postcards. "You went back to the temple."

"It was stupid, I know. Stupidest thing I ever could have done. But now that my superiors had seen the footage, they no longer wanted me involved. I was a lieutenant; this had become a job for the very best. I was desperate to prove myself, to get the answers they needed, to figure out what was going on before I was shipped home without so much as a 'Good work, soldier.'" He exhaled heavily, deflated. "Pride goeth before a fall, as they say.

"Incredibly, the Egyptians were still letting people visit the site, even after what had happened, but the shrine was roped off. It was easy enough to slip away from the crowd and sneak into the chamber. The figurines were gone, of course, but the statue was there. I ran my hands over its base, crouching down so the guards wouldn't see me. I kept thinking there had to be something else, some clue as to what those figurines were."

Bill paled then, his words catching in his throat. "At first I thought I was hearing tourists, or some of the local kids, but eventually I realized the voices were coming from the back wall of the chamber. I couldn't understand what they were saying, but it sounded like they were calling for help. I pressed my ear to the rock, with my hands braced against the wall. That's when it happened."

The soldier described how something had shot through the stone and seized him by the arms, pulling him through solid rock while he screamed and struggled. Fatima went to him and he clung to her as if she were a lifeline. It had to have been unsettling for her to be touched by a strange man, but if it was, she didn't show it. She whispered comforting words to him, stroking his hair.

Jacks raised an eyebrow at me. Bill's story, while incredible, wasn't as difficult for me to believe. I'd seen the spirits on the other side of that wall. The soldier was telling the truth, weird as it may have sounded.

"Sorry," Bill said, pulling away from Fatima to wipe his eyes on his sleeve. "This is really hard for me to talk about."

"No need to apologize. It had to be terrifying for you."
I sent Fatima a silent thank-you for giving Bill the comfort
he so obviously needed.

"I'm not sure how I survived. Nothing I've experienced during my years in the service prepared me for it."

He told of regaining consciousness in an underground
structure that appeared to be an elaborately decorated cave.
No matter the time of day, his surroundings remained dim,
dry, and cool. Young women dressed like extras from a
Cleopatra movie brought him food and drink. He tried to
speak Egyptian Arabic to them, but they lowered their eyes
and stayed silent.

"I'm not sure if they didn't understand me or were
afraid to speak to me. They were deferential to an extreme,
as if something had scared the hell out of them."

He soon found out what that something was.

"I never slept well there. I had enough to eat and drink,
and the ladies treated me with kindness, but it was obvious
I was a prisoner. Only, a prisoner of whom? And where
was I? Then one night I had a nightmare, a vision of monsters. It was so intense, so disturbing, I opened my eyes.
And there they were, circling me, staring at me."

As Bill described the creatures in detail—creatures with
the bodies of muscular human men and the heads of animals, I recalled the names of the ancient gods of Egypt—
Set, Horus, Thoth, Sobek, Anubis. All present and ac-
counted for.

"I have to say I agree with your superiors here. They
had to be dudes in costumes," Jackson said, but Bill shook
his head.

"No, no—it was too real. The one with the head of a
falcon could ruffle its feathers, and the way its eyes darted

around, like a bird's…no man could pull that off, no matter how good an actor he was. And then there was their size. At the very least, they were ten feet tall. They emanated power like a lightning storm. I could *feel* it. No, these weren't ordinary men. I would swear to it."

"Remember that thing in Lily's hospital room, Jacks. That wasn't a man in a costume."

"Yeah, but that was different. That was a dog's head appearing from a tornado. No way that was a costume."

I would have sworn Bill couldn't have gotten any paler, but he did, his skin taking on the color of cottage cheese. "What are you talking about? Why is Lily in the hospital? And what's this about a dog's head? Is she all right?"

"We hope she will be." Rushing to speak before Jackson gave a less than diplomatic answer, I squeezed my partner's hand. It was clear he blamed the soldier, but the more Bill told us, the less I was sure what had happened to Lily's family was his fault. Yes, he'd been blindly ambitious and stupid, but who could ever have imagined this would result? "That's why we're here, to help Lily. A dog-headed figure has shown up in Nightridge. We think whatever it is took control of your brother and used him to attack Lily. Thankfully, Jackson managed to intervene before any harm was done."

Any *physical* harm, at least. I couldn't speak to the psychological damage that had resulted. Would Lily ever be able to trust her dad again?

"I should have known they'd go after her." Bill ran his hands through his hair, his pale face glistening with sweat. "Jesus, what a mess."

I pictured the young woman as I'd last seen her, terrified and distraught in her hospital bed, dwarfed by the machines that monitored her every breath and heartbeat.

"I never told them about her, I swear. I never gave them any information, at least not willingly, but—"

"Go on, Bill. We know you love Lily and would never intentionally harm her." I glanced at Jackson to see if he needed another pinch, but he leaned forward, listening to Bill's story. The animosity appeared to have faded—for the time being, at least.

"There were days when my head felt like it was going to split apart. I got blinding headaches whenever those monsters were around, and sometimes it was as if a million spiders were crawling around in there. I screamed, but they just laughed. They…I think they might have had some way of accessing my thoughts.

"After a while, they got bored with me. They came around less and less, which was a relief, but I wondered if they were going to kill me. Then the servant girls led me through this tunnel that ended in a wall of stone. I remember a powerful push, like being shot out of a canon, and all of a sudden I was back in the temple. And you were there. That's all I know. I wish I could tell you more." He straightened in his chair. "Now that I'm back, I have to get home. If Lily is in danger, we need to go to her. We need to protect her. Please. My family is everything. I can't bear to have anything happen to them, especially because of me."

Hesitating, I wondered how and if I should break the news. The soldier had already been through too much, enough to drive a lesser man mad.

You need to tell him.

I heard Fatima's calm, soothing voice in my head. As I met her eyes, she nodded. "It's the right thing to do," she said.

"You girls are freaking me out."

But Bill paid Jacks no attention. His eyes widened as he stared at me, and then Fatima. "What is it? Please don't tell me I'm too late."

"It's not that." Taking a deep breath, I decided he deserved the truth. "The thing is, Bill—everyone thinks you're dead."

~ CHAPTER SIXTEEN ~

Jackson

FOR A DUDE WHO'D JUST FOUND OUT HE WAS dead, the guy handled it pretty well—I'd give him that. Still didn't like him, but that was probably my own "issues," as Kate would say. Anyone who put Lily in harm's way, inadvertently or not, ended up on my bad side.

"I don't understand it. I'm sorry; I can't make sense of this." Bill paced the room, as much as it was possible to in such a small space. "How could they have buried me? I'm right here." He cast a frightened look at Kate. "I'm not a ghost, am I?"

"No, you're definitely not a ghost. You are very much alive." Her face twisted with guilt, no doubt at causing the soldier additional turmoil, but what was the alternative? The guy had to know what was going on before he showed up back home and everyone ran from him screaming.

"Imagine our surprise," I said. "Isn't it obvious what's going on here? It's a cover-up. The military couldn't admit some dog-faced dude was going around ripping people apart, let alone that they'd tossed one of their own to it like raw steak, so they made shit up. Haven't you guys ever watched *The X-Files*? Sometimes I think I'm the only one here with any imagination."

"With all due respect, *The X-Files* is fiction. This is my life. I returned to the temple on my own; the military didn't even know I was there. How could they tell my family I was dead without bothering to do an investigation?" Bill tugged at his hair with a viciousness that made me wince. If the dude wasn't careful, male pattern baldness was definitely in his future.

It was no wonder this guy hadn't been promoted to colonel. *Sheesh.* "Of course they knew. You're telling me they witnessed something that powerful and entrusted it with a bunch of Arabs?" Inwardly wincing when I remembered Fatima, I felt my cheeks grow hot. "Sorry."

She waved a hand in the air. "No apologies necessary. I agree with you. Muslims are the new scapegoats, the bad guys and the boogeymen. The Americans don't trust us. It has always been an uneasy truce, and it is getting more difficult all the time."

Kate rolled her eyes, making that hostile little huffing sound she made when she wanted to hit somebody. "Our xenophobia knows no bounds. It's beyond ridiculous. I'm so sorry, Fatima."

"Hey, it is not only the Americans. It is everyone—it is human nature to fear what we do not understand, to divide and conquer." She shrugged. "But, returning to the matter at hand, I agree with Jackson. The army would not have left the temple unguarded entirely, not while the statue remained. They must have had some type of surveillance."

"I'm sure they have people who specialize in human behavior. They probably predicted you'd go back. Maybe they even planted that story about removing you from your duties because they wanted to see what happened when you returned," I said. Picturing a gathering of white-haired men with brush cuts staring at a video feed, I wondered what their reaction had been when Bill got dragged through the wall. I would have paid good money to see it.

"No, no, sir…they wouldn't do that. They wouldn't set me up that way. Talk about bad guys and boogeymen." Bill shook his head. "Why is everyone so quick to think the worst of the military?"

Was this guy for real? "Gee, I don't know, Bill. Past experience?"

"What I don't understand is the exploded-heart business. Why claim such a bizarre cause of death? Wouldn't it be better to say he died of an ordinary heart attack, especially if they didn't want to attract attention?" Kate asked. "And what about the vendors? They *saw* Bill run out of the temple screaming, his skin covered with sores. How is that possible if he'd been held hostage all that time?"

Bill whirled to face her. "They saw what?"

"We talked to some of the men who sold you postcards. They saw you leave the temple that same day you arrived, and said your skin was covered in sores. You collapsed on the steps in front of them."

The soldier thrust out his arms, all the better for us to examine his blemish-free skin. Aside from a few freckles, he was completely unmarked. "But that's impossible. I never left the temple until today."

I raised an eyebrow at Kate. "You sure he's not dead?"

"Not funny, Jacks."

"Not trying to be." Not entirely, anyway. "How else could he be in two places at once? I'm willing to bet the Bill who fled the temple screaming is the same one whose heart exploded. But then who's this? How can there be two of him?"

Even my extensive experience with *The X-Files* couldn't help this time. Then again, hadn't they done a show on doppelgängers?

"*Ka*," Fatima said, sounding like some strange and exotic bird.

"Come again?" I asked, not sure if *ka* was a random expression of frustration or disgust or what. I'd grown to like the psychic well enough, but I'd never pretend to understand her.

To my surprise, it was Kate who answered. "The ancient Egyptians believed that everyone has a *ka*. A spirit double, more or less, who would have the same memories and emotions as the actual person."

The psychic smiled. "I'm impressed. You know our mythology very well."

"She takes a ton of courses at the university for fun. Hell, one of her friends is an Egyptologist." At the mention of Eden, Kate grimaced and I took her hand. "But isn't mythology a fancy word for fairy tales? You don't believe this *ka* actually exists, do you?"

Kate sighed. "Jacks, we've seen Anubis in a hospital in Vermont. We just saw him on the streets of modern-day Luxor. How is *ka* any more strange or difficult to accept than that?"

"You have a point."

"Sorry to interrupt, but can someone please explain this to me in plain English? What are you saying, exactly?" Poor Bill looked ready to pull out his hair by the roots, and I didn't blame him.

"Lieutenant Bill Walkins died in Egypt. That much we know. The coroner's report lists the cause of death as an exploded heart. A group of vendors witnessed him leaving the Temple of Waset in a panic, covered in sores. There was a funeral, and there is a gravesite. And yet here you are, very much alive," Kate said, drawing a blanket tighter around her shoulders. Even with the soldier's makeshift barrier on the window, it was getting downright chilly in here again.

"So, I'm what? A spirit? I thought we'd already established I'm not a ghost." Bill rapped his knuckles against his head. "See? Hard as ever."

"Perhaps it was your *ka*—your spirit double—who died," Fatima suggested.

"Is a spirit double like a soul? How could my soul have died? Wouldn't that kill me too?"

"Eden would know." Kate thrummed her ankles against the bedframe. "I wish she were here to ask."

"Eden?" Bill's eyes widened until they threatened to swallow his face.

What was going on now? I wasn't sure my poor heart could take much more.

"She's my friend. She's an Egyptologist, the one Jacks mentioned. Problem is, she's missing."

"Is she fairly tall? Slim? Pretty face, dark hair in a ponytail?"

Now Kate was the one who looked like she was in shock. "Yes, why?"

"I've seen her. She isn't missing—she's *there*." Bill glanced at each of us in turn, as if hoping for a reaction that didn't come. "Don't you get it? She's being held in the same place I was."

The bulb above our heads shattered, plunging us into darkness.

Someone shuffled over to the window, and as the blanket was pushed aside, a sliver of moonlight allowed me to see the slight figure of Fatima peering out. "It is not just us," she said. "Look."

The street below, normally alive with activity at all hours of the night, was cloaked in shadows. Faint cries of distress wafted up on air that felt mysteriously thick in spite of the evening's chill.

"Darkness," Kate said, so close her breath warmed my ear. "The ninth plague of Egypt."

"I'm guessing this isn't a good thing."

"It could mean we're on the right track. Seems like whenever we're onto something, we're hit with another plague."

It was true, but it was hard to take comfort from that when I couldn't see my hand in front of my face. "How long is it supposed to last?"

Kate hesitated, and I could tell she was biting her lip even though I was unable to see it. "Three days."

"Three *days*? How are we going to get home and back to Lily in time?" The need to check on her, to make sure the kid was all right, had intensified until it was a ceaseless ache, forever nagging at me. Was it psychosomatic, inspired by Fatima's talk about my being Lily's guardian? Or was there something more to it? The not knowing haunted me.

"During the original plagues, the people called on Moses to end their suffering…something we're obviously not able to do. So it might last even longer."

"Can't you end it?" In my frustration, I blurted out the question without thinking, and the resulting silence was heavier than the darkness. "Like you and Laura did with the frogs."

"This isn't the same, Jacks. It feels different. I don't think this is localized to our hotel. We're on their turf now. The rules have changed."

"It sure didn't seem that way when you made him crawl back under his rock a few hours ago."

"Is that what you think happened? He was toying with me. He could have crushed my skull like an egg if he'd wanted to. For some reason, he decided we weren't worth the energy." Kate's voice had a slight tremor to it that I was pretty sure no one else would pick up. "We got lucky, that's all. Maybe conjuring the fiery hail tired him out, who knows?"

"Do not underestimate yourself," Fatima said before I could. "You are capable of tremendous power. Anubis is aware of that, even if you are not. Remember what Mister Bill told us, about those poor scientists who were torn to pieces. Anubis, he is a monster. He would have done the same to us without hesitation if he believed he could."

Mister Bill. Okay, that was pretty fucking cute. "That's exactly what I'm saying. He looked like a whipped puppy dog running off with his tail between his legs." I made some pitiful yipping sounds, and was rewarded by a laugh from Fatima, but not the woman I so desperately wanted to reassure.

"Besides, what's the big deal? Sure, he killed the lights, but we're in a hotel room, not a cave. What's the worst that could happen?"

Kate groaned. "Jacks, how many times do I have to tell you not to tempt fate?"

"When the sun doesn't rise tomorrow, it's going to get

interesting. So much for getting out of here," Bill said. "The airport is going to be chaos."

Something akin to panic wrapped its thick fingers around my ribcage and squeezed. I had to get back to Lily. "There has to be something you two could do. We have to at least try."

"Well, maybe there is something," Fatima said. "*If* you help."

"If I help? I'm just a…" *What was it Kate called me?* "A mainstreamer. What am I supposed to do, hold your hair?"

This time Kate sighed so deeply, I could feel it. "Jacks…"

"No, it is okay. I like his humor, very much. He is a very confident man. It is good. We will need his confidence."

"Cocky is a better word for it," Kate said.

"Nah, I like Fatima's. From now on, she does all of my PR."

"You and Jackson balance each other. Where you are afraid to tread, he rushes in."

"That's certainly true."

"She must be psychic or something," I said. Kate proved to have some abilities of her own in that department, as she pegged me pretty good on the arm despite the impenetrable darkness.

"I don't mean to be a wet blanket, but if you've got a plan, let's hear it. Our dog-faced friend may be gone for now, but he'll return before too long. We'll need to be ready."

For once I agreed with Bill. "Sorry, Fatima. What do you want me to do?"

"Only what comes naturally. That will be more than enough."

Say what?

"I will explain tomorrow," she said, stepping away from the window. "First, we need some rest. All of us. In the morning, we will return to the temple."

The temple? "I don't mean to argue, but that place was creepy enough during daylight hours. I'm not sure going there in the dark is the best idea."

I felt Fatima's hand pat my back as she passed. "Not to worry. We won't have to actually go *inside* the temple. We'll make what's inside come out to us."

Oh. Well. That made it *so* much better.

~ CHAPTER SEVENTEEN ~

Kate

IT HAD TO HAVE BEEN ONE OF THE STRANGEST sleepovers in history: an Egyptian psychic, an American soldier, a medium, and a professional bullshit artist. Sorry, I mean a writer. Could be the start of a really good joke. A *Jackson*-style joke.

I'd been listening to the man in question snore for over an hour but was unable to drift off myself. Not for the first time, I envied Jackson's ability to relax and go with the flow. So what if the earth was cloaked in supernatural darkness and the gods of ancient Egypt roamed the streets? Everything would be fine, as far as he was concerned. In spite of Fatima's talk of how we balanced each other, I wished I had more of his confidence.

Click.

The sound was a mere whisper in the night, but it could have been a gunshot. My eyes flew open, my heart thudding in my chest. At least when I'd pretended to sleep, I could forget how dark it was. It was like being miles underground, like being buried alive.

The first thing I'd done once we'd gotten the room was banish the lingering spirits, but now I regretted it. Some company, especially someone who could guide me through this inky blackness to the door, would have been welcome. For years, I'd felt the seething resentment of Isabelle's ghost swirling around me, and now, thanks to Fatima, she was gone too.

The thinnest streak of light appeared under the hotel room door, an answer to my unspoken prayer. Easing myself off the bed, careful not to wake Jackson or Fatima, I tiptoed toward it.

Bill sat on the floor outside the door, holding up a lighter to read from a small, leather-bound book. He didn't seem surprised to see me.

"Did I wake you, ma'am?" he whispered.

"No. Couldn't sleep. Am I disturbing you?"

"Not at all. Please." He gestured to the carpet beside him. "I'm going to have to let go soon, though. This fucker's burning my fingers. Sorry."

"No need to apologize. I'm the last person you should be censoring yourself around. I live with Jacks, remember?" The words felt strange on my tongue. Guess that was to be expected, since we'd barely spent a night at the house since he'd moved from Minneapolis to be with me.

Sliding down the wall, I lowered myself to the ground. Although I understood why he had to let go of the lighter, my heart grew heavier when it went out.

"What were you reading?" I asked to distract myself.

"Bible. I've been reading it an awful lot lately."

"Funny, I didn't take you for a religious man."

"I'm not. Or, at least, I wasn't. But they say some experiences change you, and what happened to me definitely did." He chuckled. "I was raised Catholic, but I probably would have said I was an atheist before all this occurred."

"Me too. The raised Catholic part, I mean."

"It's different for you, though, right? You can speak with the dead."

Shifting on the hard floor, I played dumb out of habit, though I knew exactly what he was getting at. "What do you mean?"

"They must have told you something. Obviously, the very fact you can communicate with them means that there's something more to us than this…something *beyond*. You're one of the few people in the world, certainly the only one I've ever met, who has concrete proof that heaven exists."

Ugh. Along with "Can you contact so-and-so?" the most common question people asked me was, "What happens when we die?" I shouldn't beat myself up for not having the answer everyone wanted—that was hardly my fault. But knowing that didn't do much to alleviate my guilt. "Sorry to disappoint you, but I don't have any more proof than you do. I don't have any idea what happens after we die. I just know that, for whatever reason, some of us stick around."

"Surely you must have asked at some point. At least once?"

The hope in his voice was enough to make me wince. And the truth was, when I was a child, I *had* asked. I'd asked my grandmother's ghost, and she'd given me the same bullshit answer any grandmother would give a kid, stuff about angels and harps and loved ones waiting for me on the other side.

It was a nice story. Unfortunately for both of us, The Gift told me that this was all it was—a story. I don't think my grandmother knew what happens afterward, and she was dead. I wasn't about to tell Bill a fable.

"Honestly, I don't think we're supposed to know. I think we find out when we get there for a reason, and I have no desire to mess with that. Where you were in terms of religion...well, that's about where I am now, though the term *atheist* has always sounded so final to me. I prefer to think of myself as agnostic. Keeping an open mind."

Bill was quiet for a moment, no doubt digesting this new information and swallowing his disappointment. I had time to marvel again at how dark it was, and how only the solidity of the wall behind me and the floor below kept me from feeling like I was floating in space. That, and the sound of the soldier's breathing.

"If ultimate evil exists, why not divine good? One can't exist without the other, right? There has to be a balance."

This was false logic, but I didn't see the point in saying so. Or bringing up the fact that nature falls out of balance all the time. Usually with our help, but sometimes even without. "Is that what you think they are? Ultimate evil?" It sounded like the name of a video game, and I felt a crazy urge to burst out laughing.

"Yes, I do. I can feel it, emanating off them. Can't you?"

Now that was interesting, but was it based in fact or fantasy? "No, I don't think so. I'm not sure. What does evil feel like?"

"It's...dread. It's this sinking feeling in the pit of your stomach, like you're going to lose your lunch and shit your pants at the same time—sorry. It's the absence of hope, feeling terror beyond anything you've ever experienced before."

"It sounds like a panic attack. Do you have anxiety?"

"Never. At least, I didn't before. Now, who knows?"

"Bill, I need you to tell me the truth about something."

"I'll do my best."

A deliberately light-hearted response, but troubling. Either the soldier told the truth or he continued to lie. How does one "do their best" to tell the truth? Either you did or you didn't. "I need you to be completely honest with me. If I'm going to help Lily, I have to understand what's really going on."

When he responded, his tone was nonchalant, but I could tell I'd rattled him. "What are you getting at, Kate? I've told you everything I know."

"See, right there. That's a lie. You haven't told us the truth about the military's involvement in this."

"What are you talking about? I told you, I'm a flunky. If I withheld anything from you, it's because I'm not aware of it."

"I don't believe that either."

"I can't control whether you believe me or not. It's the truth. Have Fatima read my mind if it makes you feel better."

"Bill, you were there. You heard what Anubis said to me. There was an experiment of some sort, and Lily was offered in exchange for his participation. He told us this, and I can't see any reason for him to lie." The soldier took a breath, but I hurried on before he could dig himself in deeper. "You're a good person. I know you didn't willingly sacrifice Lily, no matter what Anubis said. But there's more to it than you're telling, and if I'm going to help your family, I have to have all the facts."

The soldier sighed. "You don't understand. It's not a matter of lying or not lying. Some things are classified."

"Isn't death considered an unconditional discharge? The

military buried you, Bill. Twenty-one-gun salute, the works. You're not beholden to them anymore."

He cleared his throat. "That's not entirely accurate."

"Start talking. Now. Either you tell me what's really going on, or I'll call Vittoria first thing and tell her we're off the case and why. You can deal with the fallout on your own." It was an empty threat. We were too involved. There was no way we could turn our backs on this now, not with Anubis and his buddies wandering the planet and unleashing random plagues at will. And Jacks would never abandon Lily, even if I could. I just hoped *Bill* wasn't aware it was an empty threat.

"Remember I told you that a team of archaeologists found the temple? That wasn't a lie. Not a complete lie, anyway. They did find something, only it wasn't a temple. It was a scroll."

"A scroll?"

The soldier took a deep breath, his shoulder brushing against mine in the dark. "Your friend was helping us decipher it when she disappeared."

No wonder Eden had been jumpy. Classified government work wasn't her usual duties as assigned. "So you don't know what it says."

"Oh, we know enough. It gave the location of the temple, along with where we could find another scroll. And *that* scroll, well…it was supposed to reveal the secret to eternal life."

I laughed. "Are you kidding me?"

"I promise you, Kate—I'm entirely serious. And unfortunately, your friend Eden was quite bright. *Very* bright. Much better than any translator we'd worked with before. She was able to translate most of the second scroll as well."

"All of this was about some quest for the fountain of youth?" I couldn't believe it, even after every bizarre thing I'd seen. It was too ridiculous.

"It's not like that. It's a lot darker. You were talking around it earlier, so I thought you knew. You guys figured out a lot more than I thought you would."

"You mean *ka*."

"Yeah. I mean *ka*." He sighed again. "Believe me, I've paid a huge price for my involvement, and I suspect I'll always be paying for it. If I could go back, do it differently, I would, but it's too late for that."

Cold sweat trailed down my spine. "What happened?"

"There were always signs we were messing with something we shouldn't. The locusts, the frogs, water turning to blood, fire from the sky—everything you experienced, we experienced, only a hundred times worse. But my superiors didn't care." Bill snorted. "If anything, it made them more excited, convinced they were onto something. So they gave Eden a raise and urged her to keep going."

"And then what?"

"Then she vanished. That night was the first time we met Anubis. I've already told you what happened to our team—that wasn't a lie. He was furious, said we were meddling in gods' business. He threatened to wipe out every living thing on Earth, and we were in no position to bargain. We didn't have a weapon that could defeat him."

"But you had something he wanted."

"Yes."

"What was it? What was the experiment?"

"Please don't hate me, Kate. I swear, I never in a million years thought it would come to this or I never would have gotten her involved."

Pain stabbed my heart. *Lily.* The anguish in the soldier's voice was genuine. I could feel him trembling. He'd been a victim too. I wasn't sure how, but I figured I was about to find out. "I don't hate you. Go on. Tell me what happened."

"The military has been experimenting with parapsychology for years. Since the '60s, if not before. I'm sure that doesn't surprise you."

"No." There had always been rumors about stuff like that. Conspiracy theorists went nuts over it. "But I don't understand. Lily is a medium. What on earth would the government use that for?"

"Maybe she has some mediumistic abilities, I don't know. You'd have a better idea of that than me. That's not what we were interested in."

"If not that, then what?" For the most part, Lily was an ordinary kid. Perhaps more insecure than most, but aside from her talents as a medium, I hadn't noticed anything the military would find interesting.

"Kate, Lily is telekinetic. She doesn't know how to control it yet, and maybe she'll lose her abilities when she's older. But as of now, believe me when I say that girl can do things that will blow your mind."

Telekinetic? I'd heard of such people, of course, but had believed most, if not all of them, were scammers intent on separating the public from their hard-earned cash.

"I kept it pretty casual. Last thing I wanted was to scare her. Every now and then I would take her with me to the lab and we'd play games. At least, that's what she thought we were doing. But in reality, the army was measuring her abilities. Monitoring her."

"She's not stupid, Bill." I couldn't help but think of

Lily's emotional issues, so numerous and severe for a girl that young. Did any of it stem from the fact her own beloved uncle, her country, had used her as a guinea pig? It certainly wouldn't have helped.

"I get that. The last thing I ever wanted was to hurt her. It was such a small thing at first. I'd take her to the lab, we'd play a few games, and then we'd go home. What would be the harm?"

"But something went wrong, didn't it?"

For a moment, the soldier was quiet. The seconds dragged by so slowly I feared he wouldn't answer me at all. I heard him swallow, hard.

"Yeah, you could say that."

I waited for him to continue, and finally he did.

"The experiments were going well, better than I could have hoped. I was amazed by what Lily could do, and she seemed to be too…until she got bored. I figured it would be okay, you know? My superiors never made a big deal out of what we were doing. It was only an experiment, nothing to lose sleep over. Until Lily wanted to go and they decided not to let her."

I'd often wondered about the sanity of the men who run this country. Lily was a twelve-year-old girl. For all her precociousness, she was still a child. And children get tired of games.

"I tried my best to reason with her, to bargain with her. We'd always rewarded her when she performed well, but we upped the ante. By then, though, it was too late. Some of my superiors had tried to bully her, and her back was up. She missed her parents. She wanted to go home. She was fed up with the 'stupid games' and my 'loser friends,' as she called them. She was done."

Bill's voice cracked, and I knew I should comfort him, but I felt rooted to the spot, afraid to move lest I break his momentum.

"I wanted to intervene, but they wouldn't let me. They told her she'd be able to return home someday, if she co-operated, but not yet. If they'd said that months before, it might have worked, but there had been too much praise, too much encouragement. A lot of those guys were afraid of Lily, and she knew it—what kid wouldn't get off on that kind of power? I'm sure she didn't mean for it to go down the way it did."

As he spoke, I could picture her. She wasn't twelve yet, but ten. Her face had that childish softness, her legs and arms were unmarked. When her fury built, the energy crackled in the air, sending sparks. Her hair swirled in a dark cloud around her head.

"What did she do?"

"She only meant to scare them, I'm sure of it. Some of them, the ones who'd had little to no contact with her— the lurkers, the gawkers—she sent flying around the room. There were a few hard landings, bumps and bruises and maybe even some fractures, but they got off easy."

I held my breath, not daring to make a sound, trying desperately to reconcile the girl in Bill's story with the timid, wounded soul I'd met in Poveglia.

"The ones who'd bullied her, who'd threatened to keep her from her mother, got the worst of it. She threw them together as if they were in a Newton's cradle. Their skulls made contact at high speed." His voice lowered to a whisper, and I could feel his shoulders shaking. "It was a mess, such a horrible, horrible mess. But I swear to you she didn't mean it. She was a kid having a temper tantrum that spun out of control. She'd had no idea what she was capable of."

There was no need to ask if the men had died. "What happened then?"

"That was the end of the experiment, at least as far as I was aware. Arrangements had to be made, explanations concocted. Somehow, they had to account for the men's deaths, as working in a lab on that side of the pond should have been as non-lethal as it gets. For a while, some people tried to convince Lily it wasn't her fault, cajole her into cooperating again, but she never would. She hated herself for what had happened, and as far as I know, she hasn't so much as flipped a playing card since. But that doesn't mean her abilities are gone. She's just not using them."

Poor Lily. Her self-loathing, the cutting. It made sense now. "There's something I don't understand. If the experiment ended, how did Anubis find out about her?"

"Your guess is as good as mine. As far as I can figure out the timeframe, the archaeologists discovered the shrine while Lily and I played around in the lab. Maybe they'd even found the first scroll by then. If Anubis was summoned, either deliberately or accidentally, while my niece was active, he would have been drawn to her like a divining rod's drawn to water."

"But why? I'm not doubting Lily's powers are impressive, especially in light of what you've told me, but Anubis is no slouch on his own. He can control the elements. What would he need with a twelve-year-old telekinetic?"

"He wants to use her to rip a hole between our world and theirs. Anubis is tired of living in the past, surrounded by old ghosts and irrelevant gods. He wants to remain here.

"Ultimately, his goal is to destroy us."

~ CHAPTER EIGHTEEN ~

Jackson

IT'S FAIR TO SAY WE SCARED QUITE A FEW
tourists that day. What with battling an ancient Egyptian
god, trashing a perfectly decent hotel room, and subsisting
on little to no sleep or food, we were a sorry-looking
bunch when we arrived at the Temple of Waset the next
morning. At least the sun was out. Whatever had caused
the blackout the night before had passed. Guess our good
buddy Anubis thought he'd gotten his point across.

Something had changed between Kate and Bill—that
was pretty obvious. I hadn't told her I'd woken up in the
middle of the night and found them both gone. There
hadn't been a chance. I did my best to keep the paranoia in
check, but it bugged me how solicitous she acted toward
him all of a sudden, like the soldier was a victim instead of
the reason for this whole bloody mess. *Would you like some
more* fuul, *Bill? You need to get your strength back. Some tea?
How about some hibiscus?*

It wasn't unusual for Kate to be kind, but why the
fawning? It was as if he had some power over her now, and
it was getting hard to stomach. As soon as we had a second
to ourselves—assuming we ever did—I'd get her to tell me

what the hell was going on.

If anything could distract me from the strange new relationship between my girlfriend and the soldier, it was the gigantic figures of Anubis looming over the desert sand. Now that I'd seen the real thing, the statues took on ominous meaning.

We were a good two hundred feet away from the entrance when Bill stopped, scuffing his boots in the sand. "This is as far as I go. I'll wait for you here."

Before I could say a word, Fatima intervened, giving me a warning look. It didn't take psychic ability to see I wanted to throttle the guy, but it certainly didn't hurt. "We need to stay together, Bill. It is important we are not separated."

The man twisted away, but not before I caught a glimpse of how glassy his eyes were. *What the fuck is his problem?* A moment before, he'd been fine. Now his Adam's apple was bobbing up and down in his throat like he was seconds away from falling apart. "I can't."

That was, as they say, the proverbial last straw. Never the most patient person, I'd been working on my final nerve as it was. "Can you please cut the shit? The last time Kate and I visited this place, it almost came down around our ears. If anyone has a reason for pussying out, it's us, not you."

"Jacks—" Kate started, but she didn't manage anything else before Bill turned on me.

"Really? Did you die in there? Were you set up, murdered by the very people you'd dedicated your entire adult life to?" His eyes glowed with contempt. "I didn't think so, so watch who you're calling a pussy, you loudmouthed, know-it-all piece of shit."

"What the fuck are you talking about?" Though I fought valiantly to hold on to my anger, my curiosity had gotten the best of me. Bill was no ghost—he was as solid as the rest of us. Kate had confirmed he wasn't part of the spirit realm. Was this more of his bull crap? More lies?

"Boys, please. This isn't helping anything." Kate reached for me, but I moved away before she could make contact, not ready to be calmed down. If the soldier had something to say, we'd better hear it.

"I'm talking about being ordered to retrieve something from the shrine. Another scroll," he said, his eyes flicking to Kate's. This was the first I'd heard about scrolls, but I was willing to bet it was one of the subjects they'd covered in the hallway last night. "Classified business, they told me. I was the best man for the job, they said. They buttered me up good, and I was stupid enough to fall for it. Once I was where they wanted, they gassed me."

Fatima gasped, but I wasn't buying it—yet. The soldier had told us too many stories.

"What do you mean, they gassed you?"

"I mean, they shot me full of poison. My skin erupted into sores. The pain was so bad, I almost clawed my eyes out. I don't think they expected me to leave the temple, let alone make it back to my hotel, but that's where I was when my heart stopped."

Kate's eyes widened. "So you *did* die."

"My physical body did, yeah. I guess they decided they needed someone to test their new formula on, and who better than me? If everything went wrong, I'd take a lot of loose ends with me."

"You're not making sense. If you died, how are you standing here having this conversation? Are you saying

someone brought you back?" Assessing the soldier, I couldn't
see any indication that he'd undergone such trauma. His
skin was weathered and freckled in the way of white dudes
who liked their sun, but other than that, it was clear. No
weeping sores to be found.

"Jacks, you do not understand." Fatima gazed at Bill as
if in awe. "The experiment worked, didn't it? This is your
ka."

"Glad to see someone's using their brain for something other than taking up space. That's about the size
of it. I may look normal to you, but the truth is, I'm not.
Everything that made me human, that made me real, has
been destroyed."

"That is not true. You still have your soul," the psychic
said. "That is what is most important."

"I appreciate what you're trying to do, Fatima, but I've
already made my peace with it. At least I've tried. I didn't
have much else to do while Anubis and his fellow shitheads
held me captive. But I hope everyone understands why I
can't go back in there. I can't risk getting captured again."

Before I could say a word, the psychic slipped her hand
into the soldier's and smiled at him. "You do not have to.
We are not going inside. What we need is outside."

Glancing at Kate, I managed to catch her eye. She
nodded at me, just enough to confirm she believed Bill was
telling the truth. I still wasn't sure why the United States
government was messing around with an Egyptian temple,
or why killing Bill would have cleared up loose ends rather
than create more. And now I didn't even know what the
hell we were doing there. What on earth could we need
outside the temple? I was getting pretty damn tired of being in the dark, literally and figuratively.

Fatima watched me, her head tilted like a curious pup's, and I was careful to shield my mind the way Laura had shown me. The last thing I needed was anyone digging around in there right now. "Jacks, you are obviously troubled. For this to work, we have to be on the same page. Why don't you tell us what is bothering you?"

It was almost laughable how much Kate squirmed. She was the one person there who knew asking me to speak my mind was not for the faint of heart. Ask me for two cents, and you're going to get at least a buck.

But nothing wrong with learning the hard way, right?

"I'm glad you asked. It's difficult for me to be on the 'same page' without having read the book. Hell, I don't even know what the book *is*. I realize I'm not privy to the same information as the rest of you…" I paused to give Kate a *look* to communicate I was well aware of her clandestine meeting with the soldier. "But none of this makes a lick of sense. Why is the US Army remotely interested in this temple? What does Anubis have to do with it, or for that matter, Lily? And what good was killing Bill off? Seems to me that would create more attention—case in point, our conversation with the postcard sellers. Everyone remembers him running out of the temple, covered in sores. We're supposedly dealing with the world's top military minds here, but they're acting like the Keystone Kops."

My outburst was too much for the soldier, who'd never had much patience for me. "That was the whole point—don't you get it? They wanted my death to be memorable. They wanted no one to have any doubt what happened to me."

"Then wouldn't, say, a quiet heart attack be better? Rather than having your skin erupt in sores. They're never going to stop talking about it," I said, indicating the sellers, whom we could see in the distance. "Your death scarred them for life. They're not going to forget it."

Bill shuffled, scuffing the toe of his boot in the sand again. "I can only hope my superiors didn't realize how I'd be affected by the gas."

"Which leads us back to the Keystone Kops. Shouldn't they have known? And talk about attracting attention— here you are, returned from the dead. Those vendors know you. You're their American buddy; they've memorized your face. How will they react when they see you're a modern-day Lazarus? You'll be front page news."

"Guess everyone thought Anubis would take care of the problem. The last thing the military would have ex-pected is to have to deal with me here on solid ground again."

"They trusted the dog-headed creature who massacred their best scientists? Again, brilliant. I'm blown away by their stunning aptitude for troubleshooting."

"Jacks…" Kate shook her head at me, but not before I saw her hide a smile.

"What? You have to admit, it's ridiculous. If they wanted you dead, there were a million ways to accom-plish that which wouldn't result in your *ka*, or whatever you want to call it, walking around. Why not poison your falafel, or run you off the road? With the way people drive around here, no one would have questioned it."

"Because they needed me to be a test case. They were willing to sacrifice me for the greater good."

As flustered as the soldier appeared, he didn't know from frustrated. Talking to him was like trying to have a conversation with the fucking Cat in the Hat. Always more riddles and gibberish, but no answers. Was it deliberate? Could anyone be this irritating by accident? "A test case for *what*?"

Fatima stepped in, probably because she could see the top of Bill's head was about to blow. I'd fully expect to get showered with cotton candy if it did. "Anubis and his kind have immortality, which is something the military wants. By separating soldiers from their *ka,* the Americans planned to raise an army of immortal soldiers. They thought they could play chess with the gods of ancient Egypt and win."

"And how does that not make them the Keystone Kops? This just keeps getting better and better. Anyone else want to defend the brilliance of the US military to me?" Only Fatima made eye contact, though she said nothing further. Kate bit her lip, scanning the growing crowds of tourists around the temple, while Bill continued to pace like he was determined to wear a permanent groove in the sand. "I didn't think so. My questions remain: what the hell are we doing here? And how do we keep everyone from seeing Bill and contacting the *National Enquirer*?"

"Jacks has a point. We can't walk in there like this. Everyone will recognize Bill, and once that happens, it'll be chaos. The last thing we want is people watching our every move, correct?" Kate directed her question at Fatima, and I was relieved to see I wasn't the only one who had no idea why we were here.

In the silence that followed, we looked at Bill. Even if he weren't in combat fatigues, the man was most definitely a soldier. A small child would be able to pick him out of a crowd. I had a hoodie in my duffel with a hood big enough to cover his buzz cut and conceal part of his face, but who wore a sweatshirt when it was a hundred degrees?

Might as well wear a sign saying, "I'm hiding something."

"I'm big enough to admit when I'm wrong. You're right, Jackson," Bill said. He sounded a bit stiff, but a lot more respectful than usual. "It was a stupid idea, coming here. I'm bound to get recognized if I go any closer. I never stopped to think about what people's reactions might be."

"What about the café? Would they know you there?" Kate gestured to the place where we'd enjoyed a mint tea before everything went to hell. If only life came with a *rewind* option.

"Most likely. I've dropped enough Egyptian pounds there. Guess I'd better head back."

"To the hotel? But you don't have a key. We never registered you as a guest."

I didn't like the idea of the soldier hanging out in our room, either, but what else could he do? He was taking a chance just standing around with us.

"That's perfectly all right, ma'am. I can wait for you in the lobby."

"Maybe I should go with him. Fatima, whatever you have planned—do you need me for it?" I asked.

"Bill is right. It is better if he goes before anyone recognizes him, but I'd like you to stay. We need at least one person with their feet firmly planted in this realm."

Shit. I didn't trust the guy. What if he took off and we never saw him again? There was still so much we didn't know.

"I'll see y'all back at the ranch then," the soldier said, clapping me on the back. "Good luck."

Before I could think of a better alternative, he was gone, striding away from us across the sand. "I hope we did the right thing."

"What do you mean, Jacks?" Fatima said, adopting Kate's nickname for me. Any other time, it would have made me grin. "What is troubling you now?"

"What if he doesn't go to the hotel? What if he disappears?"

"To what end?" Kate exhaled in a huff. "I get that you don't trust him, but he has no reason to take off. No one forced him to talk to us. If he wants to help Lily, it's in his own best interests to tell us what he knows."

"You know him better than I do." I strived to sound casual, but the edge must have been evident in my voice, since Kate rolled her eyes.

"It helps when you're not biting his head off every time he turns around. All right, Fatima, what's next? Let's get this over with. The sooner we can chill out with some coffee and a decent breakfast, the better. I think our tempers are growing a bit...frayed."

"What I have in mind is not without its dangers. This is why I thought it best Jackson remain with us."

"I'm listening," Kate said. She looked weary enough to collapse where she stood. I hoped Fatima's definition of danger wouldn't completely drain her, but I suspected that's why the psychic needed me—to carry my girl out of there after her grand plan had been executed.

"Let us walk and talk," Fatima said. "We have already wasted too much time."

As we set off toward the temple, the psychic asked if Kate had already become acquainted with the slaves who'd been trapped within its walls, the same tortured souls who had supposedly yanked Bill's *ka* into the realm of Anubis.

"Somewhat, but thankfully there was a barrier between

us. There's too many of them, too much torture and death. My life would be at risk."

"Remember what I taught you. When you feel their suffering, do not resist it as you normally would. Bring it toward you; absorb it. Let it fill you, here." Fatima tapped her abdomen. "When the time is right, you will release it with astonishing power."

That was exactly what I'd been afraid of. Well, something like that, at least. "With all due respect, when Kate says getting too close would put her at risk, she's understating things a bit. What she really means is that it would fucking kill her."

Kate sighed. "Jacks…"

"No, it's okay. I like Jackson's honesty. I find it refreshing." Fatima stopped walking long enough to make eye contact with me. "Nothing I am about to do will kill her, I promise. But it might exhaust her. I anticipate we will need your help getting her back to the hotel."

"You mean well, but you have no idea what it's like. I've seen it, and I'm not going to let her die on my watch." The thought of Kate getting an unnecessary blister would be too much for me at this point.

"Of course not. You're the Guardian."

"I thought that only applied to Lily."

"It applies to anyone you care deeply for. As you mature, it could expand until you have it within you to care for the whole world."

"Whatever. For the time being, I have enough to worry about just keeping an eye on you two."

"Like that's such a hardship," Kate said, and it was nice to hear her laugh again. Hoping to milk it for all it was worth, I rolled my eyes heavenward.

"Nobody knows the trouble I've seen…"

"You are teasing us, Jacks, but that is an excellent reminder. You have seen Kate at her most vulnerable. Therefore, you will know when she is in danger and will be able to pull her out of the trance before it becomes too much. Correct?"

Fatima's faith in me was flattering, but perhaps misplaced. If Kate collapsed at my feet, unable to hold herself up, I'd know enough to get her out of there. But what if it wasn't that cut-and-dried? What if I didn't see the signs before it was too late?

Kate squeezed my hand. "You've got this," she said. "I trust you."

"I'm glad someone does." I entwined my fingers with hers and didn't let go until we reached the temple.

By now, the sun was scorching, even though it was still early. A few busloads of Chinese tourists waited at the entrance, using umbrellas as parasols. The sight made me smile, remembering the trip where I'd first met Kate—the trip that had started it all.

The vendors prepared as well, arranging gaudy necklaces along their arms and scarves and shawls over their shoulders. I wondered how they could stand to wear that much fabric in this heat. When they saw us, they jumped to attention, and rushed us en masse until Fatima raised her hand and spoke a few words in Arabic. Chuckling and shaking their heads, the men moved on to their next victims.

"What did you say?" I asked, curious as to what could have possibly caused such a miraculous result.

"*Filmishmish.*"

When I raised an eyebrow, she continued. "It means 'in apricot season.' Oh, never mind. I can see by your expression that it is one of those things that is lost in translation."

"I guess." *In apricot season? Those are the magic words?* Sometimes life is indeed stranger than fiction.

When we approached the temple, we attracted more than our share of inquisitive glances. We were an unusual sight—my dark skin, a diminutive Muslim woman wearing a shocking pink headscarf, and Kate with her vivid red hair.

"You are feeling it, aren't you?" Fatima asked when we were still a good distance away.

Kate grimaced, curling her arm around her abdomen as if she had a stomachache. "Yes, I can feel it. It's worse this time."

"I am not surprised; on this side, the barrier you felt before is not as strong. The slaves who died here suffered a lot. The torture, the cramped conditions, the starvation. The ones who weren't crushed or worked to death died of their wounds, or of hunger."

"Wait—I thought slaves didn't build the pyramids or the temples. Eden told me that was an old myth Egyptologists have been trying to correct for years." Kate frowned, but I wasn't sure if it was from the thought of the slaves' suffering or from physical discomfort. "Was she wrong?"

"No, that is correct. However, that doesn't mean Anubis was above kidnapping Egyptians and forcing them to do his bidding. These spirits are the former slaves of Anubis, not of any pharaoh."

"Wait a minute." I held up a hand. "Are you telling me you always knew Anubis was real?"

"Of course. His kind has terrorized our people since the beginning. That is why they must be stopped from permanently crossing over. No one would survive."

"But you're Muslim. I thought you only believed in one god."

Fatima's nose wrinkled in disgust. "They are not gods to us. They are monsters. They are evil. I have no respect for them. But, I do fear them."

Studying the towering limestone structures of Anubis, I remembered the first time I'd seen the dude himself, in Lily's hospital room. It was enough to make me shudder. "I can understand that."

The psychic tucked her arm through Kate's, veering toward the right side of the temple, away from the lines at the entrance. "Now Kate, I realize you are scared. But you do not have to worry. This is going to be very different from your past experiences. This time, you will not allow the spirits' pain to assault you. You will not resist them, but instead, welcome them in."

Kate gritted her teeth. "What if I'm not strong enough?"

"Then we would not be here. Trust me, you are much stronger than you think. And Jackson is here. You know he would not let anything happen to you."

My girl looked at me, and my heart ached to see the pain and terror in her eyes. "I do know that."

"You're sure this is safe?" I was worried at how quickly we'd trusted the psychic. How well did we really know Fatima? I mean, sure, she'd pretty much saved our collective asses during the flaming sky incident, but what if the confidence she instilled in us was one of her abilities? What if she were leading us into a trap? I'd trusted the wrong people before. Nothing said I couldn't do it again.

"I understand your hesitation, Jackson, and the wariness, the suspicion you are feeling toward me now—that is the Guardian in you, speaking up. In this instance, your primary concern is Kate, and I assure you, she is mine as well. The only proof I can give you is what you have seen of my character during the last twenty-four hours. Beyond that, you will have to trust me, as difficult as that may be. What does your gut tell you?"

Kate winced, and a wave of rage crashed over me. "That I can't stand seeing her in pain. That anything that makes her cringe like that is wrong."

"I understand. But I am about to show you both the way through the pain. Once Kate learns how to do this, she will never fear spirits again. Isn't that worth some temporary discomfort?"

Before I could snap that it seemed like a lot more than "discomfort" to me, Kate squeezed my hand. "I'm all right, Jacks. I trust her. Let's get this over with."

I turned her by the shoulders so she had no choice but to look at me. Her eyes were glassy with unshed tears. "You're sure?"

She nodded. "Yes, I'm sure. Let's go."

~ CHAPTER NINETEEN ~

Kate

MY FINGERNAILS WERE YANKED OUT, SENDING searing pain down my arms. My tormentor, a man in a hideously realistic crocodile mask, grinned at me. The screaming of my jangled nerves was unbearable, and I staggered, half-mad with agony, as he laughed.

"Hold steady, Kate. You've got this." Jackson's voice, his strong arms lifting me off the ground, helping me walk, pulled me out of the horrible vision.

"I don't think I can do this. They've suffered too much."

"You can." Fatima's confidence overrode the lack of mine, giving me another boost of determination. "The next time one of them tells you their story, bring them to you. Imagine you are gathering them in instead of resisting."

It sounded so simple, but it would be the most difficult thing I'd ever done...*if* I managed to do it. I'd survived this long by keeping walls between myself and the spirit world, holding the specters at arm's length, pretending their pain had nothing to do with me.

And now I was supposed to let that go? Break down barriers that had been in place for nearly all of my thirty-five years?

"Put her hands against the temple wall, right there. The closer she is, the better she will be able to channel them."

I could hear Fatima, but I could no longer see her. Surrounding me was a darkened chamber, full of the shrieks and moans of the dying. I saw what Bill had described.

"That's too close," Jackson said.

"Trust me."

For a moment, this side of reality was silent, and then I felt smooth, warm stone under my fingers. Digging into the grooves between stones with my nails, I hung on as wave after wave of anguish assaulted me. My head flung back on my neck; my teeth chattered.

"Let them in, Kate," Fatima yelled. "Welcome them."

Sensing weakness, or perhaps an escape, the spirits came rushing out of the walls at me. Their faces were ravaged with decay and twisted beyond recognition, unrecognizable as anything human. Squeezing my eyes shut didn't help—they assaulted my brain, and I was unable to hide from their rotting noses and blackened teeth.

You are resisting, Fatima's voice said in my mind. *Stop fighting it. Let them in. Trust me, Kate.*

"We're losing her. We need to pull back." Jackson. His terror brought tears to my eyes. I'd tried and failed. Fatima had been wrong. I wasn't strong enough for this. I wasn't brave enough.

Then I noticed someone among the shrieking, wailing mass. It was a child. Her huge, dark eyes stared at me, silently pleading for help. She raised her hands, fingers clutching at the air. *Save me. Get me out of this place.*

With my last bit of strength, I reached for her, gathering her to me. My body shook as her essence melded with mine, becoming one.

Thank you.

And where there had been anguish and suffering, there was peace.

"She's doing it," Fatima cried. "It's happening. Jackson, you can relax. She's got it."

There was a power shift even I could feel. Instead of rushing me, the spirits approached tentatively, one by one. They were no longer wailing ghouls. I could see their humanity now, as I'd seen the girl's. Some of them caressed my hair before joining their essence to mine. Some kissed my forehead.

Thank you, they whispered in a dozen different languages, but it didn't matter how they said it. I understood them all. And with each one, I became stronger. My neck straightened until I could hold my head up again. New energy streamed through my arms so I could grip the stone, pressing my palms flat against it. There were so many. Hundreds and hundreds, lending the power of their pain to mine. We had a common enemy, and together, we would bring him to his knees.

When the temple was drained of souls, my vision cleared. I turned to see Jackson gaping at me with an expression of amazement so comical it made me giggle. He ran to me, gathering me in his arms and kissing my hair, my neck, my face. "You're a goddess. I'm almost afraid to touch you."

"I can tell." I wasn't used to his being so affectionate. Usually he played it cool, but this was a nice change. "Wasn't it amazing?"

"Yeah. It was." He smoothed my hair back from my forehead, and I leaned into his touch, holding his palm against my cheek. "*You're* amazing. I was so afraid we were going to lose you. That *I* was going to lose you."

"No chance of that. How are you feeling, Kate?"

Bending down, I hugged the Muslim woman to me. "I feel wonderful. I can't get over it. Ordinarily, contact with spirits makes me feel so drained, so weak. But I've never felt this good. It's like I've just gotten back from a week-long vacation."

She nodded. "They believe in you, in your ability to avenge them. They have given you their strength, their will. And their will is strong. Otherwise, they never would have survived as long as they did. And their spirits would not have remained, all these thousands of years, to bear testament to Anubis's evil."

"Not only Anubis. I saw another one, the crocodile-headed one." I shivered, recalling the stink of his breath on my face.

"Sobek. If anyone is worse than Anubis, it's him." Fatima spat on the sand.

"Hey, I hate to break up this party, but we're starting to attract attention. I suggest we move on."

At Jackson's words, I looked up to see two guards eying us with suspicion, a small crowd of tourists snapping photos behind them. Great. At least these were different guards, not our friends from the other night.

"What's next?" I asked Fatima.

"*Koshari.*" Her face split in a broad grin.

"Ko-sa-whatta?" Jackson, always the diplomat.

"*Koshari.* You can't leave Egypt without trying our national dish."

❦

Bill poked tentatively at the care package we'd brought him, as if afraid it would bite. Couldn't say I blamed him. I'd had the same reaction upon seeing koshari—a bizarre combination of macaroni, rice, lentils, and chickpeas smothered in tomato sauce and topped with fried onions. Truly the Egyptian version of "everything but the kitchen sink."

"It looks odd, but it's strangely delicious. Try it," I said, surprised he hadn't experienced koshari yet, with all his Operation Bright Star tours. I'd expected him to greet this last Egyptian meal with relish.

"I had two helpings." Jackson patted his enviably flat stomach and collapsed on the bed. "That is some good shit. We'll have to figure out how to make it at home."

"I'll get right on that." If I ate that carb fest on a regular basis, my own stomach wouldn't stay flat, that's for sure. I didn't have Jackson's metabolism.

"I am glad you enjoyed our national dish." Fatima's smile lit up her face, and in that moment, I was grateful for Jackson's endless capacity for food. Nothing had made her happier than when he'd asked for seconds.

"I'll miss you, Fatima." I walked over to give her a hug, feeling the tears threatening. In such a short time, she'd become a good friend and irreplaceable part of our group. If she'd lived in the States, I would have hired her in a second. One can never have too many great psychics on staff, and Laura would love her too.

"Not yet, you won't." Pulling back, I saw her dark eyes gleamed with mischief. "I am coming with you."

"To the States? But you can't. It's so expensive."

"I have some money saved. I have the visa, a valid passport, and I have never gone anywhere. It is time I got a stamp, don't you think?"

"But what about your family? Will they allow it?"

Fatima smiled. "I am a grown woman, Kate. My parents will be concerned, of course, but they will respect my decision. Besides, I am not planning on becoming an American citizen. This is only a visit. You need me, and I will stay until we have fulfilled our destiny."

"And what *is* our destiny, pray tell?" Jackson asked. He was already throwing T-shirts into his duffel bag.

"Sending Anubis and his cronies back to hell."

"I'm down with that." He paused his packing long enough to sling an arm around her shoulders, enveloping her in a half hug. "You can stay, as far as I'm concerned. You're a pretty cool chick."

"Thanks, Jacks. Kate?"

"Of course you're welcome to come with us. We definitely need your help—you and Bill are the only two people in the world who get what we're dealing with. I just don't want this to cause problems for you."

"Don't worry; it won't."

"Speaking of Bill…how are we supposed to get him back? Are we smuggling him in our suitcase?" Jackson asked.

At the sound of his name, the soldier straightened in his chair. "I do have a passport, you know. I can travel legally."

I hadn't even considered that his ID might be missing. Once again, Jackson was proving to be the brains of the operation, God help us all. "You still have your identification?"

"Everything is exactly how I had it before I was…split. It's right here." He patted a pocket on the leg of his cargo pants. "Unless they can tell the difference between human and *ka*, we should be good to go."

Before I could breathe a sigh of relief, Jackson had to chime in with his pesky logic again. "Aren't you forgetting something? Won't using your passport alert the military?"

"I'm pretty sure the military thinks I'm dead. I'm a failed experiment."

"Pretty sure, but not positive. Imagine the repercussions if you survived and were able to tell the media what happened to you. I bet they're monitoring that passport, just in case. I would, if I were them."

The celebratory mood vanished, and an uncomfortable silence settled over the room. Bill was the first to break it. "What do you suggest we do? I'm not able to teleport, sadly."

"I guess we'll have to chance it, unless anyone has an idea how to get you a new passport." Jackson looked at Fatima and me. I shook my head. *Shit.* He was right. If Bill had survived, the government would expect him to return to the States and his family. What if they'd been watching the Walkinses all this time? What if they'd been watching us?

"Fatima, is there anything you can do?" Jackson asked.

"What would you like me to do?"

"I don't know. Could you make the security agents see a different name when they check his passport, or something? Or put them in some kind of a fog so they shuffle us through without looking too closely?"

"That is witchcraft, Jackson. I am a psychic, not a witch. I may be able to tell you what they are thinking, but that will only give us an early warning. It will not solve the problem."

"Does anyone know any witches?" he asked, and the

hope in his voice would have made me smile under better circumstances.

"Sadly, no." I was about to say there wasn't any such thing, but based on what we'd experienced lately, that didn't seem wise. Now that we'd seen Anubis, and Set and Sobek were real, accepting the existence of witches would be tame in comparison.

"Well, I guess the early warning is better than nothing. It'll buy us time. Can you do that, Fatima?"

"Of course. I will do my best to read the minds of the security officers."

"Good. That's all we can do. Hope for the best, plan for the worst. And be ready to run like hell."

"There is another alternative," Bill said. "I can stay here."

"Bill, no! You need to get back to your family. They've missed you so much." I thought of Dennis, who had never been the same since his brother's death, according to his wife. And what about Lily? Was there a chance she blamed herself for what had happened to Bill?

"But how can I? They think I'm dead. Everyone thinks I'm dead. How can I waltz in there and resume my normal life? I can't."

"You'll have to explain what happened. They'll understand."

"Are you serious, Kate? How is anyone going to understand what happened to me? I barely understand it myself."

"Not to mention the military will shut that shit down like yesterday," Jackson added.

"I must have taken a few too many knocks to the head, because I'm actually starting to agree with this guy. I'll stay here. It makes the most sense. You don't need me, anyway. Any information I had that would be of use I've already given you."

"That's ridiculous. Of course we need you. We're a team."

"That's very sweet of you to say, Kate, but you'll be singing a different tune if having me along results in everyone getting detained."

"He's right, Kate. He needs to stay."

I was about to bite off a sharp retort, but then I looked into Jackson's eyes and saw that, for once, he wasn't doing this out of dislike for the soldier. He honestly believed it was the best course of action, and he wasn't happy about it.

"Where will you go? You can't let yourself be recognized here, either." Sadness filled me at the thought of leaving Bill behind. I'd been so excited at the prospect of reuniting the soldier with his family. They were long overdue for some good news.

"I was thinking of going back."

"To the States?" Now I was thoroughly confused. "You mean on your own?"

"No, back to where I was before you met me. I think I understand how to get there again."

"Why would you want to return to that horrible place?" The idea of Bill being stuck in that hellhole was enough to make me weep.

"It was only horrible because I was a prisoner. This time, I'd be going back on my own terms." He tipped his chin at me. "And your girl is still there. When you send Anubis and the boys back, they're not going to be happy. Eden will need all the help she can get."

Eden. With everything that had happened, I'd almost

forgotten my friend. "We can't leave her there."

"I had a feeling you'd say that. When you figure out how to get to her, I'll be there too, waiting for you. Perhaps your friend can teach me how to teleport. She seems to have managed it, even though she isn't able to leave."

"I hate the idea of you staying behind," I said. "I really *hate* it. It feels like we're abandoning you. What if something goes wrong?"

"It won't. I know what I'm doing, Kate. And this is my choice, my decision. You're not abandoning me. I'm deciding to stay where I can be of the most use. That's what a good soldier does."

I threw my arms around him, holding him tight. I could feel pressure building in my chest, but I refused to cry. Still, I'd grown to love Bill. We'd been through so much together, and maybe it was the fact that he was a soul rather than a person, but I felt like I'd known him forever.

"You'll be fine," he said, hugging me back. "You have a good group here. And this guy is never going to let anything happen to you."

Pulling away to look into his eyes, I committed his face to memory. "You promise me you'll be careful?"

"I'm immortal, remember? But yes, I'll be careful. You know what you need to summon Anubis to the States, don't you?"

I hadn't thought of it, but once asked, the answer came to me immediately. "The figurines from the shrine."

"And you know where to find them?"

"Eden's office. She was working on some project that made her nervous. I'm willing to bet those statues were at the center of it."

"Yes. Do you think you can get in there?"

"Pretty sure, yes. A friend of mine will let me in, especially if I tell him we were working on a project together."

"Good. You're going to be just fine. And Kate?"

"Yes?"

"See you on the other side."

~ CHAPTER TWENTY ~

Kate

"**I** COULD GET IN BIG TROUBLE FOR THIS." THE entomologist's hand paused on the doorknob.

"You know I'm not going to tell anyone, Ben. And I really think it could help find Eden."

His brow furrowed. "If you have information about her disappearance, you need to go to the police. She's been gone for weeks."

"I get that. And I will talk to them, I promise. I just need to figure out how to protect her privacy. She didn't want anyone to know about our work together."

"Hey, no one understands better than me how private Eden is, but all bets are off once a person goes missing. What if she's been killed? What if she's hurt, and she needs help?"

"She's okay. She's alive and well, at least for now. That much I can promise you."

He stared hard at me, his gray eyes suspicious. *Shit.* I'd said too much. "How do you know? Do you know where she is, Kate?"

"No, of course not. If I did, I would have gone to the police. But I'm a medium, Ben. If she was dead, I'd know, wouldn't I?"

Ben stared at me a moment longer, but then his expression softened. "She could be hurt."

"I feel very strongly that she's okay. It's this gut feeling I have, like a psychic link." The great thing about what I do is that no one but other mediums understands it, which gives me the ability to bullshit freely.

"I didn't realize you were so close." This time he was wearing a Green Hornet T-shirt under his lab coat. Jackson would have approved. "I thought I was your favorite professor."

"You are. Now are you going to let me in, or what?"

"I guess it's not that big a deal, considering you were working together. The police have trashed her privacy, anyway."

"What are you talk—?"

My question died in my throat as the door swung open and I saw what remained of Eden's formerly neat, organized office. Smudges of fingerprint dust coated her desk, the walls, the windowsill. Her computer was missing, cables dangling across her desk like nerves from a recently pulled tooth.

Drawers stood open. Papers and files were scattered everywhere. Maybe it would be best if Eden stayed where she was. If she ever saw this mess, she'd have a heart attack.

"The police did this?"

"Yeah." Ben leaned against the doorframe, cleaning his glasses. "They said they had to treat it like a crime scene, in case she was kidnapped." Replacing his glasses, he narrowed his eyes at me. "She *wasn't* kidnapped, was she?"

"I don't think so." However Eden had ended up where she was, I was willing to bet it was an accident. I didn't believe Anubis had anything to do with it.

"I don't think so, either. There hasn't been any ransom note. And who would kidnap a university prof, anyway? She hadn't even made tenure."

My heart sank as I surveyed the cluttered space. What if the police had taken the figurines? That was something I hadn't considered. What if our plans were doomed?

"Do you know where she kept it? Whatever 'classified' thing you were working on?"

"No. I wish I did." Taking a deep breath, I decided to trust him. "You didn't happen to see four Egyptian figurines, did you? About yea high?"

He sucked in a breath. "Those are *artifacts*, Kate."

"I realize that. But that's what we were working with. Have you seen them, then?" My nails dug into my palms as I awaited his answer.

"We put them in the vault for safekeeping before the police stampeded in here and tore things apart. Come with me."

As I followed Ben down the quiet halls and stairways that led to the temperature-controlled vaults, my pulse quickened. I'd been allowed near them once before, with Eden, and for a history geek like me, getting a glimpse of that many ancient treasures in one spot was always a thrill.

The STAFF ONLY sign glared at me as the entomologist unlocked the door. He led the way to the so-called classical collections, where the Roman, Greek, and Egyptian artifacts were stored, his shoes squeaking on the polished linoleum tiles.

Barely giving the tiny handwritten labels a glance, Ben pulled open a drawer seemingly at random. "Is that what you're looking for?"

I rose onto my tiptoes and peered into the drawer.

There, nestled inside, were four figurines, just as Bill had described. Anubis, Set, Sobek, and Horus. The face of the jackal caught the light and appeared to grin at me. It was enough to make me queasy. "That's them. I'm so glad the police didn't take them."

"The day I let civilians get their grubby paws on priceless antiquities will be a cold day in hell." Ben sniffed. "They probably would have broken them."

"Probably. Hey, I don't count as a civilian, do I? Since I was Eden's research partner? Because I'll need to spend some time with these if I'm going to help her."

Ben couldn't have looked more shocked if I'd slapped him. His eyebrows shot up to his hairline. "What are we talking about, Kate? I thought you needed to *see* them. You're not thinking about taking them off the grounds, are you?"

"Simply seeing them isn't going to help me figure out how Eden disappeared. I'm going to need to spend some time studying them, and there's only so long I can stand on my tiptoes."

The entomologist paced in the tiny aisle, forcing me to press myself against the row of cabinets so he wouldn't bash right into me. "I'm not comfortable with this. It's not right. These jars are thousands of years old. What if something happens to them? You're not insured."

"Figurines."

"What?"

"They're figurines. They look like canopic jars, but they're not."

Ben shrugged. "Whatever. Not my department. I still don't feel comfortable letting you take them off university property. Especially without Eden's permission."

"How is Eden supposed to give me permission when she's not here? I want to use them to help her. I can't see how she'd have a problem with that."

"Maybe she wouldn't. But I have to rely on your word for it, don't I? Eden never said a thing to any of us about working with you, let alone your becoming one of her research assistants, and I'm willing to bet she never filed any official paperwork. There are processes, Kate. Try to see it from my point of view. How am I supposed to know you're telling the truth?"

"You know how private she was. You said so yourself." I cursed myself for believing this would be easy. Had I actually thought I could waltz into Eden's office and remove four priceless Egyptian figurines without a problem? My connection to Eden was tenuous at best, especially as far as the university was concerned. They knew me as an overeager adult student who audited a ton of classes, and that was as far as it went.

"Yes, well, perhaps this is the one time it's going to come back to bite her. I'm sorry." He pushed the drawer closed. "I'm afraid I can't let you take them."

"Wait! There has to be something we can do. What if I studied them here?"

Ben raised an eyebrow. "Here, in the vault?"

"I was thinking Eden's office would be more practical." How could I possibly summon Anubis and force him into a confrontation here at the university? We were talking about someone capable of making *fire* rain from the sky. What if he trashed the entire place? He certainly wouldn't go quietly.

"You want to study the artifacts in Eden's office? For how long?"

The simple fact that he was asking gave me hope. "I'm not sure how long I'll need. Several hours? Her door locks automatically, doesn't it? So I could let myself out when I'm finished."

"That's not the issue. I can't leave you in her office, Kate. Not without supervision."

So much for that idea. Nothing was going to be easy today, apparently. "Come on, Ben. We've been friends for a while. What do you think I'm going to do, trash the place?"

"It's not that." He pushed his glasses back up his nose again. "It's the principle of the thing. If Eden let someone into my office without my permission, I'd freak."

"But you have actual living creatures in yours. The only thing that will be at risk in Eden's is a bunch of papers and file folders."

"And four priceless artifacts." He rubbed his chin. "Tell you what. I have a ton of grading to do. I was going to take it home, but I could just as easily do it here. Why don't I grab a burger or something, and then you can examine the artifacts while I grade?"

"You want to be my chaperone? Are you serious?"

"Hey, take it or leave it. It's not like spending half the night here is my idea of a good time. I'm trying to do you a favor."

"I know, I know. I'm sorry. But I'm not sure how well I'll be able to concentrate with someone watching me."

"It's not like I'm going to be *watching* you. I'll be working on my own stuff." Ben folded his arms. "It's the best I can do. Your call."

"Can you at least work in your office? It's right across the hall. Surely you'd be able to hear if I started destroying stuff. *Please*, Ben. This project was supposed to be kept quiet. I'll need some privacy."

The entomologist sighed. "Okay. Fair enough. But you have to sign in with security, and I'm going to check in on you from time to time. For Eden's sake."

"Deal." I shook his hand while wondering what the hell I was going to do. Keeping Ben out of Eden's office was a minor victory, but how on earth would I summon Anubis with the entomologist across the hall, or worse, peeking his head in every ten minutes? I wasn't even sure how to summon the jackal again, for that matter. I'd been hoping that part of the equation would work itself out.

Ben handed me a pair of cotton gloves. Wheeling a small plastic cart to where we were standing, he pulled another pair of the gloves over his own hands before gently placing each figurine in a sponge-lined case. Unless it was my imagination, there was something different about the Anubis one. It was the most lifelike, as if at any moment the jackal was going to bare its teeth and snarl. I averted my eyes.

"Let's get this party started. I'm starving." Ben took control of the cart, of course, ushering me ahead of him while he turned off the lights and locked up. I felt like a child who'd been reprimanded. Out of all the professors, Ben knew me the best, probably even better than Eden. His hesitancy had more to do with his professionalism than it did with me, but his lack of trust still smarted.

Unlocking Eden's office, he pushed the cart inside. I'd have to clear off a space on her desk in order to have any room to work. The office was a disaster. I hoped someone had a chance to reorganize it before she came back…*if* she came back.

"Do you think it would be all right if I moved these files and papers somewhere else? Like, on top of the cabinet?"

"I don't see why not. You could hardly make it look worse." Ben shook his head, surveying the ruin. "It's actually a good thing Eden can't see this. She'd freak."

I tried to picture the cool, self-contained Egyptologist freaking out and failed. If she had a dramatic side to her personality, she'd kept it from me.

"Well. You have everything you need?"

Glancing at the figurines, I nodded. What else could I do? Ben had made himself clear—either work with the artifacts here, under his supervision, or not at all. "I think so."

"Great. I'm going to run out for that burger now. I shouldn't be more than ten, fifteen minutes. I'll sign you in before I leave and explain the situation, so you shouldn't run into any trouble with security. Can I grab anything for you?"

Even though I couldn't remember the last time I'd eaten, food was the last thing on my mind. "No thanks."

"Suit yourself. See you in a bit."

"You bet. Thanks, Ben." Taking a deep breath, I tackled the mess on Eden's desk, gathering the papers and folders into neat piles and stacking them on top of a filing cabinet. But as soon as I heard the entomologist's office door close and his shoes squeak down the hallway, I pulled my phone out of my jacket.

Please pick up. Please pick up. Please be there.

Jackson answered on the second ring. "Kate! We've been waiting to hear from you. How's it going?"

"Not good, I'm afraid. We've got a problem." Removing some books and papers from Eden's chair, I slumped into it.

"Couldn't find the statues?"

"No, I've got them, but Ben insists I work with them here. He won't let them leave the university. And even worse, he's going to 'keep an eye on me.' Which means he's probably going to be popping in every ten minutes. What should I do?"

"Where is he now?"

"He went to grab a burger. I've probably got ten minutes before he returns, if that. That's not enough time to get you, Fatima, and Laura here, even if I could get you past security, which is doubtful." I moaned as the magnitude of the problem hit me. "We're screwed. I don't know how I ever thought this would work. The university thinks these things are priceless artifacts—of course they aren't going to let me take them off the grounds. They probably wouldn't have let Eden take them. I wasn't thinking straight."

"Kate, you've got to get out of there."

"What do you mean? Just leave? Forget about it?"

"No, take those statues and get the hell out of there before he comes back."

"I can't do that." The idea of stealing the artifacts made my forehead break out in a sweat. "He trusts me. I can't betray him."

"Fuck that shit. What's more important? Saving the world, saving Lily, and getting Eden back, or not pissing off the bug guy?"

My heart was pounding so hard my head ached, which meant I was about to do something crazy. But Jackson was right. I had no choice. And Ben would understand. If not now, then eventually. "What if he calls the police?"

"We'll meet you at the beach like we planned. No one will look for you there. But you need to *go*, Kate. Now. Okay?"

"Okay. I'll see you in ten minutes."

Taking an old memo from the clutter on Eden's desk, I flipped it over and began to write.

Ben,

I'm sorry, but I had to go. I can't say why, but please trust me it's the best way of helping Eden. I promise I'll return the artifacts tomorrow and that they'll still be in perfect condition.

If you could hold off calling the police, that would really help, but if you can't I'll understand.

Please trust me. I promise to explain later.

Kate

Hands shaking, I hurriedly wrapped each figurine in paper before shoving it in my purse. The leather bag strained as I slung it over my shoulder, and I prayed the strap would hold. Closing the door behind me, I rushed down the hall, trying my best to appear frazzled instead of scared for the benefit of the security cameras.

On the main floor, the corridors were empty. Praying I wouldn't bump into Ben, I made my way to the door.

"Hey, hey, hey—where are you going so fast?"

I flinched, a small *yelp* escaping before I could help it.

A large black man smiled at me from behind a Plexiglas shield. "Sorry, didn't mean to scare you. But you have to sign out."

"Oh, I just need to grab a notebook from my car. I'll be right back."

The man studied my expression, assessing me. Could he see how terrified I was, how my nerves were about to explode? Finally, he nodded. "Okay. Five minutes."

"Thank you!" Before he could change his mind, I was through the doors and sprinting to the parking lot. My hands shook so badly as I unlocked the Mini that I nearly dropped my keys. How long had it been? Ben must already be on his way back. What if he saw me leave?

No time to worry about that now. As quickly as I could without screeching my tires, I left the university. Wiping my forehead with one hand, I gripped the wheel with the other, squinting at the road.

Once I'd escaped, I had to admit I felt strangely exhilarated. I'd never done anything truly bad in my life.

And now my life of crime had begun.

God help me.

~ CHAPTER TWENTY-ONE ~

Jackson

GALE-FORCE WINDS BLASTED ACROSS THE beach, sending fine particles of sand into my eyes and mouth. I hunkered down into a crouch beside Fatima, feeling nervous. The psychic had her headscarf pulled over her nose so only her eyes were visible. Vermont's fall temperatures had been a rude awakening for our Egyptian friend, who was bundled up in one of Kate's winter coats. The nylon billowed around her like a parachute, and I would have laughed if I weren't so damn anxious.

What was wrong with me? I was normally the first one leaping into the action, not doing everything I could to put it off. Was it the jet lag? Or some premonition of impending doom?

"Are you feeling all right, Jackson?" Fatima raised her voice to be heard over the rising wind.

"I'm never going to get used to your reading my mind."

"I wasn't this time—not really. It was just a hunch."

"Well, your hunch was a good one. We're crazy to challenge this guy on our own. He can make fire rain from the sky. How can we compete with that?"

"Your fear is understandable, but that isn't what is bothering you."

I raised an eyebrow at her. "By all means, enlighten me."

As usual, she ignored my jab. "You are uncomfortable because you are not sure what your role is. We have two accomplished psychics and Kate, a formidable medium who's recently discovered a new source of power."

"Thanks for the recap. Unnecessary, but succinct."

"So, what do we need you for? You are an ordinary guy."

"Ouch. That's cold."

"But that is what you are thinking, is it not?"

"You're not far off." It had started in Poveglia, feeling like Kate's shadow. I'd hoped this would change—*needed* it to change, but so far, there hadn't been time to do anything about it. We'd barely landed on American soil before finding ourselves in the midst of a new crisis, and I suspected this would always be the case. *What am I doing here? Did I make a mistake moving to Nightridge?* These were the ugly thoughts that piped up in quieter moments, but even when I wasn't listening, they nagged at me.

"But you are not an ordinary guy. You are as important as any of us, maybe more so. You are—"

"I know, I know. I'm the Guardian." Already I was tired of hearing it. It made me sound ridiculous, like some guy who liked to hide out in basements with his buddies, rolling twenty-sided dice and pretending to be an elf. "Whatever the heck that means."

"You will find out."

"Who are you, anyway? Yoda? Mr. Miyagi? 'I will find out'? Is this a premonition or just another hunch?"

Fatima crinkled her nose. "Mr. Miyagi?"

"Never mind. Before your time. Before mine too, come to think of it."

"Some things you do not need to be psychic for. I have always seen greatness in you. You do not quite believe in it yet, but it is there. And when needed, it will make itself apparent. I promise."

Touched, I put an arm around her, giving her a hug. "Thanks, Fatima."

"No problem."

Laura knelt in front of us, her face paler than usual. "Guys, I'm really getting worried. She should be here by now. I wonder if Ben came back early and caught her."

"Nope, she got out. She's almost here."

She stared at me. "How do you know?"

"I actually have no idea. I just do. She's about a block away." The thought that Kate would soon arrive made me feel a bit better. "She's driving too fast. That girl always did have a heavy foot."

"Is there something I should know, Jacks? The last time I checked, you weren't psychic."

"Jackson is a Guardian, and the abilities of a Guardian reveal themselves in times of crisis," Fatima said, blowing on her hands to warm them. Though she'd had to raise her voice to join our conversation, her tone was matter-of-fact, as if she said shit like this every day. Come to think of it, she probably did. I was going to have to cultivate some normal friends in Nightridge soon or I'd start sounding the same way.

"What does—I'm sorry, but I don't understand what that means."

Poor Laura. There had been no opportunity to fill her in

on all the new developments. No wonder she was confused.

"It means he has a link with Kate. And Lily. And whomever else he needs to protect."

"Were you aware of this?" Laura gaped at me like I'd grown two heads, and I had to chuckle at her shocked expression.

"Are you kidding? Hells no. This is a whole new world for me. Maybe this is what happens when you confront an ancient Egyptian god and live to tell the tale."

"Monster," Fatima corrected. "Not god, monster."

I shrugged. "Whatever. It's all-powerful, mean as hell, and wants to rule the world. Both monikers fit."

"We'll probably want to hold off on the sacrilegious stuff for now, Jacks. Just in case. We're going to need all the help we can get." Laura patted my back.

"True dat. I'll rein it in."

"Speaking of help, there's one thing I never got the chance to tell you guys. I've—"

Kate.

Laura stopped speaking as we all turned to stare at the familiar redhead sprinting toward us. The full moon gave her hair an unearthly silver glow. "Already? That was quick."

"Told you—girl has a heavy foot."

There was no time for a happy reunion. When Kate flung herself into my arms, gasping and wheezing, the panic in her eyes was clear.

"I messed up. I'm sorry, Jacks. I was sure no one saw me leave, but somebody must have. An SUV has been following me for the last few blocks, and it pulled into the parking lot behind me. I figure I have a ten-minute head start on them, if that."

"Fuck. We're screwed."

Laura rested her hands on Kate's shoulders. "Not so fast. Is this SUV black with stars painted on the sides, by any chance?"

"Yes...why? What's going on, Lore?" Kate's chest heaved with her exertion, and my heart went out to her. Poor girl looked spent. I removed the heavy purse from her shoulder, careful of the priceless artifacts, and retrieved the inhaler that was tucked inside. Ever since Doctor Death had told her that her asthma was psychosomatic, she'd tried her best to wean herself off the medication, but the girl was whistling like a teapot. Exceptions needed to be made.

I gave the purse to Fatima for safekeeping in case I had to deal with the driver of the SUV, but I didn't feel the usual anxiety I had when Kate was in danger. Whoever this person in the star-festooned van was, I had a feeling they were on our side.

"That's what I was about to explain before you showed up," Laura said. "I called for reinforcements."

Fatima looked as confused as I felt.

"What do you mean, reinforcements?" I asked, since Kate was using her inhaler and temporarily incapable of speech.

"I mean, well, *them*."

Six people strode toward us. As they moved closer, one broke rank and sped in our direction, sneakers kicking up clouds of sand. We'd find out what this was about soon enough.

"I asked the best girls I know to pitch in. I thought we might need help. I hope that's okay," Laura said.

The best girls? So that meant—

"Best girls? I take offense at that, honey." A slim,

good-looking guy with dark wavy hair launched himself at Laura, nearly succeeding in knocking both of them off their feet. Kate got out of the way just in time.

"Sorry, Daniel. I wasn't sure you'd be able to make it."

"Of course I made it. When your friend tells you an ancient demon from Egypt is going to destroy the world, you come. There's really no decision to make." He pulled away from Laura long enough to acknowledge the rest of us with a nod. He gave me a huge smile, and I couldn't help but notice his teeth were as startlingly perfect as the rest of him. "Well, hel-lo there. You must be Jackson."

He moved past Laura to shake my hand while she emphasized, "*Kate's* Jackson."

"Oh well." Daniel winked. "Can't win 'em all."

"Is this where the party's at?" A heavyset woman, her silver pixie cut streaked with purple, smiled at us, though she was breathing hard.

Laura beamed. "Hey, Star. I'm glad you could make it."

"Star?" I still hadn't processed Daniel. These two were making Laura look almost normal in comparison.

Star flapped a hand at me. "My parents were hippies," she said before enveloping both Kate and Laura in a hug. "So I kind of went with it. Can't beat 'em, join 'em, you know?"

Her black dress flapped in the wind like a sail, and I noticed it was covered with hundreds of tiny stars. I was willing to bet she was the owner of the star-spangled SUV.

"Fatima, Jackson, and Kate, I'd like you to meet Star, Daniel, Jean, Suzanne, Beth and David. They're incredibly talented, and some of them have experience doing energy work," Laura said. Since her friends had arrived, some color had returned to her cheeks. The place had acquired an almost festive air despite the ominous weather, rather than the waiting-for-the-firing-squad feel we'd enjoyed before.

"David's my twin. He's a man's man. You will love him," Daniel said to me with another wink while a man who could have been his carbon copy rolled his eyes.

"I'm...sure I will. So you're psychics, then?"

"Only the best of the best," Star added. "Not a fraud among us."

Her charisma was infectious, but I could tell her in-your-face personality would end up irritating the hell out of me by the end of the night. Laura, Fatima, and Kate had a kind of quiet seriousness about them, and with these new arrivals, the atmosphere seemed too chaotic, too celebratory, for what we had planned. This was the potential end of the world, not New Year's Eve.

"We may be flamboyant, but we're a lot stronger than we look." Star patted my arm. "Not to worry, honey. We like to have fun, but we know how to work."

At my expression, Laura laughed. "Better guard your thoughts like I showed you, Jacks, or you won't have a private moment all night. These people are *good*."

"Thanks for the warning," I said, which resulted in peals of laughter. Was I imagining things, or did Kate give me a sympathetic look?

"Don't worry," she breathed in my ear. "Laura would never sabotage this."

"I know." If Laura claimed this Psychic Friends Network was the real deal, I was willing to go along with it. What choice did we have? They were here now.

Besides, reinforcements were probably a good thing. Judging by what I'd already seen of Anubis, we would need all the help we could get.

~ CHAPTER TWENTY-TWO ~

Kate

I KNEW JACKS WELL ENOUGH TO GUESS WHAT HE was thinking. He'd written Laura's friends off as a bunch of kooks. Didn't he get that *we* were the kooks now? Me more than him, certainly, but we'd both left the illusion of normalcy far behind.

As much as I'd attempted to reassure him, I wasn't confident about this new ragtag band of helpers, either. Beyond my friendship with Laura, and now Fatima, I hadn't worked with psychics before. Their help was bound to come in handy, but what if I failed? What if Anubis didn't come, or worse—what if he massacred our group like he had the scientists? What then?

"We're well aware of the risks, Kate. And we're here to help and support, not to judge," Star said.

Fucking psychics. I could stand a refresher on mind-blocking techniques myself.

From the older woman's grin, I could see she'd caught that thought too.

"We might not have much time, so let's get started," I said, after filling them in on the phenomena we'd experienced in Egypt.

"Psychics, form a circle." Star's group responded immediately, linking hands around me and the figurine of Anubis. Jackson hesitated when Daniel reached for his hand, but then shrugged and took Fatima's on his other side. So many people staring at me, looking to me for answers, added to my unease. Unlike the hapless military scientists, we knew what to expect. We had our abilities to protect us. But what if it wasn't enough?

My grandmother had never had to deal with this shit, and until recently, neither had I. I communicated with the dead. Summoning angry Egyptian gods was never part of the deal.

"He wants something you have, Kate. He will come here to negotiate, not to kill—at least at first," Fatima said. "What he did to the US military was a show of strength, payment for their impertinence, but as long as he believes there is a chance you will hand over Lily, he will hear you out."

"How do you know?" Jackson asked, echoing my own thoughts, which also included, *What if you're wrong?*

"It is an educated guess," the Egyptian said. "Besides, what choice do we have? We must end this, or die trying."

"I'm...I'm not sure how to summon him," I admitted. *Or if I should.* The psychics had said they understood the risks, but they hadn't seen Bill's face when he talked about watching the scientists get torn apart.

"What about 'Anubis, I summon thee'?"

"This isn't *The Exorcist*, Jacks."

"The scientists tried to study the statue, didn't they? Maybe there is something on it that might give us a clue," Fatima said. Standing between Jackson and David, who both towered over her, she appeared even tinier than usual.

Deciding it was worth a try, I turned the figure over in my hands. It resembled a miniature replica of a canopic jar. There was a ridge under the statue's head, as if it were a lid or topper of some kind, meant to come off. I seized Anubis around the snout and twisted.

A loud rumbling noise made me freeze. The psychics looked at the sky, the color going out of Laura's cheeks again. *Please let us survive this. Please let me be worthy of Fatima's faith.*

"What was that? Thunder?" one of the women asked. I thought her name was Beth. Or maybe Jean.

"That wasn't thunder. It was *him*. You're on the right track, Kate. Keep going," Star said. "The rest of you, focus. We're not going to get much warning—we need to be ready."

Most of the psychics lowered their heads as if in prayer. After a moment, Fatima followed suit, but Jackson looked puzzled. *I don't belong here*, his expression said. Poor guy. He must wonder what on earth he'd gotten himself into.

Wiping my palms off on my jeans, I steeled myself before grasping the figurine's head again. This time I used more strength. The head moved under my hand.

The wind gathered force until it felt like it would tear my hair from my scalp. It shrieked like a wild animal, and a few of the psychics winced. A cloud passed over the moon, plunging us into darkness.

"Hold tight, hold tight. Stay strong—it's happening. Do *not* lose your focus. Hang on to each other." The confidence in Star's voice was reassuring, as was the energy that now hummed around me, making my skin tingle. Still, standing alone in the dark, unable to see anyone or anything, was terrifying. When Anubis arrived, I'd be easy pickings. He'd snap my neck before anyone knew I was in trouble.

Have faith. All of these people believe in you. It's time to believe in yourself.

"Jacks?" My voice trembled, revealing more fear than I'd intended.

"I'm here." His hand steadied me, the warmth radiating through the fabric of my T-shirt. "You've got this, Kate. I'm right here with you."

Something else was as well. There was a stirring deep inside me, a sinister power that whispered of rage and revenge, much like the spirit of Isabelle had before she lashed out. But Isabelle was gone; I'd released her. These were the slaves of Anubis. Perhaps they felt their vengeance was coming.

He'd enslaved them before; why should he fear them now? What would stop him from capturing them again and sending them back to that prison in the desert? How absurd we must seem, this silly group of mortals with our half-assed abilities and me, armed with a cargo of tortured souls. How had we ever thought this would work? We were going to die.

My hands trembled and the statue slipped. Jackson snatched it out of midair, replacing it in my hands and curling his fingers over mine.

"You can feel that, can't you?"

The air was thicker now, heavier, like it had been when Laura and I stopped the frogs from falling, only much more intense. Whatever the psychics were doing, it was working. The atmosphere crackled with energy. "The psychics? Yes."

"No, not the psychics. You, Kate. It's coming from

you. You don't even realize it, do you? The fear you're feeling—it's his, not yours. So reel the bastard in, and let's finish this, once and for all."

I didn't argue for a change. His confidence in me, his unwavering belief, was all I needed to give the jackal's head one final twist.

Thick smoke poured from the statue. The wind stilled, allowing the haze to hang over our group. I heard some of the psychics coughing and Star yelling at them to stay strong, but it sounded like they were a million miles away. It was Jackson and I against whatever this was, against whatever was to come.

The cloying stench of incense was overpowering. My lungs worked uselessly in my chest, and my partner in crime pressed my inhaler into my now-empty hands. The statue had vanished in the smoke. Tramping down my panic, I allowed myself two shots of the medicine before returning it to Jackson, trusting him to keep it safe.

And then we waited.

Orange-gold eyes flashed in the darkness, an impossibly long way off, as if the beach stretched on forever.

The eyes narrowed as they focused on us, and Jackson moved to stand beside me, holding tight to my hand, his foot pressed against mine. "You've got this, Kate. Never forget that. Send him back to hell."

On the streets of Luxor there had been more places to hide, to resist. And Fatima had been with me, guiding us through every step, every new horror.

"I am still here," her familiar voice called, and the circle drew in close again, no longer miles away. The humming of our combined power grew louder, surrounding us. I tightened my grip on Jackson's hand.

Fatima yelled something in a language I didn't recognize, and I heard an answering snarl that made me shiver.

Then he was there, looming above us, his eyes glowing bright enough to illuminate the darkness. He stood outside the circle, just beyond Star and two of her friends, a twisted sneer of amusement on his face. Poor Star. With her eyes clenched shut, she continued to chant, but I could see how violently she trembled.

Instead of snarling, the jackal smirked. *Smirked* at us. Somehow, that was worse.

"What did I tell you about meddling with gods, mortal?" His breath was a stinking furnace blast, carrying with it the odor of death. Terrifying as he was, a faint hope blossomed within me. He was confident enough to think he could handle us on his own. That might prove to be his downfall.

"Did you actually believe you could stop me? That your pathetic little plan would work?"

"You don't belong here, Anubis. And you can't have Lily."

His fangs flashed at me and I saw my death in them. "I find it amusing you still presume to tell me what I can or cannot do. But my amusement only lasts for so long, I'm afraid. As you will soon see, I have quite the temper."

"Do it, Kate! Banish him," Fatima shouted, and the dog's head swiveled in her direction. Her cry of pain cut through me like an arrow.

"Fatima!"

"No. You have to stay here. Don't lose your focus." Jackson held me fast, forcing me to face the hateful, slavering thing in front of us. Anubis grinned.

"That is all it takes, mortal. One look from me, one

thought, and you will all be dead. Is that what you desire?"

Oh no, not Fatima. I couldn't bear the thought of losing her, the woman who had become such a dear friend to us both.

Star's voice rose above Anubis's snarling. "Everyone, send your energy to Jackson. Do it *NOW.*"

Jackson? Why Jackson and not me?

In the fraction of a second my mind had drifted to the psychic, Anubis lunged. His muzzle lowered, teeth snapping shut right above my neck, close enough to snag my shirt. The dog-headed god withdrew, an expression of confusion on his face that was almost comical.

"Nice trick, mortal, but there are only so many places you can hide. I will find you, and when I do, you will join your friend in the afterlife."

Hide? What was he talking about? I hadn't moved.

"We're running out of time," Jackson said. "Do it, Kate. End this fucker."

That's when I saw Jacks's skin was shimmering. Somehow, he was protecting me. But how long could it last?

Anubis lunged again, and this time his claws found my skin, slicing open my arm. Fire blazed through my veins as I wailed, unable to bear the agony. Through my anguish, I heard the hateful creature howl, but this time in distress. A swarm of golden bees swirled around his head, the drone growing louder and louder.

"Hurry," Jackson called. Impossibly, the bees were coming from the shimmering aura that surrounded him. His arms were outstretched, his fingers pressed against an invisible wall, literally holding Anubis back. "Come on, Kate."

Before I had a moment to think, Anubis shook off Jackson's assault, appearing to notice him for the first time. "*You!*" His teeth bared as he reared over the man I loved most in the world, and this time I didn't think. I just reacted.

The immense rush I'd felt when I'd expelled Isabelle's spirit from my body was nothing compared to the ferocity of hundreds of slaves. As I propelled the souls at Anubis, the resulting force knocked me backward.

Freed from their prison and faced with the monster who'd made their existence a never-ending hell, the spirits shrieked with rage. They swirled around the jackal-headed god, faster and faster, until I couldn't see anything but a cloud of gray mist. But then I heard the sweetest sound in the world.

Anubis yelping in pain.

My ears popped and I covered my head with my hands, unable to bear the high-pitched squeals. It was like a million puppies being tortured, and even though I knew the evil of the creature being destroyed, my animal-loving heart couldn't handle it. I cringed against a psychic, needing comfort, and David or Daniel responded, patting my shoulder.

Anubis's torment seemed to last forever, until I was certain I would lose my mind. His hands turned into paws, clawing at the mist and the bees that still teemed from Jackson, stinging, stinging, stinging.

Waves of dizziness threatened to overwhelm me, and I choked back the accompanying nausea, fighting to stay strong against the ghastly thoughts that invaded my brain.

What if it wasn't enough? What if Anubis won, and came back full of murderous rage? What then?

Then I realized the mist was harder to see. It drifted with its howling, shrieking cargo, slowly at first, but then faster and faster, until it vanished into the night.

Anubis was gone, and with him, the darkness retreated. Moonlight glittered on the sand.

Something touched my head and I flinched, striking out with my good hand.

"Hey, hey. Take it easy. Good to see you haven't lost your nerve."

"Jackson!" Throwing my arms around him, I showered his face with kisses. "Are you all right?" Holding his face between my hands, I checked him for wounds. His skin was damp under my fingers, and the shoulder of his shirt was soaked with blood. "You're bleeding."

"So are you." He ripped a strip of cloth from his T-shirt and tied it tightly around my arm, making me gasp in pain. "We're going to need stitches, I think."

"You were amazing." I still couldn't quite make sense of what I'd witnessed—the shimmering light, Anubis's unexpected blindness, the bees…. "If it weren't for you, everyone on this beach would be dead."

"Um, I think that credit goes to you." But I recognized the stunned expression on his face from the days I'd first discovered my own power. He was going to need a while to come to terms with this. Hell, we all would.

"Is everyone all right?" Star's voice, exhausted and fearful, snapped me back to reality. *Fatima*.

Before I could go to her, Jackson took hold of my arm, shaking his head. "She's gone, Kate."

"No!" Shoving him away, I crawled to where she'd been standing. Laura was kneeling over her, cradling her body, tears spilling over her cheeks.

"Fatima." The psychic's dark eyes gazed past me, seeing something beyond us, beyond this world. I hoped she'd found her god, her Jannah. Gently lowering her lids, I kissed her forehead.

Her scarf had been knocked loose, and I smoothed it back into place. There was no blood, no sign of injury. She looked at peace, a slight smile upon her lips. "I'm so sorry," I whispered.

My grief crushed me. I buried my face in her shoulder and sobbed. "God, I'm so sorry, Fatima."

"Don't, Kate. It wasn't your fault." Jackson stroked my back, but I jerked away from his touch, undeserving of any comfort.

"It's *all* my fault. If only I'd been faster, if I hadn't hesitated. She'd still be alive."

"This wasn't your fault," he said again, more forcefully. "She accepted what the risks were. She wanted to do this. You remember what she told us in Egypt—Anubis was her enemy too."

Caressing Fatima's cheek, I was saddened to realize it was already cold. She was gone, and no amount of guilt or regret would ever bring her back. Maybe I'd talk to her again someday, but I hoped not. I hoped that she'd moved on to someplace so wonderful I wouldn't be able to reach her.

"She was an incredible woman," Jackson said.

"Yes, she was." Gathering her into my arms, I held her and cried until I had no tears left.

~ EPILOGUE ~

Kate

"YOU REALIZE THIS ISN'T OVER."

"I know." My bed had become a haven over the last couple days as we nursed our respective wounds and mourned our friend. The blankets were littered with magazines, newspapers, takeout containers, and half-empty pizza boxes. Nostradamus stretched out between us and yawned, waggling his front paws in the air.

"It's up to Eden and Bill now."

"Yeah." I stroked my cat's ears, letting his purr calm me. Had we truly destroyed Anubis, or sent him back to the past angrier than ever? It was an awful thought.

"Do you think you'll ever see her again?"

"Eden? I hope so. It won't be at the university, though."

Ben had been furious at me for stealing—*borrowing*—the statues, and even more so when I'd explained the Anubis one had gone missing. He was so angry that I'd expected him to press charges, but apparently banning me from the university was enough. I was too distraught over Fatima's death to care much. It would probably hit me later.

At least Lily and her family were normal again, or as

normal as they'd ever be. Everyone was home from the hospital and Dennis was acting like his old self. It would take Lily some time to trust him again, but I was confident they'd be able to repair their relationship, especially as the girl learned to manage her abilities. I wasn't strong enough to help her yet, but Laura had been working with her.

This was the first day since Fatima's death that Jackson had brought up what had happened. We'd been too numb to talk about anything serious, using bad TV and junk food as novocaine. So I risked a question I'd been yearning to ask.

"Why bees?"

He was quiet for a moment. "I'm not sure. I used to be scared of them when I was a kid, so maybe they were the worst thing I could think of in the heat of the moment."

"It's interesting. You know, some cultures believed bees could bridge the gap between our realm and the underworld."

"Really?"

"The ancient Egyptians believed bees were the tears of Ra."

"Do you think Ra—"

"Helped us? It's impossible to say." *But it made sense.* How else could mortals defeat a god? Ra represented the light, while Anubis represented darkness. Perhaps the sun god had his own reasons for preventing the jackal from running amok on earth.

"You know, before all this stuff happened, I was afraid you wouldn't need me anymore."

"Why? Of course I need you."

"Well, I was always there if you got overcome, or whatever. Once Fatima showed you how to use the spirits' pain, I figured you weren't in danger anymore. You wouldn't need me."

Leaning against his shoulder, I took a deep breath. "Jacks, I'll always need you. I hope you get that now."

"Well yeah, everything's different. I'm a Guardian. Whatever the hell that means."

"It's like Fatima said. You'll figure it out."

"*We'll* figure it out."

"I like the way you think."

Jackson wrapped his arm around me, and I let myself relax against him. We both knew the peace and quiet would be temporary, and I was determined to treasure every second. Soon, someone else would need our help.

But not yet.

Thanks so much for reading. If you enjoyed this book, please take a minute to leave a review. Reviews make a huge difference to an author's sales and rankings—the more reviews, the more books I'll be able to write.

My readers mean the world to me, and I'd love to stay in touch. You can keep up with me on Facebook, Twitter, Pinterest, or sign up for my newsletter to receive a new spooky post every week, along with access to an exclusive Hidden Library bursting with FREE books.

Facebook: www.facebook.com/jhmoncrieff

Twitter: twitter.com/JH_Moncrieff

Pinterest: www.pinterest.com/jhmoncrieff

Newsletter: bit.ly/MoncrieffLibrary

ACKNOWLEDGMENTS

Enormous thanks go to two amazing Egyptologists, Maged Bottros and Hany Mostafa of Intrepid Travel. Not only were they wonderful hosts, showing me the best of their beautiful country, they were instrumental in helping me get the details right. Exploring Egypt has been a dream of mine since I was a child, and I was so touched by the friendliness and warmth of the people, who welcomed me with open arms (and plenty of mint tea). Bill's experience in the marketplace when he was ill mirrors mine. If you're considering a trip to Egypt, please don't hesitate. My only regret is that I didn't go sooner.

I am extremely fortunate to have a large number of supportive friends and colleagues who cheer me on in this crazy writing life, encouraging me whenever I lose faith in myself. But rather than the usual lengthy list, I've decided to highlight just a few this time.

There's a moment in the movie *Under the Tuscan Sun* when Diane Lane's best friend apologizes for "screwing up her love life" by showing up right before Lane is about to go on a date. Lane responds, "Don't be ridiculous, Patti. You *are* my love life." This is exactly how I feel about Christine

Brandt, who has been my best friend and travel buddy for over twenty years. No matter what happens, she is always there for me, and I can't imagine my life without her. Thank you, dear friend, for everything.

This book would not exist without the support and encouragement of Chris Brogden, my editor and friend, who has celebrated my successes and shrugged off any failures from the beginning. Chris has made this journey possible in so many ways that mere words could never do him justice. Every writer needs a champion, and for the past eight years, he has been mine. I can never thank him enough.

Thanks to Andrew Maxwell for doing an emergency edit of the preview of my new book.

Thank you to Scott and Celeste Forman, Paul Genesse, Terra Luft, Callie Stoker, Jared Quan, Johnny Worthen, and the rest of the folks at the League of Utah Writers for welcoming me to your fall conference and showing me such incredible appreciation and warmth. I was blown away by your hospitality and hope to return. To Jared Synn, a special thank-you for wearing a million different hats, from tech guy to tour guide, ensuring the experience was an unqualified success. And to Ryan Carty, thank you for being even better in person.

More tales of spine-tingling supernatural suspense from J.H. Moncrieff and DeathZone Books! Learn more about Kate's friend Eden and her adventures in ancient Egypt when the Egyptologist's series debuts in 2018. I hope you enjoy this special sneak peek of the first book.

Book Four of the GhostWriters series should be released in May 2018.

~ CHAPTER ONE

"EDIE, YOU MUST LOOK AT THIS."

Bast meowed in irritation at the interruption. Arthur was the only one who called me Edie. As he was your typical, ever-appropriate Brit, I assumed his habit of calling me by the wrong name was deliberate, but whether it was done as a term of endearment or just to annoy me, I couldn't say.

"It's Eden," I reminded him automatically, turning to see the archaeologist was even more out of breath than usual. His face was flushed the color of autumn apples, and his stomach pushed at the buttons of his beige Oxford as he gasped for air. One thick-fingered hand grasped my door frame for support. For a moment, I worried the man was about to have a heart attack in my office, but then I saw the bundle he clutched in his other hand.

It was about the size of a Starbucks Venti, with an intriguing anthropomorphic shape. Even more exciting, it was wrapped in linen. Dirty, dusty linen. Very *old*-looking linen. I could feel my heart beat faster. Arthur had spent the past three months in Egypt, daring the usual dangers of dysentery, malaria and heatstroke, along with the new terrors of an unstable political climate and unpredictable outbreaks of violence. He also had a very bad habit of smuggling artifacts out of the country without obeying the proper protocol. In short, he gave archaeologists a bad name, but although I was an academic, that didn't concern me as much as one might think.

"Now, now, before you get your knickers in a knot, I followed the protocol." Arthur gulped for air between words. "Maybe I shouldn't have taken it with me, but everyone knows we'll probably sell it to your university anyway. And you had to see it."

He thrust the bundle toward me, and I had to struggle to maintain my air of cool disapproval. It wouldn't do for him to see a respected Egyptologist act like an excited little girl, but that's exactly what I felt like. "Is that an artifact? Tell me you didn't smuggle another..."

Arthur cut off the rest of my sentence with a wave of his hand, venturing farther into my office. Bast let out a low growl in warning. She'd never cared for Arthur. Cats were skittish creatures at the best of times, and this heavy-footed, heavy-breathing, loud-mouthed creature would have never been one of their favorite people. "It's all appropriate, I assure you. The I's have been dotted and the T's have been crossed. Just look at it, will you? Otherwise, it's a wasted trip."

He made as if to toss the artifact like a softball, and I

cried out in alarm, positioning my hands to catch it. With a grin, he placed it gently in my hands. I took a deep breath to stop my heart from racing. Sometimes I wanted to kill Arthur.

Holding the bundle to my nose, I closed my eyes, taking everything in. The item, or at least the linen in which it was wrapped, was very old indeed. It had the aroma of what I'd come to think of as *L'eau de Tomb*—that musty smell of cinnamon and cloves, topped by centuries of dust. But thankfully, the unpleasant undercurrent of decay was missing. Whatever I was holding was not the remains of a once-living organism.

It was surprisingly heavy for its small size, and quite firm in my hands. Placing it gently on my desk blotter, I reached in one of my drawers for a pair of cotton gloves. Once I'd pulled them on, I began to carefully unwrap the object, keeping a careful watch for Bast out of my peripheral vision. I'd learned from painful experience that, to a cat, ancient mummy wrappings were nothing but an unraveled ball of yarn. The university's president wasn't exactly a cat lover. Bast's position as my office mate was already tenuous at best.

When at last the wrappings were removed and the object was revealed on my desk, I gasped. It was the figure of a woman, her skin fashioned from the palest alabaster, and her hair and eyes crafted from some gleaming, dark stone I couldn't immediately identify. She wore the headdress of royalty, with Uraeus—the rearing cobra—displayed prominently upfront, but even without that marker, it was clear she had been someone important. Her dress, which was as nearly as pale as her skin, was decorated with all the symbols she'd need to prosper in the afterlife, symbols rendered in gold, silver, turquoise, lapis lazuli, and other jewels. Her eyes revealed an intelligence that was eerily lifelike, and her lips were curled in a smirk I'd seen many times before.

While she was easily the most beautiful artifact I'd ever held in my hands, it wasn't her beauty or her value that captured my attention. Those knowing eyes, that mocking curl of lip—they were all too familiar to me, and with good reason.

The artifact had my face.

The strength went out of my legs and I sank into my office chair, unable to take my eyes from the figure. "It's not possible…"

Arthur pulled out a chair and sat across from me, ignoring Bast's hiss. "It's quite extraordinary, isn't it?"

I tore my attention away from the statuette to glare at him. "Is this some kind of joke, Arthur?" It *looked* authentic, and the old wrappings were a nice touch. He'd certainly had me fooled. But he knew some of the best replica makers in the business. If he'd wanted a statue carved with my face, all he had to do was make a few calls and name the right price.

"No, no joke," he said, pointing one thick finger at the figure. "This was waiting for us in the Valley of the Kings in a tomb of an unknown queen. Not far from Tutankhamen. It's a wonder we didn't find it long before now, or that grave robbers didn't make off with it. It's obviously quite valuable."

Not a joke. The resemblance was a coincidence, then. A strange turn of events, but I'd seen stranger. Life was always playing funny little tricks, and if there's anything a historian knows, it's that history tends to repeat itself, again and again.

"And her remains?"

Arthur shook his head. "Not a single vertebra. Some priest must have smuggled her to another location a few thousand years ago. Odd that he didn't move the treasure while he was at it."

The ancient Egyptians had revered their leaders as gods. It never occurred to them that some people were so desperate they'd actually raid these precious graves. When the last fortress of the Valley of the Kings—a "new" burial chamber devised by the loyal servants of Pharaoh Thutmose I—was breached, priests moved the bodies under cover of darkness to a secret location. It made the job of the thieves that much harder, and that of the modern archaeologists as well.

"What else was in the tomb?"

"Just that, and I was hard-pressed to find it. Almost missed it, in fact. It was tucked behind this panel of stone, you see, and I only noticed that the stone was loose when I—"

Returning my attention to the statue, I let Arthur drone on about his discovery while I listened with only half an ear. To hear the man tell it, he was a master at finding things that were invisible to the naked eye. The problem came when it was time to separate myth from reality.

Who was this unknown queen who bore such an uncanny resemblance to me? I was resigned to the fact we'd probably never know. Her relocated tomb could be anywhere, buried under thousands of years of sand and rubble. Archaeologists had been digging in Egypt for over a hundred years, and there was still so much they hadn't found, so much we didn't know.

"It's a *ka* statue, isn't it?" I asked, interrupting Arthur in mid-boast.

"That's why I brought it to you. Couldn't have some wet-behind-the-ears university student fondling your soul."

His tone was jovial, but I shivered. *Ka* statues were designed to provide a resting place for the spirit after death. I'd seen photographs of the example found in Tutankhamen's tomb, of course, but this was the first one I'd personally handled. My scientific training aside, it had a realism I found positively creepy.

"Obviously my soul isn't in there, Arthur." I pushed the statue toward him, turning it so I couldn't see her mocking face any longer. "Even if I believed in such a thing, which I don't, I'm not dead."

"You're not one for reincarnation then, either, I assume?"

"Absolutely not."

"Perhaps she is an ancestor of yours. You have to admit, the resemblance is quite incredible. I don't think it could be a better likeness if you had been the model."

He picked up the figure and turned her face to me again. I hurriedly looked away, and then cursed myself for being foolish. It was nothing more than a doll made of stone and jewels. Why on earth was it having such an effect on me?

"It's a coincidence. I don't have a drop of Egyptian in my blood." Even though my brain and heart had belonged to her for as long as I could remember.

"Ah, but we were all born in Africa, Madame Professor. Surely you must know that."

Ignoring his reference to the origin of our species, I stood, indicating our meeting was over. Suddenly I wanted Arthur out of my office with a desperation that was overwhelming. And I wanted him to take his statue with him.

"Not me. I'm Greek and English, through and through. Anyway, it's been lovely to see you, as always, and this has been an interesting interlude, but I was in the middle of something that I really should get back to."

"Cleopatra was Greek, and she was the most famous Egyptian queen who ever lived."

Damn Arthur for using Cleopatra against me. I should have known he would try something like that. "Well, I'm far from Cleopatra." Walking over to the lab side of my office, I busied myself with one of the many piles of paper, hoping the archaeologist would get the hint.

"I don't know. Seeing you like this…well, royalty suits you."

He ogled the statuette with an appreciation that bordered on inappropriate. If only I had something more substantial than paper to throw at him. I exhaled with as much hostility as I could manage. "Will you go now, Arthur?"

"Okay, okay." He put the statue down on my desk so he could raise his hands in surrender. "I get the hint. Sorry I disturbed you, Your Highness."

Finally, I spied what I'd been searching for—something hard. I seized my copy of *Ancient Rituals, Vol. III* and flung it at his head. Arthur backed out the door, laughing.

As soon as he was gone, I sank onto one of the stools adjacent to the counter. My legs trembled. Seeing my own face on a relic that was probably three thousand years old had been unnerving, to say the least. Thankfully, I'd never have to see it again.

Then I looked over at my desk, and there she was. Arthur had left his damn statue behind. And even worse, I could swear she was grinning at me.

ABOUT THE AUTHOR

J.H. Moncrieff's work has been described as early Gillian Flynn with a little Ray Bradbury and Stephen King thrown in for good measure.

She won Harlequin's search for the next Gillian Flynn in 2016.

Her first published novella, *The Bear Who Wouldn't Leave*, was featured in Samhain's *Childhood Fears* collection and stayed on its horror bestsellers list for over a year. *Monsters in Our Wake,* a deep-sea thriller with Severed Press, hit the Amazon Horror bestsellers list, beating King's re-released *It* to the top spot.

When not writing, Moncrieff loves exploring the world's most haunted places, advocating for animal rights, and summoning her inner ninja in muay thai class.

To get free eBooks and a new spooky story every week, go to bit.ly/MoncrieffLibrary.

Made in the USA
Columbia, SC
25 November 2017